Mr. Neutron

Praise for *Mr. Neutron*

Joe Ponepinto's *Mr. Neutron* offers a hilarious and biting romp across the American political landscape through the eyes of beleaguered campaign operative Gray Davenport. Gray is a man accustomed to living a "slow-lane life" as an aide to a perennial office seeker, while conjuring up an imaginary alter ego, Monterey Jack, a tough hombre who bubbles with testosterone. Yet Gray's existence picks up unexpected speed when his own wife signs on to manage the mayoral campaign of an eight-foot-tall opponent, Reason Wilder—a nemesis who seems hardly human. Soon several mysterious old men have hired Gray to investigate this monstrous neophyte...and what ensues is a mad escapade that perfectly captures the ongoing derangement of our current electoral order.

Mr. Neutron is satire at its best: sharp, clever and unsettling. Ponepinto has penned the defining political comedy for our own tragicomic democracy.

–Jacob M. Appel, author of *Millard Salter's Last Day*

Inventive, trenchant, and laugh-out-loud funny, *Mr. Neutron* is reminiscent of *The Broom of the System* and *A Confederacy of Dunces*, yet Ponepinto's voice is wholly original. With its unforgettable characters and its whip-smart political satire, this novel is the catharsis we need for the America we live in today.

–Kelly Davio, author of *It's Just Nerves*

Mr. Neutron is pure fun, satire at its best, skewering American government, politics, and society with delicious humor and insight. This is a book you'll press on your friends, a book full of quotable gems and characters you won't soon forget.

–Kathy Anderson, author of *Bull and Other Stories*

A terrifically inventive romp through the insanities of small town politics delivered in high-octane prose that manages to be both mordantly funny and deeply poignant at the same time. Pitch-perfect and written with a fantastical (in every sense of the word) nod to the golem myth, *Frankenstein*, and Jerzi Kosinki's *Being There*, *Mr. Neutron* is profoundly relevant to our time. Smart, crackling with insight on every page, it is also compulsively readable. I could not put it down.

–Joan Leegant, author of
Wherever You Go and *An Hour In Paradise*

No novel has made me laugh this much since Richard Russo's *Straight Man*. Ponepinto has injected just enough of the irreal into his satire to match America's current fever-dream politics.

–Bruce Holland Rogers, author of *Forty-nine: A Square of Stories*, and two-time Nebula and World Fantasy Award winner

Just when you thought politics couldn't get any stranger, Joe Ponepinto gives us this—a madcap, comedic tale of politics as usual—or unusual, rather. You'll laugh, you'll cry, you'll read, you'll vote. And then you'll read again.

–B.J. Hollars, author of *Flock Together*

Surreal and unexpected, *Mr. Neutron* turns political satire into something haunting, strange and can't-put-down compelling.

–Libby Cudmore, author *The Big Rewind*

 Printed and distributed by 7.13 Books. First paperback edition, first printing: March 2018.

Cover design: Gigi Little
Author photo: Wesley Burk

ISBN-10: 0-9984092-4-3
ISBN-13: 978-0-9984092-4-5
Library of Congress Control Number: 2017956192

This book is available in a variety of electronic formats including EPUB for mobile devices, MOBI for Kindles, and PDFs for American and European laser printers.

7.13
BOOKS

for all you neutrons

Mr. Neutron

Joe Ponepinto

The Age of Reason

He stood in the niche of a wall in the back of the room, safe and unobserved, observing Reason, who clomped across the stage, towering over the heads of his supporters, shaking his long hair like a dog in from the rain and rambling about the great things he would do for the city. Gray watched as the giant preened, running his palm over those strands of questionable hygiene, and then offering that same hand in camaraderie. No one hesitated to take it, for in the folly born of emotion and hype, these people believed he would be Grand River's next mayor.

Gray sensed his mouth hanging open and pressed his fingers up to shut it. He'd heard the man was tall, but this dude reached at least eight feet. Each of those clomps shook the floor all the way back to where he stood. He'd infiltrated Reason Wilder's campaign fundraiser, seeking to learn about the newcomer and what made him so popular: how he looked, how he spoke, what he stood for. But what Gray discovered only raised more questions. This candidate was beyond unusual. More like unnatural. When Reason moved it came in spasms, the slab of his body stopping in mid-jerk as though posing for hidden paparazzi. His face seemed contorted in pain, even when he smiled. Time for caution, or at least hesitation. The last thing Gray wanted was for someone to notice him staring. Best to stay in his crevice and blend in among the fake flora. He could watch the action from there; watch from a distance, as he always did.

As he studied the man the strangeness of the scene began to multiply. Nothing about this event felt right. Politics was not like this. Where was the band playing the blatantly patriotic? In place of trumpets and cymbals, and too many crescendos, a guy with a beard strummed an acoustic guitar, and a woman in paisley and braids with—my God—a tambourine, slapped her hip; and they sang not of marching and war, but about dancing and drinking and—did he hear that right—sex, as in the casual kind he had hardly ever experienced. Where were the walls dripping with red and blue bunting? No stylized stripes and stars dangled above the stage. Only a mesh filled with balloons hugged the ceiling, ready to spill out onto the party. When he looked up, he saw a rainbow of hues had replaced the America colors, and those taut spheres of air quivered like sperm, as though anticipating their role in an election climax.

He watched as Reason slowed and peered into the crowd, allowing him a better look. Gray's eyes widened. In the heat of the packed hall the massive man's pasty skin did not glisten. In fact it did not glow with life at all, did not belie blood pumping vigorously beneath, but had a static look, desiccated, a look that hinted at decay. From where he stood the giant seemed disoriented, unaware of what he should do, until a supporter reached up to touch his shoulder. Then Reason twisted around and flashed a grimace of a grin, crooked and confused, as if surprised to see a long-lost comrade he'd never met before.

"My friend!" the giant slurred. "So glad you could be here for me. And what is your name?"

From within that cubbyhole reserved for statuary, Gray watched the monolith nearly stumble as he started up again, displaying coordination so lacking it might be diagnosed as an epileptic fit. He listened as Reason's speech continued to assault the air in squeals and grunts. He'd seen such afflictions before and fought to recall where. The images came back to him in grainy monochrome: a reanimated collection of body parts, a flattened head encasing a diseased brain; the whole awkward, aimless assemblage menacing villagers and little girls. But come on, Gray, childhood nightmares should remain in childhood, yes? The movie traumatized him as a boy of eight, and those fevered imaginations had stopped plaguing him long ago. Yet how easily they came back, supplanting the here and now with figments of the beyond. It couldn't be real. Just couldn't. Besides, if someone brought a cadaver to life today, it would be under controlled circumstances—in a lab at some university, with the media and religious protesters in attendance. It would go viral on the web. He would have heard about it.

Still, Gray couldn't dismiss the possibility. His timid psyche often cleaved to the supernatural, if only to explain the failures in his life. And dead men had been elected before, although they typically stayed in their graves and didn't campaign. He looked up at the hotel chandelier, its baubles now refracting light into untrustworthy images. He began to feel afraid. He began to think he shouldn't have come.

But despite not bearing an invitation, he couldn't stay away. The lure of loose lips, of campaign secrets revealed, had enticed him like a lover. At first he had only dared take a peek inside, to see if this event disappointed as badly as his own candidate's a few streets away. The dinner portion was over. No one guarded the door; no rule-obsessed matrons with glasses on chains around their necks badgered him for credentials. A few tentative steps further and still no resistance. And when he felt the energy of the crowd surrounding the huge figure, he slid along the room's perimeter as if drawn by their gravity and settled into this recess where he could spy. Who knew what nuggets he might unearth? Perhaps he'd learn how this unknown had Pied Pipered a following without a platform or a slogan.

At last Gray's curiosity subdued his reticence and encouraged him to push an inch from the wall. He sidled out, urging himself to brave the crowd to get still closer to the man. But when the giant finished blathering, his supporters regathered around him, orbiting and eclipsing the candidate in a sycophantic group hug.

Gray recognized some of them: eggheads, activists, trouble-makers. The city's radical fringe. The wearers of black on black. The ones who never ate cow because they believed the beasts sentient, who lived outside the mainstream in warrens of subversion, and came out occasionally to lecture the rest of the world about their wasted, hypocritical lives. Naturally they would back a weirdo. But there were others as well, businesspeople from downtown, shop owners from the mall's boutiques, people whose avarice was so pervasive you could smell it in their too-heavy colognes and parfums, see it in their entitled designer suits, their European cars of entitlement waiting for them at the valet outside. Typically these polar opposites never mingled, but here they were, getting along, drawn together by the colossus on stage as though they'd been chums for years. There was the head of a neighborhood association, talking to a young man who looked like the drummer in a grunge band. There stood the president of the Chamber, clinking plastic glasses with a college prof. That the object of their shared affections was so unlike any of them—so freakishly tall, so strangely uncool, so poorly dressed, poorly spoken, unaware, unattractive, so… unalive!—made no sense. Or did it? Of course the leftists would hitch their politically correct wagons to this bizarre star; of course the conservatives would proclaim their faux inclusiveness by embracing a golem of otherness.

Gray came out carefully from the potted camouflage, but kept his head down, refusing eye contact. Yet a woman, eager to share her euphoria, flitted over, blocking his path. "Isn't he wonderful?" she said. Her body undulated under a loose smock of a dress, as though she'd just come from electroshock therapy and still had trouble controlling her movements. The tattoo on her deltoid of a bird of prey nearly made him recoil. "He's going to turn this city around," she said, swooning.

"There's no doubt about that," Gray muttered. He pictured Grand River rotating on an axis, spinning out of control, its inhabitants nauseated by the centrifugal force.

The woman clasped his hands in hers. "This is an amazing night," she said.

"I couldn't agree more."

She floated away, and he began to weave a path through the few tables at the rear of the room. He didn't get far before a man seated at one waved, and then pointed at his cup, as if by doing so he could convince Gray to fetch coffee. A pitfall of his outsider status. A pitfall of his lack of tribe, lack of affluence and fashion sense—his size forty Men's Wearhouse off-the-rack special had conferred on him a waitstaff look, so that in this spectrum of lifestyles, where apparently everyone fit in, he did not. He and Reason did not. But they all adored Reason. The man waved again, more emphatically. In another time and venue Gray might have complied, but the therapy had at least helped him past such feelings of subservience and lifted, partially, his lifelong gloom over having a name like Gray. Now, with effort, he could act, go forward, rebuff that man and shelve his anxieties long enough to complete the mission he'd assigned himself.

Then the legs of the supporters onstage shifted, and he caught sight of Reason's shoe. Not so much a shoe as a leather boxcar, a size twenty-three orthopedic sarcophagus, almost as high as it was long. No human sported a clog like this. Further evidence that the life parading before him might be artificial. He leaned forward to get a better look, but just as quickly Reason's groupies re-obscured his view. If he wanted to see more, he'd have to coax himself all the way to the stage. Up there, next to the giant, he'd be able to confirm or deny these absurd imaginings. Perhaps he would find that the man was merely awkward, maybe handicapped in some way, but essentially human…unless he glimpsed a neck bolt or something.

Gray skulked past clusters of people sipping house merlot and munching hors d'oeuvres. While the guests chatted, he snuck glances at their faces. They laughed and noshed, enjoyed the goings-on, and in that respect, they bore no resemblance to his man Bob Boren's handful of supporters. Those maudlin folks had looked at first like typical campaign well-wishers, but when they listened to Gray's candidate blubber through his welcome speech, and then mangle the names of half the dignitaries attending, they abandoned Bob's sinking ship for the safe harbor of their TV melodramas. By eight o'clock, only Bob and his wife and Gray remained, and they told him they would call it a night as well. He drove them back to their home for a consoling cup of joe in Bob's study, where he eyed the gun room that contained enough firepower to arm a state militia, leafed through a stack of *Soldier of Fortune* magazines, listened to his client rationalize what had gone wrong, and then left them to their chagrin.

It was too early for Gray to retire for the night. If he went home, he'd have to watch as his wife, L'aura, with her psychedelic hairdo, pursued her psychedelic art—a combination of abstractions that made his head spin and stomach churn—and he just wasn't ready for another evening of that. Then he hit on the idea of election espionage. But he couldn't bring himself to drop by the soirée for the third candidate in the race, Elvis Vega. Yes, the event promised an open bar, and he sure could have used a belt, but the attraction stopped there. If the crowd at Reason's were tough to bear, the clique at the yacht club would have been insufferable. Those silver-haired Brahmins, slathered with the tan of venture capital, always reminded him of how many digits separated his bank balance from theirs. And the condescension of Vega's cronies—the crème of the city's crème, the one percent of the one percent—would make him feel downright puny. So it had to be Reason's. At least there he might feel less inferior to the other attendees. And if some of those people didn't know how to keep their mouths shut, they would spill strategy and secrets, and he would lap it up because he needed some kind of edge to get Bob back in the race.

Gray closed in on the candidate, step by tentative step. He saw the cockeyed grin skewered into place between Reason's nose and jaw, like a pair of wax lips on a king-sized Mr. Potato Head. He registered a pair of eyes that didn't stop moving long enough to focus. This was no challenged candidate. This was weird science. The trembling of his adolescent nights might return at any moment, but curiosity and his client's desperate situation, for now, held it in check. A few more steps and he would know for sure…

But another obstruction, this time a waiter hustling a tray of cheeses. The man had a compassionate look, as if he too saw Gray as another of the serving class. He thrust the platter under Gray's chin.

"Here. Help yourself."

It seemed like good advice.

Gray snatched a toothpick and stabbed. He lifted a cube of white, examined its geometry, and found it too perfect to be Swiss. He brought his nose—that Alp-like appendage with a sense as keen as a German Shepherd's and which his family had once hoped might have commercial possibilities á la reality TV—into play and sniffed. He tasted. Ah, Monterey Jack.

Monterey Jack? Hmm.

Now there was a name. It bubbled with testosterone and reeked of sweat. Monterey Jack, he of the three-day stubble and flower-wilting breath, the meanest, toughest hombre who ever stalked the Sierra Nevadas in search of silver, women and whiskey. A man with a name like that ate raw horseflesh; he cleaned his toenails with a Bowie knife. He feared no man, no challenge; needed no sidekick to help him through. Monterey Jack was a name a man could wear like a bandanna, a name that swaggered, that defied convention, and was so much more of a handle than his own, inanimate tag. Monterey Jack wouldn't stand in the back of the room. He wouldn't need a place to hide. He'd kick chairs and tables out of his way, and then the crowd would clear a path for him, huddling against the bar to let him pass. Monterey Jack would jangle his spurs right up to Reason, and stand, toe to boxcar.

But, no. He was Gray. Dull as a sunless, rainy afternoon. A product of his mother's promiscuity and dyslexia. She had meant to honor her father, Gary. But it went down as Gray, and burdened him with all the dreariness the word implies. And Davenport to boot, as in, Ms. Davenport, are you sure of what you wrote on the baby's registration? And when she answered yes, Gray Davenport was sentenced to a life as a blandly upholstered sofa, something to be sat upon by asses of all weights and configurations. From childhood on he endured the questions and the jokes. New acquaintances tried their best to be witty at his expense, turning his name into a weather report or an ad for cut-rate furniture. He always did his best to ignore it, sometimes laughed to show he could take the ribbing and get along with the ex-frat boys and sorority sisters who populated the halls of influence in this stratified city as he tried to claw his way up the ladder of political success. But inside, where it counted—where it hurt—he added these rubes to his "list"—an ever-lengthening mental inventory of those who'd offended him, and against whom he would someday, somehow, exact revenge in all its living-well-is-the-best-type glory. So far, however, that plan had disappointed, and Gray continued to hate them all for who they were, as they surely would have hated him for who he wasn't, had they bothered to acknowledge him at all.

By the time Gray swallowed, two of Reason's beefy handlers were guiding the candidate toward a back room. Those left on the stage began to applaud, and the rest of the crowd joined in. There was no time to deliberate, no chance to opt again for inaction. Gray moved fast, motoring around the throng just in time to block the exit. He thrust his hand toward Reason. The titan hovered over him and met the nervous fingers with a slab of dry flesh that hung limp from the wrist.

"My friend!" Reason slurred again. "So glad you could be here for me. And what is your name?"

His voice seemed different from just a few minutes ago, in a slightly higher register. When Reason spoke, his words seemed not in sync with his lips, like a movie off its soundtrack. He appeared even taller up close, with shoulders like a linebacker in pads. Gray looked higher, into the bleached teeth, into the twin wind tunnels of his nose, into the yellow eyes that scanned the room—independently, it seemed. A sharp, chemical mixture of smells wafted from the candidate. And the skin: to the touch it felt dehydrated, lacking the natural oils of living epidermis, as brittle as parchment, like the pages of an old book. Gray saw it now—a dead man walking. A dead man somehow charged back to life.

For a moment, Gray stood as tall as his body would allow, refusing intimidation. He could be the hombre: tough, proud, and filled with a bravado that would make them equal. But he only reached to the giant's sternum and realized this wall of flesh could swat him like a mosquito if provoked. He felt himself shrivel as his courage started to drain away. In a second, all he wanted was to retreat to the safety of the niche in the back of the room. But the beast had asked him a question. He had to answer. Be strong, man. Be that Monterey fellow. And he stammered, "Jack... uh, Gray."

"Well, Jack Gray, I am glad to meet you. Together we will do great things for this city."

Gray peered at him from below. There had to be a scar, an electrode, some kind of definitive proof. But before he could find it he felt himself moving away from the door. One of the handlers pushed him to the side. As they departed, the other slipped a contribution envelope into Gray's hand. The first put his palm on top of Reason's head and reminded him not to run into the doorframe.

The lights in the room flashed. Someone gave a signal, and the balloons came down. Gray ducked.

Neutrons Are Necessary

Flesh and blood reality stared Gray in the face. Bob Boren's ruddy jowls quivered despite the fact he sat, unmoving, on the couch in his living room, and they offered evidence of what might have been a life force that vibrated deep within, but was more likely the man's catastrophically high blood pressure. Either way Gray's candidate was definitely alive, not reconstituted, and listened to his consultant's report of the encounter with Reason the night before. Gray did not embellish, nor did he have to. The giant's grotesque visage had invaded his dreams, and haunted his consciousness all day, taxing his comprehension and his faith in the tangible.

Patsy Flatley, Bob's lead consultant, listened too, but the look on her face mixed disbelief with disapproval, an ironic combination coming from a puffy, middle-aged woman in cat's-eye glasses, sitting on an enormous red ball used for stability training. She said it helped her bad back. She had been saying that for seven years.

"So what?" she said. "So Wilder's a freak. How does that affect our campaign?" She rocked a little, unsteadily, and the friction of her rayon slacks against the polyvinyl sounded like she had broken wind, a sound Gray had become used to and which he registered as a symbol of his political career.

Bob changed his vapid look and followed her lead. "Yeah, give me something I can use," he said. His steak-sized hand drilled knuckle deep into a bowl of mixed nuts his wife had left, ostensibly for all. He strip-mined the bulk of them, his fist trailing cashew debris as he brought it up to feed, and continued talking despite his full mouth. "I have to beat this guy in the primary, not prove he lacks a pulse."

Bob's jaw worked the nuts like cud. He was a crew-cut steer of a man, a thick torso of low-grade beef teetering atop piano bench legs, but since there were only two instead of four, he often had trouble with balance. More than once Gray had seen him lean over to retrieve something or tie a shoe, when the weight of his massive front porch became too much to support, and he wound up sprawled on the floor, a cow of his own tipping. He was a man of indulgences, the nuts just his latest. He'd run a campaign in each of the last five cycles, trying to parlay a one-term councilship into higher office. Once he lost his bid for reelection there, he let his ambition run wild and tried Congress, then state senate, assembly, county supervisor, and now this mayoral bid, the next open rank as he approached the bottom of the electoral totem pole. Patsy stayed with him in each race, her faith in his electability unshakable. Gray came along for the ride and had never argued over tactics, until now.

"But don't you think the voters would care?" Gray asked. "If we can prove it, he'll be out of the race, and you wouldn't have to go through a runoff."

Patsy sat up a little straighter on the ball, perhaps to stretch her lumbar muscles, more likely to make her point. "Gray, haven't you learned anything in the past seven years?"

He felt he had, but considering his apprentice status, and the fact he hadn't had the guts to go out and start his own consulting practice, maybe not.

"Crime. Taxes. Repeat after me."

He stared at her as though he'd never noticed the ball before. Her left leg came off the floor as she fought to maintain a position that looked vaguely authoritative.

"Crime. Taxes," she chanted. "In a city election that's all the people want to hear. That's all they ever want to hear."

City election. Every time he thought about his work, the phrase "small potatoes" came to mind. He served a small potato candidate in a small potato city, and as lackey to Patsy, his potatoes were even smaller. Who noticed this race outside of Grand River, or outside the tiny circle of political operatives in the city? Even L'aura refused to acknowledge his job, shifting the subject whenever he tried to bring it up. Of course he'd dreamed once, like any other man. Dreamed of crafting strategies that swept his clients into office with the kind of mandates politicians salivate over. Dreamed of a string of successes that made headlines, that grabbed the lapels of the national campaigners and forced them to recognize his genius, to pick up the phone and call and ask—no, beg him to work with them on senate races, governorships, the presidency. He'd be in constant demand. His record would sparkle, with nary a loss. Elected officials everywhere would owe him. Congress would owe him. The leader of the free world would owe him. He'd have his pick of ambassadorships, consultancies, board positions, women at Beltway parties. He'd hire a ghostwriter to tell the story...

But they were only dreams, founded on nothing more than vague hope. His reality was this dead end, this broken record playing the song of failure over and over and over. Talent, drive, luck: take any one of them away and the odds of stardom become astronomical. Take two away and it's a career in the minor leagues. Take all three away and this was where that mediocrity had led. Gray stared at Patsy clinging to the handle on the ball; he watched as Bob finished off the nuts, bringing the bowl to his lips as though guzzling soup. What if this electoral backwater was where he belonged? What if the challenge and frenzy of a big-time campaign were beyond him? He had to admit he'd grown comfortable in his role as Patsy's wing boy. No risk, no reward, and no responsibility. This was his doing, as much as theirs. After all this time, nothing but a career's worth of small potatoes. He found at least some humor in it: if Bob saw it that way he might gobble them up too.

"Come on," Patsy said. "Crime. Taxes. You can do it."

"All right," he said. "I get your point."

"No, really Gray. I want you to say it."

"Why?"

"You have to believe it."

"I do."

"I don't believe you believe it."

Bob chimed in. "Say it, Gray. Taxes. Crime."

"Crime, taxes, Bob," Patsy said.

"Can we move on?" Gray said. "There has to be something more important to talk about than the level of my dedication."

"You've got to get on board, Gray. Forget about those other issues, forget about the other candidates."

He could make a farce of it—go to his knees and speak in tongues, writhe on the floor and let the spirit of her mantra infiltrate his sensibilities, replacing the knowledge he'd collected in grad school and as a councilwoman's aide, replacing common sense and the communal good. He could play the role of political zombie, like the people who worshipped Reason.

Patsy shouted now, "What's our message, Gray?"

A shockwave of frustrations radiated out from his depths, a tsunami of angst, regret over every ridiculous statement he'd had to make in the last seven years, every slogan he'd blathered, every hyperbolic press release he'd written. It was on its way to his lips, where it would renounce Patsy's ancient, clichéd campaign strategy and speak, for once, the truth, damn her twenty years of consulting and her slavish devotion to techniques that had originated during the Coolidge presidency. Right now their opponent weighed more heavily on him than Bob's platform, even with Bob on it, and they needed to take him seriously. He would refuse to parrot the standard line any longer. He would stand up to her, and the political world, and tell them proudly, "This campaign is about Reason!"

But instead it came out, "Crime and taxes!"

Patsy clapped. "Glad to see you've come to your senses," she said.

"So what are we going to say about crime?" Bob said.

"Careful, Bob," Patsy said. "You know the drill. You don't say anything about the issue. Just rephrase the question. People want to know you're aware of the problem, and that you care, like they do. They don't expect you to solve it."

"Gray said something to me about it the other day," Bob said. "Something about schools and crime..."

"Oh, you mean like armed security at schools," Patsy said. "I like it. K through twelve."

"Open carry for kids too," Bob said. "Teach 'em early, I say."

"No."

They looked surprised that Gray had spoken up. Gray did, too.

"All I said was crime and education are related."

They looked puzzled. "How so?" Bob said.

"Ninety percent of the criminals in our city are high school dropouts. What if we had greater educational opportunity? Get kids to stay through high school. Make it tougher to drop out by making it more rewarding to stay in. Study groups, achievement awards, recognize academics as well as sports. Make kids proud to get an education."

"Stop right there!" Patsy said. "What are you, a Socialist? Strike that, Bob. Forget he ever said it."

Bob shook his head. His jowls followed. Gray imagined a cowbell ringing.

"She's right, Gray. We can't be alienating anyone in this race. It's non-partisan." Bob tilted his head as if he were still thinking. "What have you got on taxes?" he asked.

"Might as well get it out of the way," Patsy said.

"All right. We've got to drop the city's income tax. People can't spend money they haven't got. They think half of what's collected goes into city staff pockets, and the other half goes to contractors, which, frankly, it does." He folded his arms across his chest, Mussolini style, proud of his stance despite knowing he was going down.

"Oh, God. Now he's going Libertarian!"

"Yeah," Bob said. "I can't use any of that."

"Then what are we going to say?"

Patsy threw her head back, as dignified as one can be straddling rubber. "Nothing that can be misquoted, misinterpreted, or misspelled. Simple as that. What we do every time."

Every time. Gray looked at Bob, Bob at Gray. Five campaigns of the same thing, the same nothing, and here they were, sitting in his living room, yet to be anointed. Bob's face had a touch of bovine sadness. Or perhaps he was just hungry again.

Patsy brought them out of their shared digression. "Let's talk about our plan."

Bob started to speak, but she cut him off. "Here's what I want to do in this election. We come out with a media blitz. Newspapers, radio, cable TV. Saturate the city with advertising. Billboards, bus benches. Then a mailing campaign. We buy lists of names and send a piece a week to every voter, then every day in the last week. Overwhelm the competition. Flood the system." She rocked hard now, back and forth. The ball started to bounce a little.

"Right," Bob said. "That's a great plan."

There was a problem with that plan, though, apart from it not being a plan. Bob had no money to pay for this offensive. With the flop of last night's fundraiser, he could only afford to post his candidacy on Craigslist. Gray was not sure if this was the time, however, to debate finances, although he'd wanted to, if only to bring up the fact that his promised consultant's downpayment had not yet materialized. Better for now to segue into questions they could answer.

Gray looked at Patsy, still vibrating on her ride. He stared at the entrance to Bob's gun room, where a mounted pair of pearl-handled Colt .45s aimed at each other. He suspected that although they'd been secured against the door they were still loaded.

"I'm going to head outside for a minute and light up," he said.

"Light up what?" Patsy said.

"I'm going to have a cigarette."

"Right. Of course," Bob said.

That he didn't smoke and never had, had somehow escaped their notice. A simple, "When did you take up smoking?" might have smoothed him over, made him eager to take another dose of Patsy's medicine. But they acted as though his nicotine habit was so profound he blew through two packs a day. So much for seven years and five campaigns together.

Outside, in the Grand River humidity, the air seemed as laden with chemicals as any unfiltered Camel. Gray breathed as deeply as he could, until his body's defenses shut down his intake to stem permanent damage. He coughed to eject airborne particulate. The city's environment, unchecked for decades, had become almost poisonous. *This* was an issue. So was the corruption at City Hall. Friends still on staff there had confided skimming and outright stealing in several departments that rivaled a South American dictatorship. They'd hoped he could raise awareness through Bob's campaign. And now this Reason and his mysterious origins—these were the issues that the public needed to know about. But what were they going to address in the campaign? Crime. Taxes. And in the most generic terms. He'd said it himself. The laws of political physics never altered. After seven years he'd worked it into a formula: $E=mc^2$, where E stood for the electorate, m for mass stupidity, and c for the craziness of politics.

He loitered in Bob's driveway now, halfway to his Civic, and turned back to face the would-be mayoral palace. A cracked walkway led past crabgrass and untrimmed hedge. Stucco walls lurked beneath vines and tree branches, sneering as their ridges poised to snatch threads from the shoulder of his aging suit if he passed too close. Above, the frayed shingles of a mansard roof angled down until they nearly touched the top of the front door. A pair of upstairs windows poked out like eyes peeping through bangs—the architectural equivalent of a bad hair day. Gray reached into his pocket for his keys. But where would he go? Home to his wife to be ignored in favor of her art projects, or maybe to a bar where he could get sloshed and at least get the campaign off his mind—maybe someplace in the gay part of town now touted as the city's hottest spot. The idea stopped him. The thought of an unknown neighborhood—even a fun one—he found too frightening. He let his keys slide back into his pocket, and sat down on the curb to think.

As a consultant and a professional he should believe in his candidate's ability to run a viable campaign and should Bob be elected, in the man's capacity to serve the best interests of the public. Assuming he couldn't, he should at least display enough integrity to leave the job. If only. A guy's got to make a living, and really he's there to serve the interests of his client, not those of the people, even if the half-truths he churns out feed the public's impression of politicos as dim-witted, privileged power mongers, whose scandals and lies tear at the fabric of society, much like the ridges of the stucco wall that somehow, despite his efforts to avoid it, nicked the warp of his jacket as he wandered past. And if he did quit, how would he meet his personal responsibilities? He had a home, a wife, a car payment. He had to do his share. How easy it is to imagine independence, to visualize oneself speaking the clear and loud truth about the world. But most times, the world just doesn't care. People let you go on about how you want to change things, perhaps they even listen for a while, but once they understand the work involved, and the risk, they turn away, back to the cloister of their own lives, their own problems. Their own niche in the wall. And where are you then?

Maybe Reason wasn't the monster he'd imagined. Maybe he was just the weird guy Patsy had suggested. Maybe she was right that attacking him wouldn't help.

He got up and turned back toward the house.

Bob had opened the door and Patsy bellowed from within.

"Hurry up, Gray. Stamp out that smoke and get back in here. We've got a platform to finish building."

Shit.

Gray trudged back to the meeting, head down, the soles of his worn shoes scraping the uneven concrete. He felt small, powerless—utterly infinitesimal, as he often did. A mere particle floating in a plasma filled with objects of greater mass and energy than he. He was pathetic, unattached, not part of anything that counted. Not bonded to any set of ideas except those of the campaign he represented at the moment, and not in any real sense, because as soon as the election was complete he abandoned those notions. He was a political consultant, but not really political. Not Republican, not Democrat, but not independent enough even to be an Independent. He was not interested, not disinterested, just…there, waiting to become a part of something, and finding excuses to refuse every movement or organization that came his way. In so many settings—at fundraisers surrounded by big money, at assemblies where the elected and appointed strutted their pompous stuff through the crowds—the power of the world whizzed past, brushing by him and his little dreams of success without acknowledging his presence. In a world that pulsed with electricity, he was neither positively nor negatively charged. A neutron, if you will, a fraction of an atom, taking up an area of space so insignificant that it was no surprise to be regularly ignored. He lived in a universe of despair, where the physics of random chance had conspired to render him moot, to keep him down, and where nothing he could do would change that destiny. But sometimes, his intellect fought back. There had to be some logic to it, some hope in which he could invest. Perhaps neutrons were necessary. Perhaps there was a higher calling for them, even if they appeared to be little more than ballast for the universe, stabilizing the floor so the baryons, hadrons, quarks and the rest of the subatomics could get it on. He just had to deduce what that purpose was. But in the meantime he would keep quiet. He'd sing the praises of crime and taxes, and acquiesce to Bob and Patsy's insanity, and try to help raise a few bucks so he could at least get paid. In short, he'd get along.

As he always did.

He walked back to Bob's front door under the scrutiny of the mansard gaze and his own conscience. Would it be any different if he worked for Reason? The giant's physical anomalies faced off against the arrested intellects of Bob and Patsy: claymation skin and yellow eyes. A big red ball and loaded guns. Size twenty-three footwear. Crime and taxes.

He coughed again, this time to add credence to his cigarette ruse.

A Reason to Believe

He almost didn't come at all, and now that he'd showed up late he would pay a price. Attending a debate among mayoral candidates was de rigueur for any political animal; the chance to watch an opponent sweat, or catch one in a gaffe might mean ammo in the media, points in the next poll. But Gray, feeling jaded and chastened, had procrastinated, and by the time he arrived, the elementary school auditorium—the only venue the local chapter of the Women's League of Voters could secure for the first of their municipal debates—was packed. Once squeezed through the door, he scanned the arena. The crowd filled every row and lined the walls on each side. He could tell they'd come for Reason, somehow invigorated by his charisma. People, most of whom he felt sure had not voted in the last few elections, crammed even the tiny walkway behind the seats. They laughed, they chatted, filled with glee over this carnival come to town. Democracy, if not yet fully breathing in Grand River, had at least inhaled.

He would turn and go, and lie to Bob and Patsy later that he'd seen his candidate's winning performance. But as he pivoted, Gray saw an open seat. Way down front, in the first row, in the center, in sprained-neck, I-forgot-my-glasses territory, just feet from where the candidates would sit on stage. It took a few minutes of side-stepping and pardon-begging for him to get there, and when he did he found himself shoehorned into a wooden fold-up, in a space barely wide enough for a ten-year-old's ass, stuck between two older women, one of whom had brought her knitting. Gray's hips were clamped, and in just a couple of minutes his butt went numb.

Before he could exchange pleasantries, a matron led the candidates, like ponies, to kids' chairs behind portable tables set up on the stage. Elvis Vega, the favorite in the race, bobbed his head and tossed his coal-colored mane like any good frontrunner. Bob followed, shuffling like a nag on its way to the glue factory. He sat on the tiny chair, threatening to obliterate it, picked up his cup of water and checked its bottom, as if he might find a hidden snack. He leaned a little too close to his microphone as he mumbled, "They said there would be crackers," to which the crowd responded with muffled laughter.

Reason stepped out last, his draft horse footsteps reverberating over the hum of the audience. He stopped at his assigned seat and looked down, and then out into the crowd as if for guidance on how to get into that chair without turning it into kindling. To Gray he seemed stymied, clueless, unable to continue until this problem was solved—but not by him, for him.

What perverse luck. He'd rationalized excuses to miss this event; he'd planned to stay in the back. Yet here he was now close enough to Reason to study the man's every movement, to look into his jaundiced sclera and determine for himself the level of consciousness, if any, present in the monster. Maybe now he could get the proof he needed to convince others.

Reason stood, wavering, transfixed on a point in the middle of the gathering. Then he nodded and stumbled out around the tables, down in front of the stage, less than a foot from where Gray sat. Those boxcars nearly touched his shoes. Reason's belt buckle glinted into his eyes. "I will stand here," the giant said, his voice an amalgam of pitches this time, like its own Greek chorus. "The seat is for a child, and I am not a child."

He still smelled funny too. Others might not have noticed the odor, but Gray's olfactory had gone on alert. The scent was subtle, but unmistakable. Not typical B.O., but something raw, although not altogether unpleasant. Reason had used a deodorant, and Gray sensed some kind of body wash as well, but they couldn't mask the man's natural tang. It reminded him of something old—very old—primordial, reeking of science.

Gray craned his head back like he was in the first row of a movie house to take in the length and breadth of the being before him. Reason's pants presented a canvas nearly wide enough to show a film, and blocked Gray from seeing the other candidates. And Reason's head loomed so high above him that he couldn't analyze its workings, as he'd hoped. He checked to his left and right for support. If his neighbors found Reason's closeness as irritating, they might convince him to go back to the stage. But the two women who bracketed him showed no annoyance, instead smiling contentedly as if watching TV.

The scrape of Vega's chair told Gray that he'd risen too. "My opponent makes sense," Vega said. "At least this one time." He paused to let the crowd laugh, but no one did. "That chair is demeaning, no disrespect intended to the fine women of the Women's League. I'll stand as well." He thumbed the vest under his Zegna suit and strutted around to join Reason, who took one more step forward.

Bob apparently was content to be demeaned. He continued to sit while Reason glared and Vega conducted a political posedown in front of the stage, turning and grinning, and making sure the crowd admired him from every angle. Gray tried to signal his man, but Reason's awesome body made visual contact impossible. He couldn't even get up now without head-butting the giant's stomach. What if one of the press photographers took a picture from the side? From the right angle it might look like he was giving Reason a blowjob.

Well, then, he had to move, never mind the consequences. He tried to brace his hands against the arms of the chair, but instead grabbed the wrists of the two women, causing one to gasp and the other to swat him as though he were a lecherous bug, and he sat back again.

From the back of the hall came a voice to the rescue. Patsy hollered, "Get up Bob," to which she might have added, "You horse's patoot," and no one in the crowd would have blamed her. But the message made it through, and Bob grabbed his water and hoisted himself from the seat. When he finally maneuvered to the stage front, Reason said, "It is good to see that they stand for something."

The crowd loved it, and Reason threw his mane back and let out a laugh with a pitch somewhere between a donkey's bray and the death throes of an elephant. And the crowd loved that, too. He took a half step forward to connect with the audience, and if Gray hadn't turned his head, those photographers would have had that scandalous image in the next day's paper.

Reason backed off a few inches, but not enough to afford Gray a view of the proceedings. Gray squirmed, but not much, since his butt was still crammed into the kiddie seat, and he couldn't move his arms for fear of being pegged a molester and having the cops summoned. It had seemed like such a perfect, unexpected opportunity, sitting there so close to the beast, close enough to hear him breathe, to see the cracking skin, to maybe glimpse a butchered scar along the wrist that thrust from his too-tight sports jacket. Give him some time while the giant paid him no attention and he'd have enough proof to drive Reason from the race, and then he would turn his sights on Vega and get the dirt on the slickster, which he'd wanted to do ever since his City Hall days when the man routinely belittled him, and then Bob would be the last candidate standing and take the mayor's office, probably the only way his client could win the election.

But now, too close to see a freaking thing. Gray could only sit in Reason's shadow and listen—and smell—and he wouldn't be able to see how well Bob did in front of the live audience, whether he looked competent and mayoral next to his opponents, or at least presentable, and wouldn't be able to advise him on how to improve, which was just as well, since Patsy would overrule his suggestions. He closed his eyes and let his mind wander...

There Gray sat, on one of the dollhouse-sized chairs, holding a perfect six inches from the mic—him, not Bob—a waking dream in which he snapped off clever answers to the moderator's collection of index card queries. He talked and smiled, relaxed while the other candidates avoided issues, rolled his eyes when they tripped over their misspoken answers. Vega babbled doubletalk so obscure it had to be code for his country club cronies. Reason contorted in the schoolhouse seat, which forced his knees into his jaw, garbling his pronunciation more than usual. The debate wasn't half over and Gray knew he had wowed the voters so thoroughly they had already decided to switch their allegiance to him. As he spoke, groupies queued near the stage to volunteer for his campaign. Men sat transfixed. Women swooned. Vega sweated. Reason did whatever zombies do to show fear. And then Gray commandeered the lectern, easing the Women's Leaguer aside to fill a dual role in his election drama. He fired heat-seeking, investigative missiles that his opponents couldn't avoid and couldn't answer to his, or the audience's satisfaction. He was the Monterey Jack of journalism. Meet this press, boys!

A voice, a woman's—overloaded with feedback from the school's sound system—introduced itself as president of the league. Gray daydreamed his podium dream through the obligatory applause and disclaimers and introduction of guests and outline of the format.

"Our first topic..." Mrs. Abernathy said.

Gray awoke from his stupor.

"...Crime"

Christ.

"The crime rate in Grand River rose point three percent last year, and residents are concerned. As mayor, what would you do to bring the crime rate down? Mr. Vega, we'll start with you."

Gray could see a sliver of Vega just past Reason's girth. The candidate thumbed his vest again and started pacing in his little space in front of the stage, like a lawyer summing up. He had so much confidence, and why not? He was the outgoing city chief of staff. He had the mayor's endorsement, the city council's, the Chamber's, the police and fire unions', and the nod from big contributors in Island Retreat, the city's moneyed enclave. So if he didn't have someone's vote, he would eventually buy it through smarmy campaign ads plastered in newspapers and on building sides, and that ran twenty-four seven on local cable. For Vega, this debate—the entire election, in fact—was just a formality.

His answer seemed a formality too. He spoke about cooperation and vigilance, city pride and more cops on the street, and making sure they had the tools they needed, and did he mention more cops on the street? It was the answer every candidate who'd run for municipal office since Jamestown had used, and Gray tuned him out after a few sentences.

"We will hear from Reason next."

Gray began to sweat from the giant's proximity. If the big man became demonstrative he might get clobbered. But Reason stood perfectly still. "I have heard," he said, "the statements of my opponent. He makes promises he cannot keep. His language is designed to deceive." A few gasps came from the audience, and one from Vega as well, but Reason kept speaking, his high pitch a counter to the depth of his argument. "The special interests in Grand River control this man, and if elected, he will do their bidding. This you know. And this other..." He gestured toward Bob. "This other is irrelevant."

Some in the crowd voiced approval, but Gray thought the speech robotic, as though someone fed him the words via wireless.

But then, the giant's shoulders relaxed. His register approached a human level. "I offer another way," he said, "separate from the influence of money and politics. A way of the people. A way that reflects us all."

What did that mean? Another way? More like another planet.

Just as quickly, Reason stood erect again and returned to his automaton delivery. "Together we will do great things for this city."

Reason stepped back when he was done, looked down, and saw, at last, Gray. "Well, Mr. Jack Gray, so glad you could be here for me," he said.

Gray bolted. Left, past Vega and to the side wall, where those forced to stand barricaded the walkway. He contorted himself past bellies and breasts, careful not to touch, except for a step on someone's toe, which nearly pitched him into the seats. But he made it to the back of the hall, where Patsy had cleared out an area so she could rock on her ball. The motion produced those flatulent tones again, which explained the extra space.

"Jack Gray?" she asked.

"Long story."

From the rear Gray could finally see the dais, as well as the rest of the crowd. In the center was a woman with long, straight hair the color of a fresh lime. L'aura. She'd been apolitical with a capital A since his decision to give consulting a try. She was sitting next to a man whose hair shone arctic white and cascaded over his shoulders. Some kind of wanna-be composer or more likely another of Reason's egghead supporters. They appeared to be conversing. And what was this new color? She'd been violet and persimmon and goldenrod, but always some color that could be at least considered a fashion statement. And what was she doing at the debate? This was a woman who believed politicians were scum, and the people who worked with them were schmucks, and what did that say about him and his long efforts to change her mind about his career? He would confront her after the meeting, ask why she had come without telling him, and about the strange man. It might not be pleasant, but at least it would be an excuse for them to hold a discussion, a rarity in recent months.

With order restored, Mrs. Abernathy continued, "Lastly, Mr. Boren. Two minutes."

Bob cleared his throat. "Well, that sounds about right," he said.

What did?

He seemed to have lost his train of thought without the train leaving the station.

"My opponents. They have some good things to say." He paused again and took a sip of water.

"Of course, I'm against crime."

He had nothing. He hadn't practiced, as Gray had suggested. He would have relied on the same blather that Vega used, but Vega said it first, and Bob wasn't quick enough to ad lib or rephrase. So he stood, apparently in deep thought, more likely in panic.

Gray watched the tragedy unfold. The yellow light—the ten-second warning—would come on soon, and then the red, and then Bob would be a laughing stock and would have to start looking for a sixth office for which to run.

Desperate, Bob looked to the back of the room. Gray thought he was looking at him for once, not Patsy. Why would he do that?

The candidate took a deep breath. He blurted, "Crime is related to education." He looked surprised at his own statement. Had Bob really said that?

No one laughed. There were no boos. Emboldened, Bob went on. "Ninety percent of the criminals in our city are high school dropouts. What if we had greater educational opportunity? Make school more rewarding and kids won't drop out. How about making our kids proud to get an education?"

Gray swelled with pride.

"That's our Bob," Patsy said, as if she had thought of the idea. Maybe by now she believed she had.

"Maybe even make graduation from high school mandatory in Grand River," Bob said.

Someone in the crowd muttered that it wasn't fair to force kids to stay in school. But more than a few applauded his answer. Vega chuckled, as if to dismiss the comment as a gimmick. It was risky, but it was different. It was something, although whether the voters wanted something beside slogans wouldn't be determined for a few months. Gray watched Bob, who seemed anxious at his own remarks.

Mrs. Abernathy shuffled through her index cards as she spoke: "We'll take one from the audience this time. A random question, so I hope you candidates are prepared."

Vega smiled with the confidence of a man who could avoid any query posed to him. Reason continued not to move, as though waiting for some button to be pushed to activate his brain.

"Let's start with Bob Boren this time," she said. "Taxes…"

Gray tried to hold back a laugh, and snorted a little.

"'We are overtaxed,' this person writes. 'As mayor, what would you do to get the tax burden off our backs?' Two minutes."

Bob looked at the ceiling, as though inspiration were about to be dispensed.

Gray grinned. It's not coming from there, Bob. Then he looked down at his shoes to keep his grin to himself.

A Traitor in His Midst

Congratulations were in order. She said so.

The post-debate crush around the candidates had kept Gray from catching up to L'aura. But he was still jazzed when he pulled into the condo garage and took the elevator up. Those ideas Bob had proposed were his, and they had accomplished what he always thought debates should: get new thinking into the political forum and put his man in the game. What Bob repeated had created a buzz and legitimized his campaign. And Gray, of all people, had done it.

But how did L'aura know?

"What do you mean, 'Thank you?'" she said. She put down her fume blanc, and flicked green strands over her left shoulder as though she'd found a piece of seaweed after surfacing in the ocean. She put a hand on her hip and shifted in what he thought was a seductive manner, reminding him that once upon a time, early in their marriage, it had been. He couldn't help remembering. Were it not for her coral reef of hair, L'aura might still be an oh-so-typical urban spouse: blond, blue, workout freak, ready to embark on the transition from babe to cougar. She was all that until a year ago.

"For the sentiment," he said. "But I don't remember telling you—"

She lifted her glass in a toast and took a sip of wine. "Congratulations to *me*."

His words of triumph stuck before they reached his vocal chords. Instead he said, "What did *you* do?"

"You'll be very proud," she said. "I'm the new campaign manager for Reason Wilder for Mayor."

She took the last splash of her wine in one gulp and went into the kitchen to pour another. Gray watched as her Capri pants swiveled away. He tried to focus on her, but as usual, was distracted by the condo's walls, painted in a curious combination of drippings and splotches, her artiste's contribution to the world of mural and her homage to Jackson Pollock.

When she'd finished she turned to look at him and raised an eyebrow. "Well? What do you think?"

"You volunteered to help my opponent?"

"Have you seen how tall he is? He'll make such a great mayor. And I'm not a volunteer. They're paying me."

As Bob hadn't yet paid him, it meant L'aura out-earned Gray at his profession, despite her lack of experience, training, or contacts. It had to be the white-haired man in the audience; not just a Reason supporter, but a part of the campaign braintrust, maybe the treasurer. More likely, he decided, an old lech on the prowl. No doubt the man had deduced the giant had no real chance against Vega and opted to blow Reason's wad on the first campaign floozie who showed interest. What was it about politics that made men believe they could abandon their responsibilities in favor of a quickie, that prompted them to abnegate the public's trust for the immorality of an affair? FDR had no legs and he got laid; Clinton put the presidency on hold to get some head. And so many others: Eisenhower, Kennedy, Gary Hart, that guy in the airport men's room. From school board on up, politicians dallying with women, men, boys, pages, livestock. The only way to insure fidelity in office was to restrict candidacy to the clergy… oh, scratch that. Gray reviewed his seven years in the cauldron—no offers of flesh for influence had come his way. But then, he had no influence. Now L'aura had it, and for sure she wouldn't trade. Not Reason's secrets for Bob's, not secrets of any kind for sex. She'd cut him off when she morphed her hair color to correspond with her artistic intentions, except for the once-a-season sympathy fuck she permitted, or as she put it, endured. And as it was the end of March, the next one would be months in coming—as would Gray.

"Does this have anything to do with that man you sat next to?"

"The Reverend Hand? It was an incredible coincidence. I was at the gallery helping prepare for the show Friday night, and he came in, looking for a reporter from the *News-Press* that he was supposed to meet, and he thought I was her, and instead we got into this great conversation about art and how he was a collector, and that led to politics, and Reason, and the next thing we were at the debate and he offered me the position." She finished her wine and moved toward a celebratory third glass. "I couldn't turn it down."

All this time Gray had one eye closed. "Hand?" he said.

"Inchoate."

"Huh? You mean, like a baby's hand?"

"What?"

"Inchoate?"

"The Reverend Inchoate Hand."

He looked at his own hand and decided to let that one go.

"L'aura, don't you think it's a little unusual for a stranger to offer you such an important job at a first meeting? Not to mention how weird it is that they didn't even have a manager at this point in the race."

"The reverend and Reason know politics. They'll come up with the ideas. I'm the person to make it all happen. They wanted someone with a lot of energy, and well, there I am."

So the monster needs energy...

"And it's not like there was no one doing it before. They had a manager."

"What happened to him?"

"Her. He said she left. Moved out of the state or something."

The "or something" part made him nervous. "I don't like this," he said. "Don't like it at all."

"Too bad. There isn't much you can do about it."

"Yeah. It's bad enough we don't do anything together anymore. But now you're working against me."

"Not true. I'm working *for* Reason."

Maybe it was Reason himself she was interested in. Gray fought the idea of the monster's possible sexual aptitude, but she had noticed his height; and he'd noticed the size of those feet, the mythical predictors of male prowess. The man was a conglomerate of oversized parts; and whoever had planned his architecture probably hadn't skimped on the infrastructure.

"I don't think he's real," he said. "Have you looked closely at him?"

"He's like a god from what I can tell."

"No, I mean really not real. Not like you and me." Her green hair almost made him take that back. But he had a point to make.

"You've noticed too. So powerful-looking. So in charge. He has all these great ideas about how to fix the city. It's like he's from the future and was sent here to save us." Something girlish lit her face as she said that, like a freshman with a crush on the high school senior. "You should hear Reverend Hand talk about him. He's the answer that Grand River needs."

He wanted to tell her to ask a few more questions, but it was clear she'd made up her mind about this campaign business, and by extension, his. Gray felt this was all a pretense for her to laugh at him, ridicule his slow rise through the political ranks by moving up faster in a day than he had in seven years. He determined to stand up for himself, to fight back, the hell with June's scheduled sex date.

"As far as I'm concerned this puts us on opposite sides."

"Do I look like I'm afraid?" she said. She slurred the sentence a little. She was getting drunk. "You do your work and I'll do mine. We don't have to compare notes."

He his anger wavered. "Are you sure? That might be kind of fun. We could be like Tracy and Hepburn—"

"See, Gray," she said. "That's why you've never gotten anywhere with this political business. You don't have standards. Work on the campaign is supposed to be kept private."

"But you're my wife. We're supposed to share those things. There's supposed to be trust." A forgotten concept in the public, and now private arenas.

"Not on something this important. Not when it's politics."

She was lecturing him on political protocol? Cancel the September liaison too.

"What do you know about politics?" he said. "You're an artist. Or at least, you call yourself one. But I haven't heard of your work hanging anywhere outside this room." He shielded his eyes as though gazing too long at the dappled walls might turn him into Reason-like stone.

She slammed the base of the wine glass against the marble counter hard enough for the stem to crack. The bowl began to teeter, but she caught it in time and threw the entire mess shattering into the sink, where the shards were sure to lodge in the disposal. The damage didn't diffuse her budding anger.

"It takes time to create art. I've only just started."

Artist. Sure. The public extent of her art was displayed in the condo's foyer, on the card affixed to the little mailbox door. A year ago it had looked like all the rest, an ink-jet "Davenport" in fourteen-point Arial, aligned with its two dozen neighbors in lockstep condo association conformity. Gray and Laura, as far as he knew, were an upscale—okay, bourgeois—couple, who ate out once a week, had maxed out one credit card and were nearing the limit on a second, and yet still cultivated that vague American confidence that they would someday rise above their peers and join the truly rich—just like all the other couples they lived next to, under and over. This unremarkable reality was okay with him. But in secret, she pried the card from its brass frame and went calligraphic, squeezing below the name, "& L'aura," the apostrophe embellished with a little pigtail of a swirl, at once marking the beginning of what she called her individuality, and the end of what he'd seen as a conventional, if not always comfortable, marriage. The old Laura was too bland, too uninspired, too predictable, she explained. Her aura ached to be set free.

"You gave up a good job at the newspaper to go into politics," she'd said. "Why can't I change too?"

Art to L'aura, like politics, required no experience, no training, no contacts. Maybe those things helped, but, she said, she had neither the time nor the inclination to go the traditional, and therefore, superfluous educational route. No Art History for L'aura. No Drawing Studio I. She would be a "real" artist, free and uncorrupted by trends and schools. She would open her soul and art would pour organically out, and it would be clear and beautiful and of a creativity so profound as to stupefy the experts and enthrall the masses. Of course there would be sacrifice and suffering, and sure enough, since then, he felt he had.

It had been hard for him to watch her foray into that world. She was still beautiful to him. Doors would be, and were, opened. And although a year later she had yet to finish a painting—apart from the Pollocked condo walls—she'd been accepted into the local art community, especially by the proprietor of a seedy gallery called Tryst, in Millennial Village, that high-end part of town he'd almost driven to in his depression the other night. She'd told him the owner was gay, but Gray didn't believe it for a second, and suspected the man schemed to put the name of his business into personal practice with L'aura.

And now she had become a player in Gray's political universe. Another door opened for her while he kept waiting for opportunity to knock.

"Let's hope you adapt to the election cycle," he said. "It moves a bit faster. You won't have a year to daydream."

"Ha! We've already got plans. And so many volunteers."

So they were ahead of Bob on two counts.

"In fact, we've got two hundred people signed up for Reason's pick-up-the-trash, get-out-the-vote street cleanup and registration drive this Saturday."

"Two hundred?" Bob had two, and Gray included himself in that count since he hadn't been paid.

"Oops," she said. "I forgot we're not going to divulge campaign strategies to each other."

"That's all right. I won't tell anyone."

A selective slip, he felt sure. If Bob's performance tonight didn't gain traction, the campaign would become a series of these "accidental" jabs. Wasn't her disinterest in his career enough? He preferred the usual disdain for his profession over this, over the possibility that she, and Reason, and Indecent Hand or whatever his name was, would kick his political ass come the June primary.

Bland River

Who would expose the monster for the monster he was? Not Gray.

After the debate, after Patsy and Bob, and now after his wife's announcement, Gray had had enough. He stood on a narrow pier overlooking the puddle that was the city's marina, stagnant at the mouth of Grand River's river, where the debris of a dozen cities funneled and clogged on its way to the Pacific. He felt somewhat close to the glamorous coast and the majestic ocean views just a few miles to the north; felt there had to be a vibrant and fulfilling life just beyond his meager horizon, even if he couldn't see it.

What he could see was a gaggle of sailboats and stinkpots moored by jetsam from the north: plastic bags and bottles, the remnants of thousands of fast food lunches, the occasional mini-fridge; evidence of the economic and environmental morass from which Grand River had been unable to extract itself for the past decade. The early morning light, so dramatic, reflected off other, pristine waters, illuminating floating piles of garbage that collected in the corners and crevices formed by the gangways. Budget cuts had eliminated the trash patrol here and at other venues, and instead, the city spent a million on a marketing campaign to suggest residents change their unclean habits. It did little good, and

Gray felt ironically proud that folks had protested against the illogic of the media expense, although it meant having to bear this seascape of rubbish.

He sipped the last of his coffee from a Styrofoam cup and scanned for a receptacle. Apparently the municipal budget made no provision for those either. He looked around to ensure no one watched, and then flipped the container over the rail. It drifted out to join its kin. What was one more bit of detritus?

Gray held out his finger as though it were poised on the handle of a toilet, as though he could flick his wrist and flush away the city's ills in one great clockwise swirl, to be replenished by clean aqua trickling in from some giant tank of second chances. He pushed at the air, but the miasma did not stir. Nothing swirled in his mind either. He wanted to rip the shroud that was Reason's shirt from his body and see the scars where the mad scientist had stitched him together; see the long-dead flesh that had been stretched to its limits to accommodate the bones and muscles stolen no doubt from dozens of corpses. An evil lurked in the freak's awkward movements, and in the marble-mouthed speech; something that said the goal was more than just the mayorship—perhaps much more. But who was he to do such ripping? A bit player in a fringe campaign in a city that didn't matter, he reminded himself.

How was it that only he could see through Reason's façade? He saw himself as the magician's foil, immune to the illusion that had hypnotized the population, but incapable of breaking its trance. If only he could snap the others out of their stupor. L'aura too—and maybe by doing so reawaken her feelings for him. He was irked—nay, infuriated! He figured his chances of that were about the same as those of exposing Reason, though. But L'aura would be with the giant now, sitting in strategy meetings, accompanying him to appearances and interviews.

An abandoned cooler floated by, a seagull along for the ride, probing its latch for access to whatever spoiled food lay inside. How like this ruined city Reason was. Both barely alive, limping along, smiling awkwardly, putting the best possible face on a carcass of used-up dreams. Each had links to a long dead past: Reason, obviously to the remains of other bodies; Grand River to a brief heyday when Hollywood spread its largesse throughout the entire region. He knew about that from the reminiscences of retired folks he knew, from the pictures in this year's collection of old photos, *Grand Old Grand River,* which some amateur historian had cobbled together from forgotten library files and displayed in the city's morose independent bookstores so stingy that their owners refused even to install coffee bars. In the grayscale pictures, the city didn't look that great even then—more like Bland River. But so many people in this town were hung up on that past and maybe that was why the future had no appeal. Gray hung his head as he watched the garbage bob in the ripples of a sailboat passing by the gangway. Grand River, like his life, was in the toilet.

He heard a noise coming from a couple of slips down. A little Catalina rocked as though someone was aboard; maybe someone who shouldn't be. Some of the city's homeless had taken to breaking into unguarded boats and camping in them until discovered, and Gray walked over to investigate. As he looked behind the cabin he saw a scruffy man sitting on the boat's railing. His pants were down to his ankles, and his buttocks projected well over the water. When he saw Gray, he jumped off and hoisted his trousers, but Gray had already reached for his cell phone. "Put that away," the man said.

Gray kept dialing. "Are you supposed to be there? I don't think so."

"Well it's my boat."

"Then why are you—?"

"If I use the head I have to clean it," he said. "I didn't think anyone was looking."

Preventive maintenance, Grand River style. Let someone else handle it. Gray felt a tinge of responsibility, as if he should lecture the man about environmental impacts, but then he remembered his coffee cup, which had a half-life that would run well into the next century. He walked toward the parking lot and the Honda.

The city's condition was worse, in comparison, because to the north, affluence shone in residential towers overlooking the ocean from sheer bluffs; to the south, the population enjoyed the meticulously planned grunge of corporate-financed beach towns, complete with pre-weathered wooden piers. Formulaic, but at least these cities had identities. Meanwhile, Grand River (the city) sat in the middle of those successes, absorbing the discards thrown into Grand River (the river) by residents and businesses in the neighboring venues. He altered his previous assessment: Grand River *was* the toilet.

He drove back toward the condo to start his workday, although what he hoped to accomplish remained as mysterious to him as Reason's origins. With luck, L'aura would be out. If he focused hard on his computer monitor, he might not be distracted by the Pollock walls.

As he passed City Hall, he saw what once might have been unthinkable: a crane and workmen installing a huge billboard for a mobile device firm on the roof, defacing the nine stories below. Corporate graffiti. Everything was marketing and advertising now. But how different was that from the message the building itself had been communicating since it was built? The cliff of mirrored glass let officialdom look out, but the people they purported to serve couldn't look in. So much for the theory of transparency in government.

Why bother? The city was beyond help. Even if he unmasked Reason and changed the outcome of the election, the beneficiaries would be people like the Catalina crapper, who wouldn't know what to do with the truth if they were sitting on it.

Exit Strategy

Another meeting with Bob and Patsy, another monumental waste of time. Not to mention another ration of their condescension and stupidity. Why even go? This time, though, Gray had an inkling of what he might do.

Bob's remarks at the debate had created a buzz. There'd been articles and columns in the *News-Press* commending the candidate on getting to the heart of the issues, as well as expressing surprise at his ability, after so many years of gibberish, to articulate cogent ideas. The publicity gave Gray hope for a few days that this campaign might somehow turn out different than all the rest. Bob might have a chance. Gray's career might finally have a chance. He'd let his imagination run wild, forecasting legions of new volunteers and bundles of checks, but when he checked the rolls and the bank account he saw, so far, nada. Tonight's strategy meeting would be the usual four: Gray, Bob, Patsy, and the ball.

Why then hadn't anyone followed up the interest at the debate with a commitment? A donation of time? Money? It didn't matter to Gray. If but a handful of voters had signed on to the campaign, it would have meant validation of the last seven years of his life, and a mandate for at least seven more in service to Patsy and Bob. Yes, he was that easy.

Inside the Taj Ma-Bob, the candidate stared at him open-mouthed. Patsy looked ready to launch into her usual critique of everything Gray. Even the ball looked mean tonight. Gray had thought he'd glimpsed a political renaissance evolving in Grand River during the debate, a forum in which issues could be discussed intelligently and participants set aside their doublespeak. But now he felt everything had reverted to its typical baseline state, a pre-Cambrian morass of political greed, a yet-to-evolve competitive soup of ego-fueled candidates, each striving to be king of the muck. He looked at Bob, that bovine lump, snacking on Chex mix, compressing the cushions of his sofa into upholstered flatbread, and oblivious of his consultant's disappointment. Gray should have felt disdain for him, but instead, experienced a wave of sympathy. What else could this man do? He had no real job skills, no diploma, no talent for leadership or any other endeavor, just a decade as a mall cop and a friendship with a long-ago Grand River councilman who put him on staff as a favor, and then did him a bigger favor by dying in office. Bob ran unopposed in the special election, got the job, and finished the last eighteen months of the term, by which time the voters had wised up to his ineptitude. When he ran for reelection, he faced six opponents, and all outpolled him in the primary.

But by then Bob was stuck—jobless, futureless, yet believing (thanks to Patsy's coaching) he had the chops for command if he could only find the right constituency. He seemed pathetic sitting there, shoveling handfuls of nuts and cereal into his maw as though feeding himself another dose of naïveté, enough to keep him going until the primary vote and certain defeat.

Gray understood why Patsy stuck with him all these years. As consultant for a perennial loser, she couldn't do much else either. He had no sympathy for her, though, not after the way she'd treated him. Nor did he have any for himself. If he really had the balls he imagined he'd stop dreaming about jumping this ship and actually do it.

"Well, we tried it your way," Patsy said to him. "I say we should forget what Bob said at the debate. Just pretend he never said it and go back to the original platform. We're stronger that way."

In fact, he hated her. The inertia of her politics had held him back the entire time she supposedly schooled him to go out on his own.

"Are you sure?" Bob said. "I have to admit it was fun having people come up to me to talk after the debate. That never happened before."

And it wouldn't happen again if Patsy had control of the campaign. She wasn't so much committed to running things as keeping others from running them. Her working relationships had become co-dependencies destined to keep him and Bob in thrall, and Bob's campaigns in last place. Even the ball was a co-dependent, bending to her girth and her guilt trips. She sat on it, rocking, pontificating, self-appointed dictator of this molecule-sized republic, secure within its borders because who would care to bring it down? With Patsy calling the shots, Bob was no threat to anyone.

And Gray had bought into it. Seven years of delusion. Seven years of hopeless hoping. Tonight, though, it ended. Really. No dreams of escape this time, but the real thing. He had to go while he was still young enough to begin another career. Maybe bookkeeping or library science, something where he would come into contact with as few people as possible and thereby avoid falling into another psychological trap like this one, which had turned out to be far more psycho than logical.

His departure would begin by standing up for his beliefs: "I like to think a little honesty would work if we gave it more of a chance," he said.

"And where's the support?" Patsy said.

"People just need time to adjust to the idea. They're a little out of practice."

"A luxury we don't have. We need people. Doesn't matter if they understand anything. The stupid ones, they're the ones that get angry and then get motivated. Happens in every election."

She was right and she was wrong, but he didn't care to argue any longer. He slid the newspaper clippings and studies he'd brought with him back into his briefcase and stood. They would have to carry on without him into the primary, and then they could ignore the message the voters sent, and focus their serial office-seeking on whatever positions remained un-run for: another shot at council perhaps, or school board, or water board, or the bottom of the political barrel, sanitation board, and still they would lose and not understand why, but find a way to rationalize defeat, and motivate themselves to start all over again. But Gray was done.

"Sorry, Bob," he said, "I want you to know I take full responsibility for the lack of support and volunteers." Might as well go out like a pro.

But Bob cut him off. "That reminds me. I invited someone to attend tonight. Well, actually, she volunteered."

A volunteer? If Patsy's theory held, this would be one of those nut jobs who attended City Council meetings and tried to speak on every issue listed on the agenda. He raised his hand to salute his host. Let him get out of here before the new idiot arrived.

But a gentle knock signaled he was too late. As Gray shuffled toward the door to answer it, Bob said, "Do you know Breeze Wellington?"

"Breeze?" He'd heard the name. It had been in the paper.

Bob went on. "She's new in town, just started some kind of marketing business."

Gray's hand cupped the doorknob. Why would someone move to Grand River to start a new business when things were hopping north and south? A marketing business needed something to market, and Grand River didn't have much. Maybe it was the cheap rent she likely paid. Maybe she'd thought ahead—way ahead—to a day when the city would be vibrant again, and she'd be a local mainstay, the company everyone went to for promotion. But who in this city had that kind of forethought? She was probably just another political amateur who wanted to meddle in a campaign to feed her ego by contributing non-existent expertise on every topic. That would explain why she moved here; where else could she get away with such obstruction? She and Patsy would probably go to war with each other within an hour. But he'd already fought that battle and had finally admitted defeat. Let someone else endure, someone who wouldn't realize how she was being used. Gray would open the door, shake this Breeze's hand, exchange a brief pleasantry, and when she walked in, he would walk out—out of Bob's house, out of the insanity and out of politics for good.

He tugged on the door and swung it open.

A Gentle Breeze

There are some women who encase themselves in clothes like armor, who conceal their bodies from the world's sight for modesty's sake, or religious belief. They deny any movement that could even remotely be considered sexual. Their roomy pants, rigid undergarments and opaque, over-starched blouses preclude detection of the natural shifts of the female body as they walk and turn and bend, as though they're wearing outfits made of PVC. Breeze Wellington was not one of them. What she wore, in Gray's eyes, offered a hint, a suggestion, a come hither to the rest of the world—that sex-crazed steam bath of humanity—of intrigues that awaited just past the low neckline and sheer blouse, and beneath the clingy fabric of her tight, yet freeing skirt. He stood in the doorway transfixed, one foot on the front step, the other now anchored to Bob's carpet, the tendons in his neck ready to tear from the torque he applied in keeping his eyes on her, and watched as the parts of her body—the ones that were supposed to—seduced him through subtle motion, as though they had been motivated by a... well, by a gentle breeze.

Gray had always suspected women like her knew what they were doing. It simply couldn't be that the almost imperceptible quiver of breasts, or the tremor of buttocks, was unintentional.

Those movements confronted the mores of so-called respectable society and dared the world not to notice. Where some saw such behavior as subordination to a male-dominated ethic, he intuited that in Breeze's case it meant independence and control, whatever the business, whatever the purpose of the encounter, giving her a grip on the course of events stronger than the grip he imagined every person in the room wanting to place on her. Those others involved in the intercourse of her day—both women and men, he suspected—must have found it impossible to dedicate full focus on the agenda at hand. Attentions became distracted, whether in admiration or lust or resentment, and no doubt she used each reaction to her advantage. No feminism for this Breeze, because she didn't have to. No demands for equality. Doors were opened and chairs were held, jewelry and cars bestowed, but also, he imagined, this Breeze could speak her mind as she pleased, stand up to any corporate mogul or government official and converse on an intellectual par.

And with all this preceding her in his head, Breeze eased, like an estrogen thermal, past Gray and into the room. He took one more step toward his escape, and then stopped, weighing the cost to his soul of even a few more minutes in this political hell. He looked back again at Breeze, at the assemblage of her curves enticing him to stay. He imagined it might lead to some Faustian bargain, but could not stop himself. Freedom would have to wait.

He followed her back to the living room, offered her the seat he'd been using, and squeezed in next to Bob on the sofa. When she settled across from Gray, she made sure the girls said hello with a little pause to display her tan, buttery cleavage as she bent before him to sit, and she held the pose while apologizing for her lateness, to make sure he saw it.

Which he did. Fantasies of late night pornos overwhelmed his consciousness: Breeze in a torn dress on a deserted tropical island, Breeze entwined in satin sheets, bondaged Breeze; all of it overloading his mental circuitry and disconnecting him from the conversation. He squinted as he tried to force the tripped breaker of his thoughts back into position, and wished someone had invented a sexual surge protector to keep men like him in line. Then he realized she could see his face contort, and he experienced another swell of current, this time fear, that she would interpret his grimace as something sexual, which of course it was. He could not, for the moment, allow himself to travel further down that path, not while Bob and Patsy were watching. What kind of spell was she casting?

She likely knew what went on in the minds of those around her and used the knowledge to her advantage, and this deadly combination of brain and bod had jiggled itself into what he knew about her via the article and local gossip: two divorces, a luxury condo on the water, an E-Class Benz, and as much bling as a woman could imagine.

"It was so refreshing to hear a politician talk honestly," she said. "I was at the debate. The things Bob said... There was a kind of genius behind it." She smiled, not at Bob, but at Gray.

He opened his mouth to claim ownership of the brilliance, but Patsy cut him off. "The Genius of Grand River," she said. "That's our Bob."

Still, Breeze kept looking at him.

So quickly did this seduction threaten to envelop him that he had to pause and ponder. Years of invisibility in the eyes of the beautiful women he occasionally encountered, and suddenly the most stunning of them has a case of the hots? Perhaps the odds, so stacked against him for decades, might finally allow a point in his favor. Perhaps he might finally experience something he could label as good luck. And what about *his* reaction? Did he really want her, really want to act on this impulse, to sweat beneath his collar until after the meeting, walk and talk with her back to her car and drop the not-so-subtle clichés of the American mating ritual, or had he merely been conditioned by a lifetime of aftershave and cheap vodka commercials to believe that the search for sex was his life's work? He hated the feeling of being exploited, like some itinerant farm worker picking lettuce for less than minimum wage, but exploited he knew he was. A huge chunk of modern life, as he saw it, was a cavalcade of innuendo designed to prod an occasional biological need over the line of decency and into obsession, just so a handful of corporate fat cats could profit, ironically so they had the means to pursue their own obsessions. Of that he was sure. But knowing this didn't help because the sexual onslaught never relented. Twenty-four seven, his culture insisted he stop thinking in favor of desiring. He'd realized that by this point in life, he, like most other men, had been rendered a Pavlovian penis, disengaged from reality but still slobbering for sex.

He watched her mouth move as she spoke, but her words didn't register—his desire soon blocked any meaningful impulse from reaching his brain. Instead of reacquiring the campaign talk, he began to wonder if it wouldn't be better to seek not sex, but celibacy—not the postmodern, secretly deviant kind, but real denial of arousal, something of which Francis of Assisi would have been proud. Mind over sexual matter. How much easier life would become. And he wanted complete control over his urges, not just the paper-thin façade with which the rest of society shields its lust, ready, at the right glance, to tear off its garments for a quickie. Besides, what chance did he really have with this goddess? His thoughtful reticence—okay, his spinelessness—had always had its drawbacks around women. Like men, they'd been programmed, too—in their case to pine for muscled jerks with three-day stubble, the Monterey Jacks of the world, the crude boys in low pants and vulgar tattoos who flaunted sexual bravado. It was never more obvious than at times like these that he had no chance to thrill a woman of such erotic power. He would have to closet his feelings. There was no need for a protector to control his surges, since women like Breeze had one built right in—she could turn him on and off with a look or a word. Gray focused on Patsy, which calmed his libido. Rubbing up against Bob on the couch stifled his desires as well.

"What did I miss?" Breeze asked.

Bob stopped chewing. Patsy stopped rocking. They seemed hypnotized, and Gray, his intellect returning, seized the moment.

"I had some ideas to energize Bob's campaign," he said.

"I'd *love* to hear them," Breeze said. Her voice was tropical, suggesting trade winds, tanning oil, nude beaches. She smiled at Gray. Just the idea that she was interested in what he had to say excited him, and to use the word "love," well, it would be rude to describe how that affected Gray's Pavlovian part.

He spoke again, emboldened by the possibility of impressing this Aphrodite. She leaned forward to listen, and he fought to translate his feelings into speech. Never mind he had no new ideas to report—he would ad-lib like any lounge lizard who thought he had a shot. The important thing was to keep talking.

"We'll take advantage of technology in this election. We have an opportunity to use the latest in social networking systems to expand our base of support and take Bob's message to a far wider audience than this city has ever seen. Bob can have a blog. We'll Whatsapp and Snapchat and Xing for starters—" He stopped, hoping no one would ask what any of that meant.

Bob and Patsy were still unable to speak.

Breeze breathed, "And what about Twitter?"

Why not? Bob was already a twit. Gray said, "Yeah, that would be perfect."

Bob's wife interrupted to bring out a tray of luncheon meats, cheese and crackers, and set it on the coffee table. "I heard some commotion," she said. "I thought this might help." She loitered for a moment, staring at the new guest, as if envious of the attention Breeze commanded. Mrs. Boren was a pretty woman in her own right, Gray noticed, as trim and demure as Bob was not. The idea that she was too good for Bob lingered in his mind. She disappeared without Bob's introducing her.

Unconsciously, Gray slipped a disc of salami into his mouth and licked his lips.

Breeze licked hers, and he suspected it had nothing to do with food. How quickly his lust returned with just a flick of her tongue.

During the remainder of the meeting, she continued to eye him and deferred to his opinion as though impressed by his intelligence, all of which fed into his expanding fantasy of her coming on to him. He tried to fight the impulse, reminding himself over and over that the laws of sexual physics were constant, and that since a woman this beautiful had never been attracted to him before, it shouldn't happen now. But she kept looking, kept complimenting, and he could not help but entertain that this might be one of the as-yet-unexplainable mysteries of the universe, an anomaly, and he should accept it and deduce a theory later. Yes, why not pursue this experiment, and see where it led?

But what was he thinking? He was married. Or was he? L'aura didn't act as though their vows meant much anymore. Breeze would be the perfect woman for an affair, capable of sending each of them to opposite extremes: he to one of pleasure, she to the height of jealousy.

As the session, moved forward Gray's amazement at this woman did not diminish. She seemed to know about campaign structure and strategy, and she contributed good ideas about marketing Bob, in spite of Bob. To his equal amazement, Patsy never questioned her ideas, but only rocked contentedly on her ball, which caused her head to nod in assent of everything Breeze suggested. Gray knew also that his frustration over the election was ending. His anxiety over leaving and finding some other means of supporting himself lifted. He would stay on the job.

And when it was time to go, an event that even Bob and Patsy seemed to want to delay, Breeze waited at the door for him while Bob had a few last-minute requests. Gray met her there, and they walked in step past the stucco wall and down the driveway to the street. He asked about her business, but she ignored the question to ask about the campaign's finances. Gray accompanied her to her Benz, as much to be chivalrous as to keep her from seeing his battered Civic two spaces away. She hit the remote to open her door, and the frequency activated something in his brain as well.

He found himself staring at her again, assessing the sine wave that described the curve of her body. She was a world of her own, with mountains and valleys, dimensions, horizons. His world had always been flat, and now he seemed to be falling off the edge of it. "I'm hungry… Are you?"

He tugged at his collar, at his conscience. He could stop there, make it seem as though he'd only meant himself, tell her he was making a Taco Bell run and that he'd see her at the next meeting. But no. Come on, Monterey Jack…

"Do you want to get a drink? We could talk strategy." He stood in the damp night air. A cone of light from a streetlamp illuminated his foolishness, and he turned to go.

Breeze touched his hand. "It's okay," she said. "I'd love to."

Love, again. Gray's knees buckled.

"But it's a little late for tonight," she said. "Tell you what. Are you going to the yacht club event in Island Retreat Thursday?"

A mixer for the candidates among the snobs who'd already picked Elvis Vega as their man. Something to prove to the masses that they were committed to diversity, that the iron gates and moat that separated them from the rest of the city didn't mean they weren't inclusive. He was guaranteed not to know anyone and wouldn't care to hang at Bob's elbow all night. It would take a miracle to get him to show up at that farce.

"Of course," he said. "Wouldn't miss it."

"Good. I'll see you there."

The door was closed, and she was purring down the block before he regained his senses. He watched her taillights turn the corner.

It would serve L'aura right. Just a hint that he was seeing a woman like this would make her care. She'd beg him to come back. And if she didn't, well, it was Breeze for God's sake.

Gray opened the Civic's door. It creaked a little. He'd have to get it fixed, eventually. Better yet, he'd have to get a new car. Maybe he should rent something nice for his rendezvous Thursday night, otherwise he'd have to park out of sight. He started the car and put it in gear, already planning what they might discuss beyond the politics, how he might let her know he was as into her as she seemed to be into him. She was as hypnotic, in her way, as Reason appeared to be. It would be interesting to see the giant's reaction should they meet. Whose spell would be the most powerful?

He mulled the possibilities as he drove, and started scribbling some notes on a pad in the passenger seat with his free hand, interspersing his plans with visions of her body in various stages of undress. The hand that was writing began to shake, and he dropped his pen onto the floor. He leaned over to retrieve it, but jerked back up at the blare of an air horn that sounded like it was in the car with him. He'd drifted across the road into the path of a semi. Gray wrestled the wheel and just managed to swerve out of its way.

He let the car idle on the shoulder as he regained his composure. Things were starting to happen too fast for his slow-lane life.

A Well-Played Hand

What if he told her about Breeze tonight? The shock of it would give him an advantage on two fronts: disrupt L'aura's focus on the Reason campaign and force her to look at Gray in a totally new light.

She seemed irresistible, he would say. She was beautiful. Intelligent. Articulate. Any other man would have melted and lost his head. Then he would bare his soul, the way men do on the Hallmark Channel, and make the obligatory, melodramatic appeal, and let her guilt do the rest: I thought about it, but then I thought of you and what we had, and I told her, "No." I hope that was the right thing to do, he would say. He could be irresistible too.

If it worked, he'd turn this marriage upside down and be in control for once. No more appeasing her whims and enduring her insults. No more pining that her indifference would somehow turn into passion. She'd realize that she might lose him; realize, despite their differences, how much she needed him.

No more waiting for their quarterly sex date.

She would turn back into a wife.

He would turn back into a husband, but he wouldn't stop there. He'd keep going until he was a man—more than a man—a

Monterey Jack of a man. And if he chose to pursue Breeze on the sly and keep it from L'aura, well, maybe he'd do that too.

It was risky, though. L'aura might call his bluff. She could say she didn't care and that he could see whomever he wanted, and that would clue him in about her indiscretions with that gallery gigolo. Or she might have the opposite reaction, explode in jealousy and become violent, attempt to use him to Pollock the kitchen walls. Gray hovered in the yellow hallway outside the door to their condo, trying to run through all the possible outcomes, weighing the odds of each.

As he debated, he heard the tic of a wine glass against wood. He reached for his keys, but the door swung open. L'aura stood before him in jeans and black t-shirt, holding a goblet of chardonnay. She'd dyed her hair again, and in the diffused light, of the room it matched the color of the wine.

"How long were you going to stand out here?" she asked.

"You could hear me?"

"You breathe loud."

He put his hand to his nose. "I was trying to find my keys."

"Come and sit down," she said, swaying, barefoot, to the couch. She sat on one side and pulled her knees up until her toes dug into the crevice between the cushions, all without setting her glass down. Gray watched her drink slosh back and forth, just barely staying within the bowl. He adjusted his eyes to the Pollock-walls and joined her.

"Not here," she said. "Over there." She pointed to the sofa's matching chair, flicking her new color behind her ear.

As he sat, Gray saw that she had been busy today. Hair was just the start. L'aura had Pollocked the coffee table, and streaks and splashes of black and brown marred the surface and spilled over onto the carpeting. She was turning their home into a hallucination. "Why did you do that?" he asked, riveted by the swirling colors.

"The mood struck," she said. "I'm an artist."

He looked over his shoulder into the kitchen to see if the refrigerator or dishwasher had been assaulted. "What's next?" he asked.

"That's what I wanted to talk to you about." L'aura sipped from her chardonnay.

So she wanted to talk. The wine began to look good, even necessary.

"Mind if I get a glass first?"

"Don't."

"You're telling me I can't have a glass of wine?" He felt a twinge of nervousness in his abdomen. She had a bomb to drop.

"It's not good to drink and drive."

"I'm not going anywhere."

"You're not staying here."

"I live here."

L'aura gulped the rest of her wine and headed to the kitchen to pour another. Her hair moved like a pendulum between her shoulders.

"It looks nice like that," he said. "I didn't care for the green color. Too organic." He could hear the flow of the wine into the glass, and he got up to help himself.

She looked at him coldly, which stopped him, and then she spoke from behind the kitchen counter, as though protected by the barrier. "Don't you think it's time we took a break from each other?"

"A break?"

"We're on opposite sides of an important campaign..."

"What are you saying?"

"...and we can't afford to take the chance that details and strategy will be compromised. At least I can't."

"Aren't you taking this a little too seriously?"

"Aren't you not?"

He moved closer to face her. "A husband and wife should be able to handle this."

"Is that what we are?" L'aura sipped, and then leaned one hand on the counter and held the glass with the other. She had practiced this. She could never be that spontaneously sophisticated. "Maybe in name only," she said.

Perhaps not even that, considering what was on the mailbox downstairs.

"You have to admit, Gray, there's been a lot of changes. We're not the same couple we started out to be."

"I'm not the one who's changed," he said, beginning his defense. He knew he should be outraged and call out her behavior, and get her to admit she'd been having an affair with the gallery owner. Surely no businessman would have let her stay on for a year without her producing one way or another. He should be a brute, claim he wouldn't leave and never set her free from this marriage. He should drop to his knees and beg her for another chance. He should be the adult here, and tell her they could work it out if she would give honesty and openness a try. He looked away for a second, and the chaos of the living room walls finally became clear: the mottled drywall was neither L'aura's creative outlet nor a symptom of some repressed mania, it was the manifestation of their marriage, the product of every disagreement and doubt they'd ever had, mapped out in dark bursts, an EEG gone haywire, the explosions of their discontent rendered in twisted, cancerous lines, as though a disease had engulfed them.

Now it was obvious this had been coming ever since she dyed her hair blue last year. Longer, probably. Maybe his decision to give up his steady job for a shot at the political big time had sparked something in her mind, and it had taken the next six years to foment. Their savings had dwindled and they'd borrowed money from her father, adding to the tension. And since that first change of hair color, the graph mapping her animosity toward him had taken a hyperbolic curve. He'd fought it, but now resistance drained from him in an instant, as though it had never been there at all.

If she wanted to split, he would try it. If she asked for a divorce, he believed he could live with it, because for once, for maybe the first time in his life, he had a fallback position. He didn't have to claw for a fingerhold on the ledge of self-respect. Because he had Breeze. Waiting for him. Wanting him. Theoretically.

Nine years of marriage and another in courtship. Could he walk away from that on a whim? And to what guarantee did he hold Breeze? She'd smiled, she'd jiggled. She'd said the words he interpreted sexually. Not much to go on, really. In fact it was childish, wishful. Irrational. But he was at a point in life where the failure of rationality had pushed him to where a risk like this—a stupid, uncalculated one with almost no chance of success—seemed like the greatest opportunity he'd ever had.

Gray let his thoughts wander until it was Breeze in the kitchen, pouring wine for two, undoing the buttons of her blouse, and demanding not that he get out, but that he stay over. When she hopped up onto the counter and stretched herself across the marble surface, his decision was made easy.

"Whatever you say. If you want me to leave, I'll go."

L'aura looked surprised, no doubt expecting more of a struggle.

Gray headed toward the bedroom. "First thing in the morning," he said.

"No," she said. "It has to be now."

"But it's nighttime."

"If we're separated, you can't stay here. Then it's not a separation."

"I'll sleep on the couch."

"Get out."

Gray Davenport, a sofa of a man denied access to his own kind. It was too late to be rambling around the city, especially this one, looking for a place to stay. He had nobody he could call for a night's flop. Not Bob. And it was too soon to think of Breeze. There were a couple of decent hotels downtown.

"Let me pack a few things first," he said.

L'aura jogged into the bedroom and came back a few seconds later with two suitcases. "Everything of yours is in here," she said.

She must have crammed his suits and clothes into the bags with a steamroller to get them to fit. Gray looked at the kitchen clock. What time was the gallery guy coming over? She *did* have it all planned. He'd probably saved her an hour or two by refusing to argue. He'd been played and now he was mad.

Well, he would win this war. He would seduce Breeze and move in with her, enjoy the comforts of her wealth and her waterfront view, bask in her voluptuousness and the admiration his being with her would inevitably bring him around town. He would do a little flaunting too, and whenever the opportunity arose, would make sure L'aura heard about it.

He took the suitcases and walked them into the hallway, and then turned back to retrieve his laptop and briefcase. L'aura stood at the entrance, holding them out for him. She handed them over and shut the door before he could offer a goodbye.

She would regret this.

The Civic was balky as he guided it out of the condo garage. The transmission slipped when he hit the gas, causing the car to jerk, as though he were a high school junior learning a stick shift. Another thing he'd have to get fixed if he was going to make a play for Breeze. She wouldn't fall for a second-class man.

Yeah. But a second-class man was what he was. At best. And now he was having second thoughts. She was just being friendly, trying to get along in a new situation. Her invitation to the yacht club soirée was meant to promote the campaign's chances, not his. What seemed to be her come-ons were just the way she talked to people.

He really was a neutron, incapable of affecting change at any level, in any situation, least of all his own. What happened in his life seemed always to be dictated by another—as L'aura had done tonight, as Bob and Patsy had been doing for years, as Breeze could do in just a few seconds.

Depression set in, and the Civic's stumbling pace could not shake him free of it.

Gray headed west, for no better reason than it was a direction he had not been told to take. As he motored past the front door of the condo building, he noticed a man with white hair to his shoulders, turned toward the wall and using the security phone. It had to be that Reverend Hand from the debate. He didn't like the man, hadn't liked him from the start, and that was without having yet seen his face. So he was the secret lover, not the gallery owner.

Or maybe in addition to—

He knew so little about the reality of things.

There was still time to turn around and accost them. He pulled the car to the curb and spied as Hand stepped through the door and made for the elevator. When it closed, Gray watched the lights indicating the floors as they flashed on and off, until the one where he'd lived until a few minutes ago stayed lit.

He put the Civic back in gear, but kept his foot on the brake. What kind of a man would just drive away?

At the Boundary of a Forlorn Universe

A lone neutron doesn't take up much room, but apparently enough to be turned away from the two-star derelicts that passed for Grand River swank. How was Gray to know every available bed would be taken by a dry cleaners convention?

In the lobby of the Continental, a whiff of naphthalene carried from a queue at the registration desk as though the people in line sucked on mothball mints. He paused to assess the length of the wait, which afforded him a look at a pretty woman in a red jacket and tight skirt. She turned and eyed him the same way Breeze had, and Gray conjured thoughts of meeting her in the bar a little later. There was a placard on the counter that said the line was for pre-registers only; hotel full; welcome Southwest Association of Pressers (SAPs).

Then he noticed the woman's gaze was not at him but at his shirt and pants, creased from the long workday and wrestling his bags from the condo to the Civic's trunk. The woman pointed and said something to the man next to her, and they smiled at the wrinkly outcast in their midst. She desired only to steam his cotton twill, not his libido. Just his luck he had already paid to valet.

He motored a few blocks to the city's two other big hotels and found more of the same. And every one of the cheaper flophouses had a flickering "No" next to its misleading "Vacancy."

So downtown wasn't a good place to stay. Had he been paying attention he would have noticed the troupes of visitors, all wearing neatly ironed clothes that looked like they still hung on conveyors, negotiating Cancer Boulevard in search of a non-existent nightlife, finding instead weathered little storefronts, once quaint and now dingy, never-refurbished businesses from a decades-past economic apex, the last time Grand River resembled prosperity. Those people would soon realize that Tip-Toe Shoe Repair, and Short and Portly Suits, and anything else resembling retail closed by six. There was always Tessie's Pot Pies, though, and the line already stretched to the curb from the probably ecstatic Tessie's front door. He could almost hear the confused visitors wondering at the name of the street, and whether the run-down mom-and-pops were considered little polyps on a citywide melanoma. If they asked, he wouldn't let on that some genius in Planning had come up with the idea of an astrologically-themed downtown grid. Maybe they'd figure it out when they made it over to the convention center at the corner of Leo and Sagittarius tomorrow.

Finding lodging then would take some exploration. He pointed the Honda inland, toward Grand River's netherworld, where the streetlights had long ago been blown out by gunfire and left unrepaired as a budget-cutting measure. These were the neighborhoods that ringed the city's center like grime around a suffocating collar. A mix of Section Eight housing and manufacturing businesses that appeared to date from before the Industrial Revolution. Gray had never understood what these shops produced, apart from filth, old car parts and broken shipping pallets that piled up in the weeds behind those cockeyed brick structures. Now he was in it, craning over the steering wheel to see past the semicircle lit by the car's headlights and into the abyss that seemed to linger just beyond. Points of light, like faraway galaxies, twinkled at the ends of abandoned, pitch-black streets, indicating destinations up the coast, and the four-hundred-dollar-a-night beds that went with them. He would stay in Grand River. He needed to make sure he could afford Thursday night's rendezvous with Breeze.

The lone neutron, who often felt small, infinitesimally small, began hoping he could be smaller still, invisible to the naked eyes of the creatures who populated this ominous corner of the galaxy. He coasted into red lights, accelerated slowly so as not to draw attention. When cars approached from the other direction, he pulled to the right to show deference to whatever gangsters might be inside. A good twenty minutes of this and the expense of driving up the coast for a single room along the water began to seem reasonable. Still, he held out hope for an inexpensive and relatively neat motel not too far from civilization.

Another half hour, and having thus far not been the victim of a drive-by, Gray used his solitude to reconsider his options. There really weren't any. He resigned himself to a freeway onramp, assuming his next stop would see him max out his last credit card at some overpriced lodge. But then, turning the corner toward the freeway access, a glimmer of hope. A pinkish glow at the boundary of this forlorn universe. A quasar? A dying comet?

A star.

The Star Motel, in fact. Seventies neon and decor. Pea green shag carpeting. Bare walls embellished with shoe scuffs, as though someone had danced on them, looking a bit like the Pollock-walls at home. A sink whose pipes complained whether one called for hot or cold water, although it didn't make any difference which one he turned, since the water never got hot. There was cable, though, which made the thirteen-inch color set watchable, and might have made the room almost bearable, except that competing smells of disinfectant and urine worked on his ultra-sensitive olfactory until he could barely concentrate.

The manager, at least, had been accommodating. "Do you like to sauna?" he'd asked while Gray signed in. "I could fill up the hot tub. Just keep the hose in it because there's a leak somewhere, and it gets low after a while. Do you wear Speedos when you soak? I can loan you a pair if you need them, you know." The man, Randy, wanted to talk. Gray hoped that was all he wanted and answered questions about his work, his home, and his separation like the politician he thought he could never be, making up facts, lying without changing expression, telling Randy what he thought would make for good, but safe fiction, lamenting how much he missed his wife and how beautiful she was and even how much he enjoyed fucking her because he was a real horndog about women. Randy understood. He held Gray's hand with understanding. He held it tightly, so full of empathy and compassion, until Gray yanked it away and took the key.

He had landed in his new home, for the time being. His outpost on the edge of the cosmos. No one would find him here. No one would come looking.

Gray opened one suitcase on the caddy—L'aura hadn't bothered to pack anything neatly, and his shirts and suits were a tangle of sleeves and pant legs that had been entwined with his underwear—clean and dirty briefs together. He pulled out his suit jacket, the one he'd hoped to wear Thursday night, and held it front of him like a crumpled piece of paper. All those dry cleaners—where were they when you needed one?

He hung the suit near the shower in hopes steam would relax the threads. It was best to leave the rest of his things in the luggage, since the closet doubled as a supply locker, and the idea of his clothes hanging next to filthy mops, brooms, a moldy bucket and wringer, didn't sit well.

L'aura must really despise him to oust him so quickly, so sloppily. She was still at the condo, entertaining that reverend, and Gray felt sure this man of the cloth was only interested in how much of it he could remove from her body. Somehow he'd always been suspicious of her, and yet clueless. What other crimes had she hidden from him? What other lovers? Surely the gallery owner would drop by eventually. And why not Reason, too? Make it an orgy, and a farce, conducted at his expense.

Once he got everything into a semblance of order he sat back on the bed, clubbing his skull on the headboard, fighting against the sense it tried to knock into him. If he became logical now, in the soul-crushing depression of this purgatory, he would realize just how pathetic his situation was and lose the little hope that made him want to get up the next day and tackle it all again, despite the endless obstacles. Why did he think it would ever change? And yet it had changed, the moment Breeze walked through Bob's front door and breathed his name. And maybe her attentions were all a dream, or a misunderstanding, but they were something to hold on to tonight.

He rubbed the spot where he'd clonked himself. His awareness of the pain subsided. He smiled just thinking about her.

With nothing on cable and the hour not terribly late, he decided he would work. There was no Internet access in this void, but he could still fire up the laptop and brainstorm more strategy, more phrases for Bob, echoes of his own philosophy, which Bob, being Bob, might repeat when the incomplete thoughts that were the bases of his political foundation left him searching for coherence. He sat cross-legged, the computer wobbling on his thighs, and meditated on the campaign. He'd become acclimated enough to the room's smells to be able to write, but his thoughts oscillated between politics and his mental photographs of Breeze, both memory and fantasy. The thought of her might drive him to succeed, but right now, it kept him from the work needed to attain success. And the laptop was rubbing his crotch, disconnecting him further from the task at hand, tempting that hand to take up a different task, to bring him some relief from the conspiracy of torments he faced. Great. Now even his hand was telling him what to do.

He felt sleepy. He felt weak. A shower might calm him. He stood in the tub and waited while the pipes groaned at being asked to deliver water at this hour. The shock of the cold almost made him climb the plastic curtain. He needed this, but it would have helped if he had remembered there was no hot, and he yelled, "Don't help me!" to the showerhead, having to vent his frustrations somewhere. And before he finished soaping, a pounding at the door, as though there were an emergency. Since the water was so frigid, Gray didn't mind getting out.

Randy peered in, scanning, spying, while Gray dripped, in a towel at the door. "I saw that you were working. If you need the Internet, I have it in my room. You're welcome to come. I stay up real late."

Gray mumbled his regrets and slipped the security chain into its slot. He propped a suitcase against the door, just in case. How did Randy know he'd planned to work? A light on could have meant TV, reading, anything else. He checked in corners for some kind of webcam or peephole. Oh, what the hell; if Randy wanted to watch, let him. He'd already decided he would only stay for a day. Gray put on briefs and a t-shirt and went back to the bed and the laptop.

Night is a good time for creation. The world quiets, the pressures of the day relent until tomorrow. Challenges sharpen into focus. With his earlier lusts now chilled, and with the possibility that Randy might be watching on some kind of voyeur-o-scope, Gray had no choice but to concentrate. But night is also when even the smallest noise becomes a disturbance. The day's cacophony doesn't cover annoyances like that bubbling sound, like someone pouring water into a bucket.

He checked the closet, but the cleaning tools remained still, and then he realized it came from the next room. His neighbor was peeing. The walls were that thin. Then a phlegmy cough. Then a flush. Then the TV from behind the wall. And so many other sounds. Semis on the highway nearby, their happy rumble that they were heading somewhere else. Above, the chop of a police helicopter, no doubt swooping in to investigate the unmistakable sounds of crime that came from the street in front of the motel: men's raised voices, a woman shrieking or perhaps laughing. He worried about the Civic parked in the open.

Through the drywall, television sounds: the neighbor must have been watching a late-night talk show. Gray began typing random sentences, things Bob might say during the campaign. And after every thought he saved on the screen, a burst of laughter from the audience next door, as though they were judging what he'd written.

A Warning Ignored

A waft of salty air from the ocean beyond the private enclave reminded him that this venue stood apart from the rest of the city. Gray stopped the Civic a quarter mile from the guard shack, cranked down the window, and breathed in the relatively contaminant-free atmosphere that swaddled this portion of the coast. He checked the invitation, which he'd miraculously stuffed between some papers in his briefcase instead of trashing outright, and on which he'd managed to dribble, somehow, the mustard from yesterday's lunch. It smelled a bit—perhaps a shred of pastrami had burrowed its way down there too. With luck no one would notice the stain when he presented it, nor would they care that his suit remained crumpled from L'aura's mistreatment or that his brown shoes, the only complete pair he found in his suitcase, didn't go with the charcoal coat and pants.

Island Retreat, where Elvis Vega bunkered with his campaign financiers, and where tonight he would shine as the star of the candidates' mixer, constituted a parallel universe. It occupied the same space as the one he knew, but remained invisible to most people in Grand River. It existed, in theory, because what happened behind its huge gates affected lives outside, but as with a black hole, visibility stopped at the surface. Within this parallel universe, moguls made decisions, money appeared or disappeared, jobs were gained or lost, spirits rose and fell out here. It was a place of dark energy, that secret stuff of space. He put the car in gear and inched closer.

Those gates stood astride a narrow bridge that crossed a canal. A web of intricate waterways protected the exclusive digs and the attitudes they housed like a moat around a castle. Only one road led in and out, making the community easily defensible in case of assault by the serfs. The grates loomed fifteen feet high, were guarded by rent-a-thugs, and displayed the community's elucidating name in a florid font, one word on each enormous grille. Gray watched as a resident exited from the other side. The left side gate opened inward and the "Island" disappeared, leaving the closed side to tell him and other potential interlopers what to do.

The guard waved a Beemer in ahead of him, but when Gray tried to follow, the man made him stop for a border inspection. The burly security dude—when are such men not burly?—walked around the car as though Gray had smuggled a trunk full of illegal aliens. He examined the invitation, sniffed it, handed it back. This man, who likely was invited into the community as infrequently as Gray, had breathed in his employers' attitude along with the briny air.

A queue formed behind the Civic, and Gray could see the impatient faces of desired guests in the rearview mirror. It was all a little game. The guard made him sit and wait, but they would blame Gray, if only for being different enough to be stopped.

At last, apparently satisfied he'd irritated everyone involved, the guard let Gray through. Gray stuffed the invitation into his pocket and noticed the wrought iron warning him to "Retreat" as he passed. It was too late to comply.

The Center of Attention

Up close, Breeze would see a moiré of tiny wrinkles embedded in his jacket's pinstripes; wrinkles he had not been able to steam away because the icy waters in his motel room shower produced no steam. He could not dry clean the wrinkles away because none of the cleaners he visited would do a same day job during the convention. Bastards. And if she saw the wrinkles, she would surely see the little tear on the shoulder made by Bob's stucco, which he had tried to hide with a square of inked-over masking tape that fell off, perhaps fortunately, when he got out of the car. Still, it was the best suit he had, the other having been mashed beyond recognition when L'aura packed his bags.

He would keep a safe distance to hide the flaws in his clothing, but nothing would prevent her, or anyone else, from seeing those brown wingtips. There had been several shoes when he checked the suitcases, but since he had decided to leave everything stored, rather than risk contamination in the room's funky closet, he didn't notice that only one pair matched. He panicked as he dressed for the event, knowing he had no time to replace them. A fashion statement, if anyone asked. He would try, at least, to keep his feet moving or hidden behind legs and furniture.

The rest of the crowd wore Zegna, Prada, Lauren Black Label

and other names he couldn't afford. Such stylistic conspiracies explained one of the ways the rich maintained their distance from the rest of society. Even if his suit were crisp and his shoes the right hue, he would have felt out of place—this crowd could spot Men's Wearhouse from a half mile, and they would let him know that they knew with disdainful, confused looks that begged the question of why anyone would choose such an inferior cut over Italian microfiber.

He looked for Breeze. He'd promised he would be here and standing her up was not the way to impress a woman he had no business impressing. A circle of business types in black suits had surrounded her—men of wealth, each holding a fat glass of amber liquor and eyeing her with the uncompromising avarice that had secured their fortunes. Gray could feel their want from across the room. Breeze did not act disappointed by their attention. In fact she appeared quite at home among those posers. She smiled and laughed, enjoying her drink in flirtatious little sips.

How to break through that barrier. Gray needed an opening line that would show the other men he was as much a player as they. He turned to the bar for fortitude, but before he could move, Breeze wedged her way free from the entourage and came toward him.

"You finally made it," she said. "You see what I have to put up with when I'm by myself."

Gray tried to speak, but the spaghetti straps of her cocktail dress had somehow tied his tongue.

"Here, let me get you a drink," she said, leading him to seats at the bar.

He stopped gazing at her long enough to take in his surroundings. There was leather and tobacco, and enough rare wood adorning the club to deforest a small Central American nation, and at the bar, a display of alcohol so vast patrons could nip a different brand of Scotch every night for weeks. Breeze signaled, and the bartender poured. Gray saw they'd even managed to freeze ice cubes with an "IR" carved into the top. He imagined himself as a member of this exclusive sect, coming here each evening to be absorbed by plush things and the only decent view of the ocean to be had in Grand River. He would joke with the bartender and trade back slaps and anecdotes with the other regulars. Maybe then he would be comfortable amid these ostentatious digs.

Why wasn't he now? He'd already attained a position of some envy. Hadn't gentle Breeze abandoned her groupies to be with him? She held on to his arm like a girlfriend, the way L'aura never had, even when they were dating. He should be beaming, making a show of this, resting his hand on Breeze's sensuous knee that flexed just inches from his, and when the time was right, sliding it higher, over that fertile thigh. He tried to relax, to act casual, but he couldn't do it.

It was not the poor choice of clothing, and it was not the lack of money that kept him from enjoying this—okay, it was—but another feeling triggered discomfort. He could live with his unfamiliarity in such surroundings and could even bear the egos that suffocated the room, but something deeper gnawed at him. These people believed they deserved this luxury, and more than that, they were certain others didn't. And Gray, as one of the didn'ts, couldn't convince himself he deserved it either. So he listened to Breeze chat him up about Bob and Reason and Grand River politics, and while she talked, he made up excuses for not liking the hardwoods and the leathers and single malts the rest of the crowd took for granted. What was she doing with him anyway?

Then a hand on his shoulder, and a nudge as a thick body oozed past him to the empty barstool on Breeze's far side. "Elvis Vega. We met at the Futures luncheon." He was not talking to Gray. He skipped ahead a few minutes into the conversation. "What are you drinking?" he asked Breeze.

"Chocolate martini."

"Let me see," Vega said, and helped himself to a taste. He paused and signaled to the bartender. "Philip, the next one with the

Jean-Marc. On my tab. The lady will appreciate it." Gray was surprised Vega didn't curl the end of his Dali moustache.

He didn't even know what his glass contained. Breeze had merely pointed and the bartender somehow knew what she'd ordered.

"And who are you?" Vega asked him.

Of course he would pretend they'd never met, but to abandon civility from the start?

The look Vega offered said he really didn't remember Gray, despite the dozens of fundraisers they'd attended in the name of their offices, despite the handshakes and idle chatter when they'd been forced to sit at the same table at city functions. Vega's face was a riverboat gambler's, skewed to portray whatever emotion would suit his immediate need. His brow lowered and he squinted his eyes, and peered in at Gray, looking sincere in his amnesia, probably for Breeze's sake.

Gray peered back at the two puffy black eyes, the two chubby, tawny cheeks, and the two chins. This face screamed arrogance and indulgence and seemed to become more porcine, like a caricature in an old-fashioned political cartoon, the longer Gray looked. He turned his gaze, knowing he could never win this staring contest. "Davenport," he said, thinking it would sound more manly to go with the surname alone. Thoughts of spitting out "Monterey Jack" instead swirled in his head.

"Boren's man, right? Is that fat fuck really going to make it all the way until June?"

A quick glance toward Breeze—how dare he use language like that in front of a woman. But she hadn't flinched.

"We'll be there," Gray said, turning red. It was the first time he'd phrased his association with his client as a team, the first time pride was involved.

"Why doesn't he quit wasting everyone's time and concede now?"

"Because he has a chance to win," Breeze said.

Vega hadn't stopped looking at her. "Oh, don't tell me a goddess like you is part of the slob's campaign," he said. "How did he convince you, honey?"

Vega was two kinds of snake: a cobra charmed by Breeze, a viper for everyone else.

Breeze said, "I was curious about the election. When I went to the debate, I loved what he had to say. Bob Boren was the only candidate with an opinion."

Vega finally moved his gaze to Gray, who was busy replaying the tape of Breeze's last comment. She wouldn't have said it in public if she hadn't meant it. Vega produced a sneer like a high school bully's. Would he insult him, jump him, challenge him to a duel? Instead he only smiled and said nothing. The message was clear: Must they even hold the election? Why not turn the mixer into a coronation and save the city thousands of dollars that would only confirm what everyone knew? Vega would be the next mayor, despite anything Gray could do for Bob, despite Reason and his followers. The Island Retreat clique had dictated their choices to the electorate for decades and that was not about to change. They still had the money to ensure their candidates could overwhelm opponents with advertising.

Vega might not be one of the elite, but he had found succor in the wealth of this community by rubbing cashmere elbows with the old money that still ran the city. He picked up the donations they dropped at his feet: funds so expendable they were not worth the time to bend down and pick up themselves. He'd achieved his position as the consensus frontrunner by scaring off a half dozen other challengers more capable of campaigning than Bob. Gray shook his head. More than two hundred Vega supporters packed the bar and the dining room. Each would drop a thou, or more, on their man's campaign. He struggled to do the math. Meanwhile, Bob would have to nickel and dime his way into contention, holding maybe two dozen fundraisers to make up for what Vega might raise tonight alone.

Gray reached for his drink—now he wanted it—and almost spilled. A boom—as in fighter jet sonic type—reverberated from the entrance and caused everyone to jump. Reason had arrived, and he'd forgotten to duck coming through the threshold. Which had been damaged most, the man's head or the doorframe, was of some debate among the crowd, and one of the club staff checked the woodwork, to confirm the majority opinion.

And L'aura accompanied him. She was, after all, the campaign manager, but tonight she looked more like Reason's recently manufactured niece. She'd splashed her hair tomato red and fixed it in pigtails. She seemed paler than usual, as though she'd been spending too much time in whatever crypt the campaign held its meetings. A clingy green t-shirt with Reason's face across the chest, a black leather miniskirt, and a canvas bag with the strap slashed across her shoulder completed the look, a combination MILF and Pippi Longstocking. Reason wore an undertaker-like black suit, but it must have been something off the rack, since the sleeves came up short of his wrists, and his pant cuffs missed the tops of his boxcars by two inches.

Suddenly, Gray felt stylish.

Reverend Hand followed them in. He wore a too-long trench coat that dragged along the floor as he walked. At last Gray could see his face, which shone nearly as white as the hair that cascaded to his shoulders, and had a vampirish need about the eyes and mouth. Instead of staying with his group, the Reverend moved off into a corner by himself and gazed out at the crowd. He licked his lips non-stop.

Vega blurted, "I see the circus is in town."

Breeze put her hand on Gray's shoulder and whispered, "That woman needs a fashion intervention." She laughed and tugged on his elbow.

Gray's temperature rose a degree. It bothered him, surprisingly, that she should talk about his wife that way, even though L'aura had initiated their split. The fact that Breeze was right did not matter.

And what was with L'aura's skin tone? She'd had a healthy glow last time he saw her. The entire campaign must be staying indoors until sundown.

His wife saw him leaning against the bar and Breeze leaning against him. Theoretically, this was the moment he'd planned for, to ignite L'aura's jealousy and get her to understand the mistake she'd made, although he hadn't expected it to occur for a couple of weeks, at least. Sure enough, she came straight for them, but instead of confronting him, she extended a hand to the other woman.

"Are you familiar with Reason?"

"Yes," Breeze said. "I am."

L'aura's eyes bore no sign of regret, or even of recognition. She fixed on Breeze and did not turn toward him, or acknowledge him. She did not blink.

"Would you like to meet him?" L'aura asked her.

Now it became Gray's turn to hold on to Breeze, but she patted him on the arm and insisted she'd be right back. L'aura took her by the hand and led her through the throng that had gathered around the giant. Vega's supporters and guests were four or five deep in orbit around this sun. The wait staff and bartender had migrated his way. The cooks came out from the kitchen to watch. Even Vega took a few steps toward the crowd.

L'aura and Breeze maneuvered to the center and looked up at the mane of hair and stony visage. Reason must have noticed Breeze's approach, and he looked at her for a second, seeming to be distracted before staring back out at the crowd. He raised his arms as though about to conduct them in song. The crooked smile rippled across his face. "My friends!" he shrieked. "So glad you could be here for me."

In front of Vega, they applauded Reason.

"Together we will do great things for this city."

L'aura had a stack of flyers in her bag, and she began handing them out. No one refused, no one bothered to see if Vega minded. As for the frontrunner, he stood alone in the middle of the floor, mesmerized like everyone else, but not enough to move closer. He should have been incensed that Reason had stolen his moment. He should have grabbed a mic and made a speech to bring the guests back to political reality. He should have called for eight or ten of the staff to cart the hulk downstairs and toss him into the parking lot. Thank God Bob hadn't arrived yet, lest he be sucked into this Wilder love affair.

But Bob *was* here. When and how he'd arrived with no one noticing was understandable, considering the attention lavished on Reason. Bob remained oblivious to his competition, engrossed instead in the high-end spread of cheeses and pâtés the club had prepared to assure Vega's chums maintained the style to which they were accustomed. And he'd finally found those crackers.

Patsy, and the ball, were—thankfully—absent, or maybe just stuck at the club entrance, still trying to figure a way to bounce up the stairs.

Gray looked into a dark corner to see Reverend Hand, just waiting, just watching. He gave no gestures, no signals to the monster, but merely observed, his eyes half-closed as if in a trance.

Reason offered a high-pitched monotone about peace and community that was essentially meaningless and sounded to Gray like an alien broadcast to the people of earth. But the giant stopped in mid-sentence and jerked his head up. "You have heard enough. It is time for me to leave," he said.

With that, L'aura, Hand and he walked single-file out to the stairwell. Reason turned and said, "Consider our way, and join us." When he turned back, he was so close to the doorjamb he could not avoid crashing into it again, and this time bits of costly trim splintered off and fluttered to the floor.

As quickly as they'd been spellbound, the guests and staff went back to their pre-Reason activities. In seconds the club filled with the sounds of tinkling glass and silverware, gossipy conversation and the obnoxiously loud laughter of successful businesspeople.

Gray looked out the club's windows to watch the entourage

walk out to the parking lot. It dawned on him that he hadn't been affected like the others.

Breeze walked back and took her place on the barstool.

"Well," she said, "I don't really understand what people see in him."

Gray let out the breath he'd been holding since the group broke up. She too was unaffected by whatever magic the monster used to reduce the crowd to that zombie state. "You had me worried," he said.

She smiled. "He's quite a specimen, though. But it takes more than that to be successful in politics." She touched his shoulder. Breeze's magic definitely held more power. Through Gray's jacket, through his shirt and t-shirt, from the point of his shoulder through every cell and atom of his body, a warm feeling surged, putting him at ease again, helping him forget his troubles with L'aura and the campaign. Reason could never do that.

He had an idea.

Before he could polish it in his mind, though, Vega headed over. He'd been released from Reason's hypnosis and captured again by Breeze's. But as soon as he arrived, a group of men on the opposite side of the room beckoned to him. He turned to Breeze, a look of dread across the conceited topography of his face. "I've got to go. A strategy session." Gray watched him hustle across the floor, realizing then that Vega belonged here as much as he, which was not at all, but Vega had found a way to stay: as toady to the powerful.

A strategy session? More like someone had pushed the panic button after Reason's display of personal magnetism. The door to a side room opened and Vega slithered through. Gray imagined the rest: the yacht club junta sunk into leather chairs, exclusive Oxfords atop exclusive ottomans, sitting in front of a fireplace and downing twenty-year-old booze as a piece of fluff in a bunny leotard slipped hors d'oeuvres onto their waiting tongues like a priest delivering the Eucharist. They'd be anxious, upset that their hand-picked lackey hadn't stood up to the giant. He had let the beast and his raw, populist appeal dominate the room.

His backers would do the talking and Vega the umm-hmming. He would have a distinct look of subservience on his face. They'd tell Vega to start kicking Reason's ass or they'd boot his back to the poor side of town, which was the rest of it outside Island Retreat as far as they were concerned. They'd remind him of all the cronies they'd called in to finance him through Election Day—Vega didn't have to knock on doors or send out pleas for cash, although Gray surmised he'd have to sit through a few miserable coffees on the Island, where the gentry could congratulate themselves on finally backing a minority, even though under his olive skin, where it mattered, Vega was as corrupt, scheming, deceitful, and therefore as white, as any of them. If he played the game right, Vega could say he'd crossed the bridge to Island Retreat in style. If he were elected mayor they might even let him live there.

Breeze continued to watch the door to the room while Gray tried to sound interesting, but she was not listening. She stood and tugged at the hem of her dress to cover another millimeter of her glamorous thighs. She continued to straighten as Vega emerged from the penalty box. Damn! He'd probably come right back over and they'd be stuck for another half hour while he salivated over her.

He glared at Gray, but instead went in the opposite direction, toward the throng of business types avoiding Bob.

Then an old man—frighteningly old—vulture-necked and spotted with age, came out of the room and gestured to Gray, who pointed first to Breeze—for why would they want to talk to him—and when the ancient one shook his head, no, he pointed to himself. A single nod for yes, and Gray looked to her for permission.

The man had to be part of the cabal that had controlled Grand River's affairs for decades. Gray had heard the stories of political puppetmasters during his tenure at city hall—mountains of cash and virtually every pol in the city on the take—but no one had ever offered definitive proof. Now here, perhaps, the truth beckoned, clutching the doorframe as if holding on to life itself. Gray took a step and then turned back to Breeze.

"Will you excuse me my dear?" he said.

Agents of Change

Gray had never really considered running for office. Not that he didn't have the desire or think himself capable. Patient, level-headed, more concerned with the general welfare than the prestige of rank, he would make an exemplary mayor, congressman, senator, what have you. He would be diligent and understanding, eschewing partisanship for the rare atmosphere of collaboration, all for the benefit of his constituency. Nor would he surrender to special interests or fall for the deceits and largesse of lobbyists. He was, as he liked to remind himself several times a day, an intelligent person, above the petty games and duplicities of politics, and therefore would be targeted by the lesser, evil competition that always opts for smear tactics during a campaign, spreading their lies and false news about a worthier opponent. He would never lower himself to their level, but knew the electorate craved such dirt. And they would eventually accept the slurs as gospel and send him to defeat. It was safer, he rationalized, to participate as he always had, from the sidelines. But when the old man summoned him, he couldn't help but allow his thoughts to wander into the meadow of candidacy. The forces that controlled elections in this town, and to which this dinosaur obviously held membership, practiced vigilance in the search for talent capable of leading, and therefore pacifying the masses. They must have heard of him, of his work within the failed Boren campaigns. They had noticed, been alerted somehow. Breeze? The gears of the meritocracy for which they stood must have ground into motion, and without his knowing they had evaluated him, analyzed his character, and decided that yes, Gray Davenport would be a fine addition to their stable of political thoroughbreds.

He always knew it would happen this way.

They had dismissed Vega like a disciplined schoolboy. Could it be they had fired their candidate and wanted Gray as an emergency replacement? Only three months remained until Primary Day. The task would be difficult, almost unheard of, but with their financial guns and connections he could do it.

Okay, Gray, get a grip. Even in a dream world, candidates stayed in the race with far more baggage than Vega. His shortcoming tonight was bad, but not something that couldn't be overcome. What then, did the power brokers want Gray for?

He ran through the slate of offices to be contested in June. The council races all were full. City clerk and manager had strong, popular incumbents. An open seat on the school board remained—not the best starting point for a man with aspirations—but the lone candidate thus far was a soccer coach who'd come in third in the same race two years ago. That must be it.

He took a mental photo of the bar for his personal memoir before he went into the room: the elites he was soon to join sipped and chatted in groups of threes and fours; Vega strained to regain his stature in the eyes of his cronies; Bob stood by the buffet, disoriented by the empty tray in front of him as he waited for a staffer to replenish the nosh. And Breeze. She smiled at him, as though she understood the future that awaited. "Take your time," she said, and held up her glass to toast him as he followed the old man.

Inside the paneled cloister another old man waited. They sat him in calfskin and shut the door to the proceedings. The waitress bunny Gray had imagined stood in a corner, ready to satisfy.

"I am Mr. Fox," said one, taking a seat across from him. He looked eighty, but nodded in deference to the other, who appeared even older. "And this is Mr. Zinger. We are what you might call agents of change."

Gray sat forward in the big chair. He was so ready for change.

Fox gestured to the waitress, and she took three snifters from a cabinet, poured from a bottle of cognac, and served. Zinger pulled panatelas from a humidor and offered them around. The girl lit each one, bending sharply so the recipient had a view of her cleavage and the others of the seamed stockings clinging to her thighs. When she was done, Fox slapped her lightly on the backside and she went out to the crowd. "Life should always be such a pleasure," he said, and then took a long, contented draw. The unspoken details of that pleasure hung in the air like exhaled smoke.

The ubiquity of leather and exotic wood in this room surpassed that of outside. Gray envisioned a swath of land as seen from the air, clear cut of its forest, stripped to the soil; a phalanx of dead cattle laid side by side—all to provide these men something nice to look at. He inhaled the tobacco smoke and the cognac's vapors, and found both dizzying. Or did his mind spin from the portent of the moment? His anxiousness might kill whatever offer these men had in mind, so he rested the cigar and slid the drink away, clasping his hands together in prayer to receive their benediction. "How can I help you gentlemen?"

Fox began. "Not everyone in Island Retreat is as enamored with Mr. Vega as the people outside this room would like you to believe. Mr. Zinger and I are not convinced he would be the best man to lead this city through its crises. And we represent a significant number of people who feel the same way."

Oh God! They did want him for mayor.

"But as none of the other candidates in the race has the proper qualities for leadership, we must take steps to preclude an even more disappointing outcome in June, specifically Mr. Wilder's victory."

Gray began to imagine campaign posters and slogans: red, white, and Gray would hang on walls and beam from television screens. "So you want me—"

Fox put his hand up to silence the interruption, and Zinger added a look that made it clear additional outbursts wouldn't be tolerated. No wonder Vega had come out of the room so downcast.

"You saw the spectacle of Mr. Wilder earlier. We can't abide the idea of someone like that as mayor. But we know little about him."

The question begged: Someone like...*what?* Perhaps they suspected what he suspected.

"We wish to retain you to conduct an investigation."

Gray exhaled slowly. All they wanted was to hire him to tail the giant, like a cheap P.I. in a bad detective caper? Pop went the dream of political glory. But then, this was what he'd considered doing himself since seeing Reason at the fundraiser.

A nod from Zinger indicated he could speak.

"Why me?"

Fox sipped his drink and exhaled heavily, as though already bored with Gray's presence. "A fair question. Sad as it may be to say, you are the most qualified to do this job for us. You know as much about Grand River politics as anyone. And we understand your spouse has a position of prominence within their organization."

"Yes, but—" He almost mentioned that he'd been exiled from her world, but that revelation could kill the deal.

"And surely you noticed that Mr. Wilder had some strange hold over nearly everyone in the room, with the exception of yourself and that lovely woman you've been fawning over. And, of course, us."

"So you want me to—"

"Infiltrate," Fox continued. "Give us his weaknesses. It should be a simple matter."

"You do know that I'm working for Bob Boren."

"And we also know that you have yet to be compensated for your fine work." Zinger pulled a check from his jacket pocket. Gray saw zeroes—four of them, all in front of the decimal point. Enough to take care of his clothing, his housing, car and other financial woes, and present himself to Breeze in a fashion that reflected the confidence she seemed to have in him.

"You can terminate the charade of that employment," Zinger said. "And it would make the job easier, we imagine, if your wife did not view you as a threat."

The man had no idea.

"So in essence," Gray said, "I would be working for Mr. Vega."

"No, you would be working for us."

"Wait a minute. Who are you? Or should I say, what do you represent? I've been involved in Grand River's politics for a long time and I've never heard your names mentioned."

The old men stared with disdain at the audacity of the questions. Fox shook his head. They had given him all the information he would receive.

"Take the money, my boy," Zinger said. The check wavered a little in the old man's hand until Gray reached over to snatch it. The check began shaking again. It was made out to him and signed with the stamp of someone else's name, probably an accountant. He folded it as carefully as he could and slipped it into his jacket.

They raised their glasses and nodded at him to do the same. In this world was a toast the same as a handshake? A contract? He'd already heard more than he could walk away from. If he gave the check back and turned them down, they might call in muscle. Gray downed the last of his cognac and noticed his vision becoming blurred. He felt bones envelop his hands, his wrist moving up and down. And then he was alone in the chair.

Gray walked out of the room spinning now on three axes—smoke, drink and largesse—unsure of what, exactly, he had agreed to, but understanding he'd been elected to something after all. He saw Breeze still at the bar, surrounded again by a group of leaning, leering suits. Her auburn skin shone under the muted lighting of the club. What would she say to this? If he left Bob's campaign, would he fall from her graces? He had to talk to her.

"So what was it about?" she asked when she extricated herself from the suitors.

"Let's get out of here and go to dinner. I can't discuss it here."

"Is it that big?"

"Monstrous."

"Let me get my purse. I know a place where we can talk without being disturbed. I'll give you directions."

Original Sins

Breeze moistened the point of her serviette in Gray's water glass and aimed it at the droplet of Bordeaux on his lapel. "Come toward me," she exhaled, words he had a few nights ago hardly dared imagine her saying. But then the reality check: "I think I can get it before it sets."

"Clumsy of me, really." Gray did his best Cary Grant and fought to keep his eyes on her hand and not, from this better vantage point, welded to her cleavage. In that respect the spill was a fortunate accident. And what was one more insult to this suit, which had endured so much abuse in the last few days? At least no one could see under the table, where he had secreted his off-color wingtips from the eyes of the restaurant's patrons.

Gray couldn't decide if their waiter was being helpful or a smartass. "Another glass of wine, monsieur? A white this time, perhaps?" This place was so French he assumed the latter. Breeze ordered the sole. He opted for the duck breast, as much to drop a hint as to make sure he got some kind of boob, in case things didn't work out later. Breeze raised an eyebrow.

Better to deflect that subject. "I've driven by here a hundred times," Gray said, "but I've never been inside. What a jewel. I'll bet not many people in Grand River know it's here."

Breeze's half-smile gave the lie to that assessment. Frenchy's customers packed the house, and several parties waited near the entrance. They'd braved the rough neighborhood, a shantytown of neglected apartments and suspicious bars, and the sex shop next door, for a chance at a table. He'd meant to say that the city's elite would never bother with a restaurant not located downtown or at the yacht club, no matter how good the cuisine. "I think I know what you mean," she said. "To be honest, most of the customers come from outside the city."

It should have been obvious. The diners weren't white and wealthy. An Asian couple with three girls, all with matching bobbed haircuts, sat at the next table. Across from them an black man and white woman conversed. Farther down sat an older man and woman—he in an ascot and she in a black hat with an ostrich plume. And on every face, he saw a satisfaction that said by being here, these people knew something the rest of the world didn't: a gram of knowledge that no amount of wealth could purchase or reproduce. In the corner of the room, hiding behind a menu, a fellow ate at a table by himself. Gray waited for his slick of black hair to look up to confirm he had the look too, but the man focused on his Blackberry. Some people just don't know how to enjoy anything. Everyone else dined at ease, not at all concerned with who might be watching them, or how they might look. Gray relaxed. He tilted his chin forward and cracked a little smile, hoping it would appear self-assured so he might fit in with this new community. Unconsciously, he let his brown foot slide from beneath the long tablecloth.

Where had this place been hiding? Here was intelligent life, right alongside the supposedly advanced culture in which he'd existed, but it had gone undetected, broadcasting its position on a frequency the Grand River glitterati had never bothered to monitor. It was the kind of location L'aura, she of her own planet, might like to visit. For a second Gray envisioned her across from him, happily perusing the menu.

But enough of his wife. She'd made her choice. Here was Breeze, guiding him into a world whose purpose seemed to be to delight his senses. Her body, this food, her face. A pleasure now and what pleasures sure to come later. She'd exploded upon him like a meteor. Science would tell him she was not that different from any other woman, or any other person, that her atoms were arranged only slightly differently, yet it was that subtle rearrangement that had sent his own molecular structure into chaos. Physics be damned. In comparison to the women he'd known, she was completely alien, and he knew the chance the two of them could create a life together remained infinitely small. Still, she must have traveled the cosmos to get here, to be in that seat across from him.

She took a sip of her wine. Her eyes said she was ready to talk, to reveal her origins and desires, to get past the campaign chatter that had dominated their conversations until now. He needed more time to build up the nerve to tell her about the check and the mysterious old men, whose names, he had realized on the drive over, might be pseudonyms. He had decided to stick with Bob's campaign, however, lest he give her an excuse to quit his company, and was still working on the lie that would sound honest enough to keep her engaged in his affairs. How to explain what happened behind that menacing door?

"Where are you from?" he asked, expecting her to say something like Andromeda or the Virgo cluster. But she only said, Chicago, hardly galactic.

"Let's not waste time talking about me," Breeze said. "I want to know what you discussed in that room at the club. You said it was monstrous."

Deflect. Delay. "Did I say monstrous? It really wasn't that big. Almost not worth mentioning."

"It certainly seemed important when you asked me to dinner."

He pulled at the knot of his tie to loosen its grip. "I was worked up."

"What about?"

"You would have been angry too."

She stared at him. Another minute and she might leave him to finish dinner alone.

"It was about Bob," he said. "They wanted him to pay for the food he ate. They said he kept everyone else from enjoying the buffet."

Breeze's look said she didn't believe any of it. But her response let him slide. "No wonder. I might have called it monstrous too. Why couldn't you tell me there?"

Gray took a deep breath. "I wanted to get you away from there, away from the hordes of men that seem to be everywhere you go. I wanted to talk to you alone." He finished the rest of his wine in a gulp. "I'm sorry," he said.

"Sorry for what?"

Yes, what? Sorry he had asked a beautiful woman to dinner? He should feel sorry for feeling sorry, and he almost said that. Instead he tried to shift the topic: "Tell me about yourself."

Breeze looked as though debating whether to answer.

"You're so mysterious," he said.

"All right." For the first time since he'd met her she looked away, down at the top of the little table. She wrapped her fingers around the stem of her glass. "My father was a rich white man who lived in Barrington Hills. My mother was the black maid. I'm the bastard child."

Gray looked at the table as well. "I shouldn't have asked."

"Fortunately, my old man felt responsible."

"You don't have to—"

"The best prep schools, private high school, Loyola. Anything so his wife wouldn't have to see me."

"I didn't mean to pry," he said. "Just curious how someone so beautiful pops up in Grand River like out of nowhere." She was beautiful too. Saying so was not as much a come-on as a fact that needed to be entered into the record. He studied her as he waited for a response. There had to be a flaw in this woman. No one could be this perfect. He adjusted his eyes, searched for a blemish, a mole, a freckle even. But nothing. He realized the flaw, if he found one, would be his for perceiving it.

She sat a little straighter and touched her fingers to the hollow of her neck, as though surprised to hear his compliment. Beautiful, he'd said. He was officially flirting now, and the thought relaxed him, despite his questions having made Breeze uncomfortable. Whatever else happened he could at least say he played his role right for a few minutes.

"You wanted to know. You would have found out eventually," she said.

Eventually was a good sign. It portended a future.

"Now it's your turn," Breeze said.

Gray took another breath, ready to embellish his life with survival and triumph. A childhood on the desolate outskirts of San Bernardino would not impress. Nor, he suspected, would contrived roots in some tony seaside suburb or other bastion of easy life. Now that he knew about her, he suspected she would respect only the most unprivileged of beginnings, a mind-blowing poverty in the slums of L.A. that had been overcome by his supreme intelligence and effort, and related humbly. This was the version to which she would respond. She would drink in so hard a life like a well-aged wine, and it would excite her senses, touch her at every level—human, mother, little girl—whatever it took to gain her sympathy, her passion, enough to pique her interest, to make her see him as a fellow survivor and a budding god, and induce her to beg him for sex later that night. Sex—the possibility of sex, however remote—he saw as the foundation for every male endeavor. The making of money, the acquisition of power and knowledge: all have their basis in the belief someone will notice, be attracted, stimulated enough to hop into bed. Even men's more ridiculous pursuits—professional skateboarding, cheese rolling, NASCAR—have at their core the sentiment, "Look at me. I'm a man. A stupid man, maybe, but I'm willing to make a fool of myself if it will entice you."

He began: "I was born in—"

"No, not that," she said. "I mean the campaign. Tell me how we're going to win it."

She was still all about the campaign. But if Gray's theories were correct, he need not be discouraged. It would just take a little adjustment. If she wanted politics, he would deliver. If he could make up an entire childhood on the spot, surely he could fake the details of his unfinished campaign strategy.

"We have to get Reason out of the race," he said.

"Really?"

Of course! He could satisfy his benefactors and keep Breeze involved. "Wilder's the wild card," he said. "Bob and Vega are poles apart. Voters will choose one or the other. There's no middle ground. But Reason steals votes from both of them. And I have my suspicions about him."

"You mean the effect he seems to have over people?"

"And more."

"The way he looks like his body parts don't match?"

"You've noticed too. Thank God. I thought I was the only one."

As dinner arrived, they compared notes. Each had now seen the giant up close, had seen the anomalies that others ignored. "But how can we prove anything?" she asked.

"We have to get to him when he doesn't have his public face on. We have to go to where he lives."

"I've heard it's an old mansion out by the abandoned landfill. It's a pretty rough part of town."

Naturally.

He gazed at her perfect skin for a few seconds. The clatter of dishes in the kitchen brought him back to reality. "Then that's where I'll go," he said.

"Despite the danger?"

Danger? Monterey Jack laughs at danger. He allows nothing to stand in the way of his desires and goals. He will defeat Reason and take more of the old men's money. And when the time comes, he will lasso Breeze around her waist and pull her in. She will fight, but it is a mockery. She wants him as much as he—

"What's the first step?" Breeze was not quite ready to be taken.

"Well, we can't just walk in the front door."

"What if we disguise ourselves?"

We? Awesome. They were a team now.

They walked out to the parking lot, past the sex shop, which fit into this neighborhood far better than Frenchy's. Gray glanced through the window to the racks of bedroom toys, lingerie, and leather. A section against the wall boasted old-fashioned triple-X videos.

Restaurant patrons zipped past the shop as though it wasn't there. How curious that those who don't wish to register such ugliness can block it from their minds. They just don't see it. Gray recognized the store as neither good nor bad, but an extension of a natural urge, commercialized for profit like everything else.

The shop's neon window sign alternately flashed "open," and then, "wide." The front door beckoned like a cheap streetwalker. He decided to take a chance.

"Want to check out a few titles?" he asked.

She exhaled slowly. Her breath blew like an island wind, and he could feel its heat on his neck. She looked up at the stars. "Oh, it's tempting," she said, "but we'd better call it a night."

Gray took her by the wrist and pulled her into the cramped aisles, and didn't let go, despite her protests, until they neared the DVDs. A man in a filthy military parka, holding a stack of jewel cases in his arms, watched them—her, actually—for a minute. He stared, salivated, placed his rentals on a table, and headed off to a shelf labeled "Boobalicious."

"Gray, I really don't think this is a good idea," Breeze said.

He realized his mistake, but couldn't back out now. Not yet. Even if he'd made the wrong choice he had to play it out long enough so it might appear to have been a kinky whim, instead of the desperate maneuver it was turning out to be.

He picked up a movie, "The Whip Whisperer," and put it back before she could see the title. He grabbed another, with a photo of a dominatrix holding the spike of her stiletto against a nude, supine, bondaged man's throat. "Make Him Sorry," read the title. Oh, how he was. Breeze saw it and giggled.

He'd wanted to appear spontaneous and sexy, but had come up looking sick. "Let's get out of here," he said, dropping his plan to suggest a nightcap at her place. Before they could leave, however, the scruffy doughboy came back, this time with a pen and scrap of paper.

"Honey—" he said to Breeze.

Deranged pervert. Gray started to move closer to the bum to protect his woman.

"Could I have your autograph?"

Breeze said, "Oh!" and then laughed. She winked at Gray as though willing to humor the man. Then she took the pen, thought for a moment, and scribbled something longer than just a signature.

He walked her to the Benz and stood by as she opened the door. "What did you write?" he asked.

"Nothing, really. But I'm sure it made his night."

Whatever she'd written, it was more than Gray would get. No sexy movie. No sex, only the intimation that this might be a woman who once had engaged in sex as a profession. Still, by his standards, a success. Breeze took his hand to shake, but he raised it, Cary Grant-like, to his lips. When the door to the car closed and she started the engine, Gray saw her smile and bring her fingers to her face to cover it. She looked as though she were laughing.

He'd assumed the evening would have lasted a little longer, and he'd rather do anything besides head back to that motel room on the edge of the city's abyss. Why not another glass of wine at the bar? When her car coasted out of sight he walked back to Frenchy's. The dark-haired man he'd noticed before stood by his table, turned away so his face remained obscured, and when Gray came through the door, he headed for the men's room.

As he teetered on the stool at the end of the bar—and once he got the images of Breeze's body out of his mind, which didn't happen until his second glass—he reviewed the video of the evening in his head. She had a perfect response for everything he asked and tried. Was he that obvious?

Or was she so practiced, so experienced with men, especially naïve men like him, that she could treat them like the toys they were? Even the supposedly soul-baring revelation of her background might have been an act designed to gain his confidence, or so he now imagined. He'd been prepared to lie, why not her?

And perhaps it was Gray's imagination as well, but he never saw the dark-haired man come back out of the men's room for the hour or so he sat at the bar. Had he slipped out through the bathroom window? Damn if he didn't look a lot like Elvis Vega, at least from the angles he'd observed, but how could the slickster have wound up in the same restaurant? He imagined a scenario in which Fox and Zinger's mistrust had pushed them to order their lackey to spy on their spy, to make sure Gray wasn't thinking of some form of double-cross, but surely the old boys' tongue lashing had relegated Vega to something other than following lowly Gray around.

The Search for Flesh

It wasn't like he didn't know how to do it, how to immerse himself in the darkest regions of cyberspace to search for a dose of flesh; the babe—okay, babes—of the hour who made it possible to take his mind off the strains of life with L'aura, and the seemingly eternal delay until their next quarterly sex rendezvous. In fact, since she'd cut him off from regular contact a year ago he'd become quite good at locating whatever fetish popped into his head: naughty nurses, busty Asians, horny housewives. But nowhere in that sex crusade did he recall seeing a woman who quite resembled Breeze. Surely he would have remembered that face, that bod.

As soon as Gray got back to the room at the Star, he opened his laptop to access the Internet—with a fantasy of her in his head and the right search terms he would find out who this Breeze Wellington really was. The answers always seemed to be available by turning inward, hunching over the monitor, shutting out the world in an effort to access it, conducting his investigation the way he conducted his life—virtually. Of course he had forgotten his room was broadband-free, wired only for cable TV.

He weighed his prurience against Randy's. The manager had the link to cyberspace, but Gray couldn't imagine surfing for a porn star in the man's presence. Still, the light in the motel office burned brightly despite the late hour, and the lure of her mystique was nearly as strong as that of her body's. Computer in hand he trudged to the door, which opened before he had a chance to knock.

"It's about time you got here," Randy said.

"I didn't know I was expected."

"Don't be coy. I knew a working stiff like you would need the Internet eventually."

Gray didn't like it when anyone anticipated his moves, preferring to be thought an enigma, the way he saw himself. And he didn't care to have Randy refer to any part of him as "stiff," even his regimen. But he stepped into the Bates Motel décor of this man's apartment, past the counter that segregated the transient world from this one of clean, but unnerving permanence. Tables and chairs looked suspicious, wobbling slightly without being sat on. The bric-a-brac appeared anxious too, as though about to launch at him. Corners lurked, obligingly dark and musty.

He knew Randy would have questions, but the alternative would have him drive back to downtown and try to find an all-night Starbucks with Wi-Fi.

"Drink?"

One more pour after the bottle's worth at Frenchy's might make him pliable. "Do you have coffee?" he said.

There was a carafe next to the ledger, the motor oil it contained no doubt solidifying since morning.

"Why don't I make a fresh pot?" Randy offered. "I could use some too. It might be a long night."

Who was the enigma now? Perhaps Randy was a fan of late-night movies, but his comment smacked of ulterior motives. Gray opened the laptop and tried to communicate through body language that this visit was all business. A poor choice considering his host seemed so into bodies.

"You're tense," Randy said. "I could massage your shoulders while you work."

"I don't think—"

"Now don't get the wrong idea. I'm a licensed masseur."

Gray didn't know if that was good news or bad, only that his mind had been filled with wrong ideas since before dinner. "All right then," he said. "Maybe for a minute or two."

Randy had Gray's jacket off and was kneading flesh before he could protest again. Strands of muscle disintegrated under those fingers, and the accompanying nerves radioed waves of relaxation throughout his body that triggered something like arousal. From a man's hands? And now he was going to search the Internet for a porn star…

He opened the browser, simultaneously thinking of search terms and explanations for when Randy asked him what he was looking for. After all, his host had no clue about Breeze, and Gray decided to explain that she was part of the opposition and that he needed information to use against her. He entered "Breeze Wellington" and "porn," but aside from a few references to a New Zealand radio station, found nothing.

He widened the search—just "Breeze" and "porn," which produced nearly a million returns. Crystal Breeze, Wendy Breeze, Amanda Breeze, all kinds of decadent siroccos blew in. Could she have been one of them? Gray itched to follow the links, but not with Randy, who hadn't said a word while he surfed, watching over his shoulder.

"I'll take that coffee now, if you don't mind," Gray said.

"Of course. What do you want in it?"

His chance for privacy. "A little milk, and, oh, I really like a dash of cinnamon if you have it."

"I'll have to check the cupboard," Randy said.

Gray clicked through on Crystal Breeze, but her skin was far too pale. He heard Randy rummaging in the next room. Quickly to Wendy Breeze, who was too dark. Then Amanda. The pictures resolved small and blurry, and dated from at least a decade ago, although the woman in the shots had the tone and proportions to be a possibility. Then he remembered; the pervert in the porn shop had called her Honey. He'd thought it a term of endearment, of a depraved sort. But maybe he was calling her by name.

Gray entered "Honey Wellington." One return tantalized; a video site that advertised a flick as "Honey and friends find that an all-girls school doesn't mean a lack of..." But that was all. No picture, and the vid listed as discontinued. A couple of the other results offered more dead links from years past.

His time to try another reference ran out as Randy jogged back with a red shaker. "I had cinnamon after all. What a surprise," he said. Gray closed the laptop as Randy placed the cup at his elbow. The brew smelled better than any coffee he remembered having in recent days.

"Give up on your search so soon?" Randy asked.

"I found what I was looking for," Gray said. Did it make any difference if Breeze merely played the sexpot or actually was one? He felt all women did it to some extent—their bodies serving as collateral in a chauvinistic barter system. And Gray believed himself enough of a liberated man to understand that it was okay, commendable even, for a woman to degrade herself in porn to beat that system. If Breeze had dabbled in the genre, he wouldn't hold it against her. Whatever she'd done must have been long past and certainly would have been understandable considering her difficult psychology and male stiffening abilities. He decided not to let it matter. How enlightened.

Randy put on some music. The hip-hop throbbed and would have disturbed anyone trying to sleep for a half-dozen rooms in any direction, and it kept Gray from concentrating, which was all he wanted to do on the clues to Breeze he'd found. He folded the laptop, tucked it under his arm, and eyed the front door.

Abruptly, the music changed. Randy mixed in Brubeck and Ella Fitzgerald. Breeze music, Gray surmised. He sat back in the chair, thinking Randy might continue the massage, and that he would allow it for a few minutes more. But his host jogged into the kitchen again, returning this time with two glasses of wine. "Carmenère," he said. "From Chile. You have to try this."

"Just a sip," Gray said. But the varietal impressed; he found it as interesting as the wines he'd had at the restaurant and accepted a refill from Randy before he realized he'd finished the first glass. The man had taste. A thought worked its way through the haze brought on by an evening of alcohol and Breeze—was Randy hitting on him?

It would be poetic, sexual justice. He had made Breeze the object of his desire, leering and looking, peppering his comments with innuendo throughout their dinner. And here stood Randy, doing the same to him. If he found his host's advances laughable, then what did Breeze think of his a few hours ago? Never mind gender expectations, this whole business of desire suddenly seemed inane. Did looks count for that much? A body was a body. Attractiveness might be an illusion, enhanced by hormones running wild. Was Breeze really as beautiful as he believed, or was his urge just a physical process over which he had little control? Yes, he thought. And yes. Or was it driven by something else, a desire to prove himself to L'aura? Maybe all of it was true, in which case he had no hope of subduing his urges.

Gray postponed further contemplation of those issues until tomorrow. For the moment he didn't mind the attention. He moved across the room, plopped himself into Randy's plush easy chair, and held the glass out for more of the Chilean elixir. "Your place is very comfortable," he said. Immediately he thought his comment too encouraging.

Randy looked as though he wanted to squeeze in next to Gray, but the neutron was not so desperate as to bond with this stray particle. He spread himself as best he could to fill the chair. Randy moved to a loveseat and sat to the side, keeping possibilities open.

Gray would talk at least, and he so wanted to share his problems with someone. Randy offered a sympathetic, if a bit familiar presence, and he had good wine. "There's this woman," Gray started. "I'm sure you don't want to hear about this."

"Your wife," Randy said.

"My wife is history."

"So that makes you available."

"Don't read too much into it," Gray said.

"But I take it you're looking?"

"I wasn't. More like I was found. She walked through the door of my life and I've been swinging from the hinges ever since."

"Seriously? Pretty melodramatic…and a horrible metaphor. She's the one you were Googling?"

"Yeah. She even makes my syntax go out of control."

"And she's done porn."

"Maybe. It could have been a case of mistaken identity. There was a guy who seemed to recognize her, but he never really looked at her face."

"Undressing her with his eyes. And now you want to undress her with your computer."

Maybe so. Okay, obviously so. He was glad he'd stopped the search. He would wait for consummation and let his anticipation build. This way he could still look forward to that exquisite moment when she unzipped herself for him, when he undid her bra hooks and her breasts spilled into his waiting, sweaty palms. Even at this late hour, under the influence of so much alcohol and, with Randy sitting across from him now draped over the loveseat in a Mata Hari recline, he felt something move, down there, and hoped his host hadn't seen it. He crossed his legs, but it only made the feeling more intense.

"Restless?" Randy asked.

"Exhausted. I think I'll go back to my room and take a shower before bed." But the Arctic waters would probably keep him awake for another hour or two. He realized how much he'd missed temperature. "You don't suppose I could take a shower here? I don't have hot water in my room."

"Why didn't you say something sooner, poor boy? Of course. You can sleep on the extra bed. It's more comfortable than the one in your unit."

Gray had begun the evening entertaining a fantasy that he'd get to sleep over, but Randy's place was not what he had in mind. And even the little joke he'd told himself that there wouldn't be much sleeping going on was coming true, since he doubted he would allow his eyes to close if he stayed here. Maybe he could wait until morning to shower when frigidity might not feel so bad. He pushed himself out of the chair. "I don't want to impose."

"You're not," Randy said. "You'll be much better off here. We can keep on talking… make it a slumber party. Girls shouldn't have all the fun. We boys have to stick together."

"All right," Gray said. As long as things didn't get too sticky.

Randy poured him another glass. Before Gray finished it the room began to fade. He thought he heard Randy say something about it being time for bed. Had he slipped something into the last drink? Gray didn't remember the rest of the conversation.

He woke up, fully dressed thank God, on top of the bed in his room. He didn't want to know how.

Iterum Vives

It had been his idea, and Breeze had gone along eagerly, but as they parked their bicycles outside the gate to the crumbling mansion, Gray had doubts.

Who would believe this woman was a missionary? She wore the white shirt and dark slacks of the order, the thin, striped tie from the 1960s, the backpack, and even strapped her breasts flat—okay, sort of flat—against her body so as to appear less seductive, more devout. He'd suggested she wear a sweater over the top, despite the seventy-degree afternoon, but even that did little to mitigate the sexuality he feared would give them away to Reason and whoever else resided in the manse. She'd stuffed her hair—that tide of tresses that framed her face—under a man's wig, a helmet of hair suited to a live-with-mom engineer type. He hoped the package would be convincing, would snuff the lust she seemed to spark in everyone who met her, but in watching her precede him to the front door, and ogling the shift of her hips beneath the gabardine, he found himself more attracted than ever.

For his disguise, he felt justified going overboard. Reason had recognized him before, and for all he knew, L'aura lurked inside too, so he altered every aspect of his appearance. He wore the biggest pair of dark glasses he could find to cover his eyes and much of his nose. He sported a blond wig, with a mustache and goatee a few shades darker. If they asked he'd say he dyed up top, part of a Bleaching for Jesus campaign. He prayed no one would know that missionaries were mandated to be clean-shaven.

At least Reason's manor of gloom fit expectations. It oozed melancholy. It was a cliché of every haunted house Gray had seen in childhood. Shutters, where they remained, hung crooked from windows. Windows, like lazy eyes, hung crooked within their frames, as though the architect of the place, or the builders, or both, had been under the influence. The wrought iron gate through which they passed squealed and shuddered on cue.

The roof even sported a small belfry with a lightning rod on top. Gray scanned the sky for bats. He saw nothing, and instead caught a whiff of the chemical smell that seemed to surround Reason during the debate. It was not as strong as before, but his nose picked up a bit more rot this time. Breeze had mentioned the abandoned landfill nearby. Could be the stench originated from there and attached itself to whatever or whoever came in proximity. He made a note to shower later, to make sure it didn't stick to him, and of course, he'd have to tell Breeze to do the same, and he lost a few seconds over the idea of them doing it together.

But she had rung the bell, and someone creaked floorboards on the way to answer. The footfalls did not sound like Reason's clomps; they belonged to someone lighter. Gray took a step away from the door and pulled at Breeze's elbow. He heard the slide of a peephole opening and closing, and then deadbolts sliding. The door hinges groaned.

A white-haired man peeked through the crack made by the barely open door. He was the one who had come to the condo minutes after L'aura threw Gray out. Hand, he remembered. Something Hand. The man opened the door wider, letting the sun hit his face to reveal skin as white as chalk, nearly reflective in its absence of color. Gray recognized this as the face of death.

"Yes?" The man licked his lips.

Gray pulled a weathered book from his backpack. He held his hand over the cover to hide the fact that it was an old cookbook of Randy's—Gray had managed to take a room in the only motel in town that didn't keep Bibles in the nightstands.

"Hello, sir," he said. "My name is Gary. And this is… this is, um, Brad."

"What do you want?"

"We're here to seek the truth."

"I thought you people always brought your truth with you."

"Right," Gray said. "That's right."

"We're here to *share* the truth," Breeze said. She'd lowered her voice to sound mannish, but there was no mistaking her tropical tone. The man's eyes ran over her like a body scanner.

"Why call on me? Do you know that I am a reverend, a man of the word? You have come to a house of faith and miracles."

Breeze smiled at him. "We came to teach," she said. "But we will stay to learn."

"I am the Reverend Hand," he said, still licking. He raised a palm to welcome them.

Gray played along. "Is this the house of Reason?"

"Reason can be found here, yes. Please come in."

Whatever the outside of the house had portended, the inside refuted. Contemporary furniture—plush sofas in pastels of blue and green—lined one wall of the great room. Gray hated them for blaring such color. A huge flatscreen television, seventy-two inches at least, showed a college football game and dominated the opposite wall, and a bar that rivaled the display at Island Retreat spanned the distance between them. Reverend Hand's religion, apparently, was consumerism.

But for all the deference to the bourgeois in this room, what lay beyond hinted at the repulsive. The smell that they thought had emanated from the old dump had grown stronger. In fact, Gray's talented nose told him it originated here, in the house. He could barely breathe for the stench. He imagined someone had mixed rotted vegetables in discarded bath water and left them in the sun. Breeze smelled it too, although her diminutive nose seemed able to handle the reek more capably.

Hand offered them drinks. Gray declined, fearing the man might try to expose them by getting them to imbibe alcohol. But Breeze opted for a martini and he said nothing. Hand prepared the cocktail with the flair of a bartender at a Vegas casino. He made one for himself and brought both to where she sat—on the blue sofa—and slid in next to her.

"It's such a pleasure to have guests who share an interest in ecumenical matters. It's so rare in this city," he said.

"Reverend Hand," Breeze said. "Where is your church?"

He clasped his hands together and looked skyward. Gray followed his eyes to the ceiling and noticed a pattern of cracks in the plaster. Perhaps Reason lived in a room above them and his weight had strained the joists.

"My church is here," Hand said, gesturing to the furniture like a game show moll. "In this place. But it is not a temple you would recognize."

No doubt he'd been booted from whatever congregation had been unlucky enough to host him. Gray ran through the probable causes: embezzlement, blasphemy, pedophilia, just plain sexual impropriety. The Reverend nudged a bit closer to Breeze.

"This house is a church?" Gray asked. He stifled a laugh. The place did have pew.

"You misunderstand, my son. I'm not speaking of a church made of bricks and wood. You will see no false icons or altar here. My domain is of the body."

"All bodies? Can anyone participate in this church, or just the ones you choose?" Gray frowned as Hand continued to inch closer to Breeze. Perhaps she'd become so used to men's advances that she didn't notice him encroaching on her personal space. But Gray had. If the Rev touched her, Monterey Jack might have to get tough. Monterey Jack would have no reservations about protecting what was his, even to the point of roughing up a clergyman—if Hand really was one.

"I don't think you're ready to know that," Hand said.

"Am I?" Even Breeze's most sincere questions had a sexuality about them, and Hand's tongue finally stopped massaging his lips, only to jut out a half-inch, an epiglottal erection of sorts.

"Perhaps," the Reverend said.

From down the hall, a series of thumps, like someone trying to move a refrigerator. It had to be Reason and his size twenty-threes slamming the floorboards, or maybe his head smacking what remained of the doorframes in this house. The giant stopped at the entrance to the great room, and looked toward Hand, as if for guidance. Gray inhaled deeply, hoping to sense if the monster was the origin of the odor, but the smell was so pervasive he could no longer tell from which direction it came.

"We have guests," Hand said.

Reason leaned against the wall. He appeared worn out from a day of campaigning. He noticed the visitors, and went into his standard delivery, although it lacked the shrieking timbre of his typical outbursts. "Welcome, my friends. So glad you could be here..." He sounded exhausted, and by comparison to his usual self, almost human.

Breeze rose and approached him. "Mr. Wilder. It's an honor to meet you." She extended her hand toward his leathered, catcher's mitt of an appendage. Reason took her fingers, but barely shook them.

"Join us, my son," Hand said. "These lovely people have come to talk with us about the spirit."

Son?

Reason said, "Yes, sir." He shuffled to the green couch, turned, and let his mass fall into the cushion. When he hit the surface, he went down so far that Gray fulcrumed up, popping up an inch or two above his seat. As he stabilized, Gray at last sensed the odor of the house was concentrated on the giant's body.

He blurted out: "That cologne; it's so unusual. What do you call it?"

Reason sat back as if in surprise. "I use no scents," he said. "I am a natural man."

"And quite a man," Breeze spoke to cover Gray's miscue. "We heard you were running for mayor. An impressive man for an impressive job."

The compliment seemed to energize the monster. He sat up straighter, riveted his gaze on her, and went into his shtick: "Together we will do great things for this city."

The Reverend watched them as though anticipating a reaction. Did he expect them to move closer to Reason, to adopt the glassy-eyed pose his converts at the fundraiser and the yacht club had displayed?

"Tell us more," Gray said. He nodded at Breeze, signaling her to follow his lead.

"Yes. We want to help the city. How can we do it?" Breeze asked.

"Together," Reason said. "There is so much we can do."

"Yes, but what?"

"We will address the crime problem," Hand said. "We will lower taxes." The Reverend seemed perturbed they were not satisfied with Reason's answer.

Breeze pressed the point. "How?"

"Together," Reason said. "Do you not see?"

"Yes. Yes! It makes perfect sense," Gray said. "Right… Brad?"

"Of course," Breeze said. "Together. We must all work together and put our trust in Reason."

"Now you've got it," Gray said.

As he spoke, Gray felt the hair on his forearms rise, as though he'd experienced a rush of anxiety. But instead of straight up, the hairs seemed to be pulling toward Reason. It was as though the hulk had an electrical charge, and his magnetism had turned on full force in an effort to overcome their resistance to him. Gray knew Reason could not control him the way he seemed to dominate almost everyone else, but he would let the giant and Hand think so. For once his neutron-ness became a plus. He could absorb whatever power the monster could produce, his chargeless state serving as a black hole for the evil energy. It was all beginning to make sense.

And Breeze too. She was as immune as he, but in her case likely because her power was greater. He couldn't wait to find out. Between the two of them, they might drain Reason of his power.

As if reading his thoughts, Breeze slipped her hand to the knot of her tie and loosened it. She undid her top button and leaned forward, toward the monster. On any other woman this would have meant nothing. But she was Breeze. From that almost imperceptible opening such femininity radiated that no one could withstand its allure.

Gray began to sweat. Hand sat with his mouth agape. Reason stood from the couch, swaying like a redwood sawed at its base, holding for one last moment of dignity before letting go. "I must retire," the giant said, and he began to walk away.

Breeze dropped her faux baritone. "Where are you going?" she asked. The zephyr of her voice caressed the men in the room, rendering them speechless, and Reason stopped, the gentle wind clearly affecting him. He paused and put his hand against the wall for support. One more word might do it.

"Reason…"

The giant dipped to one knee and closed his eyes, letting his hair fall over his granite-like face. He looked ready to keel over.

She'd done it! She'd brought him down. They were the same height now, and in a few seconds, the giant would be on the floor, and Breeze would be towering over him, fists on hips, legs planted wide like the Wonder Woman she surely was. Her power of attraction proved greater than Reason's. Exponentially greater. Even bound up in the disguise, her charms had overpowered the big man's hypnotic abilities and rendered him impotent. Sex had trumped science—which was really no surprise to Gray, since it had always worked that way on him.

Gray and Reverend Hand both jumped from their seats and went to their respective fighters. But Breeze already attended to the giant. "I think he's fainted," she said.

Fools they were to dare match wits with the good guys. Gray considered warning them to be careful, lest he unleash her magic upon them again.

Hand braced himself and pushed on Reason's shoulder. "Help me stand him up," he said.

"Shouldn't we call paramedics? Or a doctor?" Breeze asked.

"He'll be fine. I just need to give him his—" The lip licking started again.

Gray and Breeze took the other side and lifted. The beast must have weighed four hundred pounds, and it took the three of them just to get his other foot far enough under him so he could stand. They spread those tree limb arms across Gray's and Hand's backs, and walked him down the hallway, to the caverns that made up the rest of the mansion. Breeze followed, voicing concern and encouragement. Reason's cool, sour breath was on Gray's neck, causing him to tear up as they trudged.

"We'll have to get him upstairs."

Hand had to be kidding.

They couldn't all fit into the stairwell at once. Gray and Hand went first, with the giant leaning on their shoulders. Thank God Reason had come to just enough to work his legs, and the size twenty-threes clomped in an agonizingly slow rhythm, accompanied by the squeaks and groans of the wooden steps. The passageway, unlike the great room, proved as macabre as Gray had hoped. The display up front must be just for show, for the media and the few guests who came by during the campaign, designed to portray this freak as an ordinary citizen, sharing the lifestyle of those he wished to represent. He knew all along it was hogwash and reveled in the realization that with every inch they traveled up this corridor, they were getting closer to solving Reason's mystery. And with each step, the stench that defined this house became stronger.

By the third story, the light from the great room had extinguished, and Gray could see no fixtures or switches that might illuminate their path. It was nearly pitch black. He remembered at last to take off his sunglasses, which helped, but night still dominated. At the top of the stairs, they took two more turns in the shadows, and then Hand reached for a knob. When the door cracked open, the light from a small window diffused into the hallway. But the smell from inside the room nearly overpowered them. Gray fell away and staggered to the far wall. Breeze covered her nose and mouth.

The Reverend eased Reason inside. Gray tried to assist, but Hand nudged him away while Reason stumbled forward, out of his view.

"Wait!" Breeze said. "We can still help."

Hand whirled and faced them, closing the door. "I will take care of Reason from here. He will be fine."

"Should we wait? What can we do?"

"You must leave." Hand's face took on an even more deathly pallor. His eyes were black in the dim light, and his tongue worked like a windshield wiper in a downpour, sending a spray of saliva onto Gray's brown shoes. "Follow the hallway back," he said. "And let yourselves out. I must attend to him now."

With that he shut the door, but not before Gray caught a glimpse of a Reason-sized tub, filled with greenish liquid. It did not look like bath water, but had a murky, foamy surface. At last, the source of the smell.

"We can't just leave them," Breeze said.

Gray took her hand. "We must. You heard him." He directed her back toward the great room, and was about to join her when he heard a loud splash from inside, as though someone—surely it was Reason—had fallen into that tub.

He pressed his ear against the door. Reverend Hand spoke, but he couldn't understand a word—the door must have been thicker than it looked. He listened harder, could make out syllables, but they weren't in English. It sounded like Latin, but since Gray had never spoken Latin, he couldn't be sure. A switch made contact and a whirring noise, like a small blender, pitched higher. Then came more splashing, more muffled chanting.

Gray turned to leave and join Breeze, but something big and metal moved. Then an arc of electricity crackled from inside the room, and Reverend Hand shouted, "Iterum vives!"

The lights went out in the rest of the house, leaving Gray in black again. He groped for the wall as he felt his way back to Breeze. He wanted to scream but didn't dare, wanted to run but feared he would stumble and alert Hand and Reason.

He made it down the stairs and to the end of the wall, hoping it meant the entrance to the great room. A girlish gasp—his—and the lights came back on. He was sweating, breathing hard. Breeze grabbed his hand. "Let's get out of here," she whispered, pulling him toward the front door.

They ran out past the gate, to the sidewalk and their bicycles. Wigs and fake facial hair and Randy's cookbook ejected as they escaped. When they unlocked their bikes from the telephone pole, Gray, still hyperventilating, said, "I know the secret. I know what Reason is!"

They pedaled out of the neighborhood, away from the landfill and the horrific smell, back toward the road where they'd met up and left their cars. They did not stop until they came to a traffic signal. Breeze turned to hear the explanation.

Gray said, "Now if only someone will believe it."

In the Doldrums

Like a change in the weather, gentle Breeze had disappeared. The cell phone number she'd given him rang on with no pickup and no voicemail to record Gray's anxiety. She stopped coming to meetings at Bob's. His emails bounced, reporting her as a fatal error, recipient unknown.

They'd pedaled back to their cars, and Gray delivered his theory with all the pomp and bluster of a right-wing blogger: Reason's bath was some kind of organic broth, a chemical concoction without which the giant couldn't continue. The blackout meant Reverend Hand had applied the electric charge necessary to rejuvenate and reanimate the monster, and it took so much voltage to power the eight-foot beast that Gray wouldn't have been surprised if the whole neighborhood had gone dark. And in that darkness he had found clarity; the light to expose Reason as undead. Like Frankenstein before him, Hand had found the secret to sparking life from lifeless tissue. He had infused it with the primordial, connected the spent lives of those who'd unknowingly donated their parts to the genesis of a single new life. He'd imbued the collection of excavated bones and flesh with enough energy to force them to live again.

The current was the key. Gray imagined Hand presiding over

the immense body as he brought it to life for the first time, high on a scaffold in the belfry, calling on thunderclouds to unleash their electricity. The lightning sizzled. The stolen heart jolted into rhythm. The body charged. Fingers and toes quivered. Arms and legs spasmed. Hand performed his magic, and Reason jerked with life. But the science, as Gray had witnessed, was imperfect. The mad reverend must have miscalculated somewhere, and poor Reason eventually ran down. Perhaps through some flaw in the arithmetic, the giant remained partly in the grip of the beyond, pulled back toward the grave by the spirits of the bodies Hand had robbed. That meant he had to find a solution to keep his experiment alive. Who knew how long it had taken him to concoct a remedy—maybe days or weeks of frantic mixing and matching potions, a desperate alchemy, until he hit on a combination that worked. And now, maybe once a week or month or so, he deep-fried Reason in that ancient, molecular soup—and the monster smelled like it.

And Gray surmised that since then the Rev had made another discovery, a by-product of his experiment—that the electricity with which he infused the monster created a polarity that attracted others to the monolith of his body, physically and psychically, as though Reason had become a giant ion. Hand must have pondered how he could use the beast's magnetism for his personal gain—never mind the pretensions of him being a man of the cloth. Gray believed preachers could be as greedy as anyone else. Televangelists made millions selling snake oil to the masses. Who could say whether the Reverend didn't harbor such desires? He'd been sneaking around with Gray's wife—and if he'd crossed that line, probably none of the other traditional clerical boundaries made much difference to him.

But Hand hadn't opted for the obvious. He didn't enroll Reason in the freak show of media attention, because as soon as he did, someone else, from the legitimate scientific community, would deduce his secret, reproduce the procedure, parade another Reason out in public. Sure, that had to be it. Reason One would soon become a forgotten prototype, and Reasons Two, Three, and beyond would take center stage, offering better programmability and function, and less of the stench since real scientists would figure a way to do without the chem-bath. Then what for Reason and Hand? A book tour? Stints at the county fair? The opening act for the Cable Guy?

No, Hand wanted more. He wanted power: real, lasting power, the kind that emanates from behind the scenes, safe from the public's lust for the minutiae of celebrity and personal lives. He wanted to pull the puppet's strings, be the fingers that worked the ventriloquist's dummy. And Gray knew that when politics came to mind, Hand understood he had the perfect candidate, the perfect solution. The monster wouldn't have to say anything coherent. He could strut and stumble and use his subatomic pull to sway the voters. And when Reason won the election, it would be four years, maybe eight, of Hand ruling Grand River from behind the curtain, sucking millions from the city's coffers and demanding tribute from contractors, business people and other supplicants. No wonder Fox and Zinger had enlisted his help. They were scared that their role as the city's bloodsuckers was in jeopardy. How interesting, Gray thought, to be in the center of this polemic struggle, privy to the extremes of power. How exciting. Exciting enough to make up for the seven years of sleepwalking through Bob and Patsy's campaigns? Okay, no, but not a bad start.

He had it all figured out. But he could not indulge in his excitement. Not until he knew what happened to Breeze.

"We'll call the media," she had said as she glided on the bike. She barely pedaled and still outpaced Gray, who huffed and chugged as if the entire trip were uphill. "We can expose them and change the course of the race."

Gray had contacts at the daily paper. He knew the political bloggers in town from his work on campaigns. He would get in touch with them as soon as he got back home, he said, not ready to reveal to her his residence at the Star. And that was the last he'd seen or heard of her.

Now he sat on the bed in his room and stared at the blank browser, preparing to ask Randy for another access to his bandwidth. It was as though she had never existed—her zephyr had blown into his life and passed just as quickly, leaving no trace. It had only been a few days but already he could scarcely remember her face—although her body remained chiseled into his cerebrum in bas-relief.

Perhaps she had been an illusion. Gray's fantasies had always served an ironic purpose: they'd kept him from desperation over his inability to achieve success, but they'd also kept him from trying. His dream world softened his desires, delayed them, rationalized them as worth waiting for, and he preferred to live in that Xanadu, rather than putting himself on the line. All the scenarios he'd imagined with Breeze—the romantic, the sexual, the hardcore—had given him an excuse to avoid pursuing her and forcing her to own up to her intimations. But now with her gone, he would never have the satisfaction of knowing that he'd tried to win her, faced the odds, given it all he had, and won. Or lost. As he squirmed on the cement slab of the motel mattress, it registered, finally, that the outcome wasn't as important as the attempt.

He had trusted his instincts, and they had failed him. As always. Did that mean he was wrong about the giant too? About Hand and his motives and the tub of green glop in that dark room? Perhaps the ridiculousness of his "theory" had scared Breeze off.

"Poor baby," Randy said after Gray spilled his guts. "So mystery woman is no more. Let's see what we can do to fix that. Maybe some tea. Earl Grey?" He laughed. "No. Earl is not gray. Gray is gray."

Time, perhaps, for another massage. "No," Gray said. "I'm going to find her."

"And how are you going to do that?"

"There's the yacht club. Everybody knows her there. And

Frenchy's restaurant. Someone will give me an address, or at least a lead."

Randy sat back on his couch, looking a touch disappointed. "You've made up your mind to go after this Breeze and forget about your wife?"

"My wife made her choice. Now I'm making mine."

"You *are* smitten, aren't you?"

He should have taken a photo of her, should have perused the triple-X store until he found a jewel case with a picture of that sapphire of a woman, bodice-ripped across the cover. He could show it to Randy and he'd understand. Even he would be unable to resist her. The trouble with Gray's life thus far, the reason he'd never moved beyond bystander, beyond neutron, was that he'd never allowed himself to become obsessed with any object or cause. It had always been too risky, too potentially embarrassing. Now, in Breeze, he had purpose. He'd been so close to possessing her; the thought of her gone from his life felt unbearable. She would be his quest, his purpose. Fuck the campaign, fuck reconciliation with L'aura, fuck...yes, that was the general idea.

"I would do anything to have her," Gray said.

"Are you sure you want to give up your freedom like that?"

"What are you saying?" Gray asked. "It's because I have freedom that I'm able to go after my dream."

"Really?" Randy moved behind the couch and pressed his fingers behind Gray's ears, swirling the tips to bring a surge of blood to the brain.

"Oh," Gray said. "That does feel good."

"I have the freedom to give you pleasure. You have the freedom to receive it."

"What?"

"No strings. No obsession. It's like a matrix."

"I think I'll take that tea now, while you explain that last sentence."

Randy went into the kitchen to heat the water, but kept talking.

"I give pleasure; you don't want it. You desire pleasure; I'm not in the mood. Or, neither of us wants anything. But then, sometimes, I'm ready and you're ready. Sometimes we both want the same thing, and when we do, there's no pressure. We can just do it. We're both comfortable with the occasional indulgence, and that's the way relationships should be."

Gray felt uncomfortable.

"That obsession business doesn't work," Randy said. "That's what kills relationships. Take it from me. One person desperate for the other, and the first person eventually resents it."

"I'm not desperate for her. I just want her," Gray said.

"And you'd do anything to have her."

"Something like that."

"Be careful, my friend."

Gray logged on to Randy's wireless. After a few days without a response from Breeze, he'd put her name on Google Alert. His email had the first notification. A political blogger's site had mentioned her that morning.

He scanned the text from the blog. "Ladykiller Candidate?" it read. "What's with Reason Wilder and his bevy of political beauties? First, the rainbow-haired L'aura Davenport and now a bombshell named Breeze Wellington." Gray's jaw dropped. He clicked through to read how the blogger had fallen under both Breeze's and Reason's spells.

She had proven her magic stronger than the monster's, hadn't she? He saw the giant go down, succumb to her sexual power. What, then, was she doing with Reason now instead of sharing in the triumph over his campaign's demise? She should be with Gray at the yacht club, describing for Messrs Fox and Zinger how they'd uncovered the horrific secret that would destroy the evil ones. The geezers would be thrilled, no doubt, and would pile a bonus onto what they'd paid—a bonus that Gray would lavish on Breeze in the form of a spectacular dinner, perhaps a bauble or two, maybe a spree at Saks. He might even indulge in some duds for himself, for

Breeze had put up with his dishevelment long enough. And then, of course, there would be no more imagining sex with her…

Randy's power—that of perception—broke through Gray's lustful fog. "You're planning something. Something stupid."

"How do you know?"

"You have that look on your face—the one that says 'I'm going to throw everything I've worked for away on some babe.'"

"You probably think I'm being pretty childish." Gray looked, for the first time, directly into Randy's eyes.

The manager paused between sips of tea and stared back. "It's not my job to judge," he said, and smiled.

"Good. Then I have to get back into that mansion," Gray said.

"Let's think about that," Randy said.

Called on the Worn Carpet

They'd summoned him to the yacht club in the morning, before the swagger of martini and ribeye lunches, while the rising sun poured through windows that looked out on the only body of clean water in Grand River. Apart from Fox and Zinger in their upholstered bank vault, no one else languished in the building, not even wait staff, but somehow each old man sloshed a crystal of intoxicating amber liquid. Had they retrieved it themselves, or had they stashed today's eye candy in a closet somewhere? Gray did not need a drink, not this early, and not with so much swirling in his mind. The vapors from their glasses were potent enough; his olfactory went on high alert, and the molecules of alcohol floating in the air began to unbalance him, making him antic in his explanation. But as he related the events of the afternoon at the mansion, the goods by which they would bring the giant down, his benefactors only stared, the gargoyles and their stony façades only slightly less impassive than usual.

"And of course you have proof," Fox said. "Something we can forward to the media to make the case?"

"I was there," Gray said. "I saw it. I'm the eyewitness."

"That," Fox said, "is insufficient."

"We trusted you, my boy," Zinger said. "Don't tell me you've let us down."

Gray had deposited the check they'd given him, but the bank had clamped a week-long hold on the funds to ensure they cleared. If Fox and Zinger asked for the money back, he'd have to comply. "There's another eyewitness," he remembered. "That woman, Breeze, was with me. She can corroborate it."

"Fine. Where is she?"

If he only knew for sure, he would fly to her. But he couldn't relate the only information he'd received. If she had really defected to Reason's camp, they'd be furious. They'd not only take the money back, they'd have him thrown into the river—the dirty part—in a sack. "Umm… She seems to have disappeared," he said. "But I'm working on a few leads."

Fox put his hand over his face and massaged its sagging skin, as if he might rejuvenate it if he rubbed hard enough. "This is what you'll do," he said.

Gray knew instantly it was not a choice.

"You'll continue to track our opponent, and, from now on, bring a video camera and record everything until you have what we need. You'll learn the meaning of the word 'proof,' and you'll bring back evidence we can forward to the newspapers and television stations."

Zinger was angry too. "Who's going to believe a man in a dark suit and brown shoes? They'll think you're a street person trying make money through fabrication."

"But you don't understand how difficult it was to get close to him the first time."

Fox took a sip of his cognac. "Excuse me," he said. "Just how much money did we pay you for this information?"

"We have a business relationship here, and we expect your end of the deal to be fulfilled," Zinger said. He tapped the base of his glass on the table next to his chair, and a bunny/waitress appeared as if from nowhere to replenish it. "And when you deliver the promised goods, you will be further compensated."

Well, at least something to look forward to. But how could he get back in that mansion? No disguise would fool Hand and Reason again, and Breeze wouldn't be with him to distract. She might even be there when he tried to infiltrate and would rat him out. Or L'aura would.

He hadn't spoken after Zinger announced this latest charge, had barely nodded his head, but found himself outside the private room, as if teleported to the middle of the club's dining area. The emptiness of the place, the lonely feeling it inspired, persuaded him to walk among the tables, peruse the accommodations to which he had never been privy, and might never be, despite the old men's largesse if he came through for them. The morning sun blazed through panes designed to frame a starlight view, and in the harsh sun he could see the wine-colored carpet looked worn, not plush as it had seemed at the political event. The tables and chairs exhibited wear, too, and some had chips and gouges in their veneers as though kids with switchblades had held an event. He shuffled to the line of windows that stretched across the back end of the building—the ones that glimpsed the boat docks and the river channel beyond—and noticed how cloudy they were, uncleaned for some time.

As the sun dodged behind a bank of clouds, he realized he had another way to bring Reason down. He might never be able to get into that room with the bath again, but maybe he didn't have to. Hand had recruited two women—both beautiful—for his purposes. And since neither had political experience, he had to have another purpose for them. Breeze, after all, had a checkered past, perhaps a lurid one. L'aura didn't, but she acted as though she did, and maybe she saw being with Reason as her chance to make up for lost opportunities. So he would stalk them, film them, catch them at something, some act still technically illegal, at least in some states, and that would create scandal enough to close down the Traveling Reason Show. Yes! Of course! How wondrous is the promise of a last, desperate chance.

Gray headed for the stairs to the parking lot. He realized that without Breeze to impress, he was pulling this entire caper for money. Money alone. He would stand outside a window and record all manner of depravity, let her whore her way to campaign success, and do nothing about it but watch. L'aura too. She was his wife still, and it meant something, even if he ridiculed her in his descriptions to others to cover his shame. But whether he could bear to watch such scenes unfold as he filmed posed a question he'd have to answer later.

He took his first step down the stairs, but was stopped by the sound of something loose and heavy crashing into a sink behind the bar. Gray turned to see a worker dumping a bucket of ice in preparation for the day's customers. The man in the white uniform, from here, looked familiar. Jet-black hair, the Dali mustache, the paunch. Could it be Vega? Had they demoted him that far? Or was this just the way Fox, Zinger, and the rest of their cabal treated anyone who worked for them?

Ridiculous. Even if they'd booted him from the campaign, which seemed unlikely, and even if they'd pointed him toward the bar and held out the apron for him to wear, even Vega had enough integrity to refuse them. Didn't he?

Gray had wondered if it had indeed been Vega lurking at Frenchy's, spying, for whatever cause, while he and Breeze dined. Maybe working for Fox and Zinger meant unconditional surrender. He tried to study the man more closely, but the worker turned and went into a back room. When he did not return, Gray gave up the vigil and continued down the stairs.

That Old Black Magic

An Election Exhibition: art of change, of choice, of new voices from within Grand River, voices that heralded a populist future for the city and had anointed Reason its leader. No red, white, and blue here either; the event at Tryst promised a spectrum of painted colors instead, a reflection of the city's diversity. The ad said part rally, part display, part party, and open to supporters and art lovers of all political persuasions, but Gray read it as an unexpected chance to get close to Reason and record some gaffe or slip on the video camera hidden under his jacket and secured by his left hand. He stood in that Napoleonic pose, with Randy at his side ready to deflect the attention of anyone curious about the bulge at Gray's midriff.

The giant stood at the other end of the gallery, pressing cold flesh and spouting what sounded like pre-recorded campaign blather. Gray felt sure Reverend Hand had tucked himself into a corner somewhere—although he couldn't yet see him—and broadcast his commands into the monster's vacuum tube cerebrum, telling him what to say and how to stand, and triggering the magnetism that pulled so many to his candidacy. Artists milled en masse—at least people who looked like artists to Gray's stereotyped thinking—wandering through the rooms, along with their flunkies and fans, creating a mixed media of personalities of which Gray had little real experience—okay, no experience.

And among the throngs of black-clad cognoscenti this night flitted L'aura, the featured artist of the evening, whose work hung in the main showroom; work that had neither been seen nor intimated when they lived together at the condo. When had she created these pieces, and how? Why hadn't she ever mentioned them to him? But then, his discomfort over her early attempts at art, his less-than-encouraging comments, must have motivated her to keep all this a secret from him.

Gray sidled up to one of her paintings and ogled an oblong of splotches in Technicolor hues, as though she'd sawed a chunk out of one of the Pollock walls at home and brought it down for framing. He didn't understand the difference between this mess and a couple of spilled cans of semi-gloss enamel. He assumed he could have done this himself if he'd been so inclined. Perhaps a room full of chimps could turn out a similar canvas given enough time.

But as he stared, lines converged into patterns, colors blended to suggest meaning. He experienced a little revelation. The painting communicated something—at the very least that his estranged wife had talent. It said he could be proud of her, if she'd let him.

"My wife did this," Gray said to Randy. "This is art."

"Nice drippings."

Gray's landlord had loaned him the camera. Randy had rustled up a pair of black shoes too, to go with the still-wrinkled suit, and Gray was relieved at not having to fret over the appearance of his feet, although they hurt like hell, the loafers being about two sizes too small.

"Do you know any of these people?" Gray said.

"What makes you ask that?"

He wished he could have withdrawn the question. Randy was gay—maybe. The gallery was located in the gay part of town. But the connection he'd made relied on yet another stereotype. He blurted a rationale and hoped it would erase the mistake: "I recognize a few faces from the other event, but I don't know their names."

Gray stood in the shop's deliberate gloom, against the ragged, mossy-colored slats that made up the walls, like the novice spy he knew himself to be. Should he mingle, act more casual, or stay plastered to the sides, believing he didn't fit in here and hoping no one would notice his presence if he stayed out of the center? Maybe it didn't matter. The gallery's overhead lights had been extinguished so the bulbs illuminating L'aura's paintings would beam like tiny spotlights. Deep shadow haunted the rest of the space.

"So is she here?" Randy asked. "I'd really like to meet her."

Gray scanned the room. Even in the dim light, her curves would stand out from the harsh angles of the crowd, like Cleopatra among the pyramids. Breeze, by definition, did not fit in here either, but wherever she went, people accepted her—virtually every gathering had room for a woman like her. The idea that she might attend the event had sealed Gray's decision to come. He could confront her, that traitor to his cause and his libido, and find out what Reason had said or done to change her mind and make her switch sides, just when he was ready to make his move—yes!—he would have done it and soon, would have made that move, never mind his years on the sidelines spent in a fantasy funk. He would have achieved a personal landmark of a move in a lifetime of moves deferred, moves planned and never enacted, but this one would be different because he actually would have gone through with it. Well, he would have. Maybe.

He continued his reconnaissance of the gallery. Reason's shoulders and head towered over the group of patrons circling him, and it came to Gray that Reason was another, like him and like her, an outsider, perhaps the ultimate outsider because he should not have fit in here or anywhere, and yet he did. She and he did, and Gray, he did not. And he began to wonder about them both, about their origins. Breeze's he knew in part, and if she had told him the truth, then he knew she had overcome obstacles—the misogyny and lust of men, the jealousy of women—and used them to her advantage so that she could fit in. Reason's he had only guessed, but if he was right, then what life had that ancient head lived before this one? What terrors might it have known?

He felt that their apartness somehow bound the three of them together.

"I'm looking," Gray said, returning his focus to Randy. "She should be easy to find."

Randy tugged on his sleeve. "Isn't that her over there? With the orange hair, talking to those people by the mural?"

"Oh, you meant L'aura," Gray said. This fixation with Breeze had to stop. It interfered with the mission, with his life. He refocused and watched L'aura escort the people admiring her work to the crowd surrounding Reason, into which they melded like drops of mercury into a silvery pool. She looked paler than usual and lethargic—not her typically manic self, and seemed to sleep-walk back to her mural, where she waited for more art lovers to approach.

Randy turned to Gray. "It's like hypnosis. Do you notice how no one leaves the group around Reason? It just keeps getting bigger."

"We should head over." Gray slid the camera a little further back behind his jacket flap.

But they had attracted attention too. An older man in a tweed sportcoat made his way to Gray. He looked sixty, but had the build of a former athlete, maybe a football player. "You're new here," he said to Gray. He took a sip of the chardonnay from a plastic cup. He had a leather patch on his elbow, which matched the swath of leather draped from his right shoulder. Perhaps he'd just come in from riding to hounds. His thick mustache brushed the rim of the plastic glass when he drank.

"I'm new everywhere," Gray said, and the man laughed.

"Buy you a drink?"

"Umm… they're free, I thought."

Randy nudged Gray's shoulder as if they should move on, but he couldn't be that rude.

"Homer Hunter. Editor of the *Journal*."

"*Grand River Journal?*" The weekly rag. A throwaway that printed more ads than news.

"Oh, and art critic. It's a small paper. I wear a lot of hats."

The weekly's popularity in Grand River had always dismayed him. The city's mid-size daily, the *News-Press*, which covered budget-wranglings and local events, was shredded after a series of acquisitions. People now preferred the homey mix of gossip and amateurism Homer and his staff of unpaid interns threw on front doorsteps. It seemed, in the Grand River scheme of things, to fit. More small potatoes for this uninspired city.

The man smiled and extended a hand. But when Gray reached for it, Hunter took only the tips of his fingers and gave them a pull, as though milking a cow. "Come on. You look like you could use some alcohol. Loosen you up a bit."

Gray looked to Randy for support, but found himself dragged toward the buffet. In a few seconds, he had a glass of white in his free hand, topped with a paper plate holding a few broccoli florettes and a pat of dressing. With his left hand on the camera, he couldn't drink or eat, so he settled for conversation.

"Are you writing this up for the paper?" he asked.

"Yes, indeed."

"What do you think of the work?"

"Beats me."

"You don't like it?"

"I'm the art critic. That doesn't mean I need to know anything about art. Makes it easier to keep the writing in layman's terms."

"I happen to think the paintings are fantastic," Gray said.

"Can I use that?"

The ersatz critic didn't take notes. He barely looked at the paintings. "Why don't you say they're raw, they're rough, but they have great promise," Gray said.

Hunter looked past Gray, as if giving the art another chance to please him. When his eyes met Gray's, Hunter said, "You're not enjoying yourself. What's wrong with your other hand?"

"Oh… ah… I sprained my wrist this afternoon. Just keeping it safe."

"Well then. I shall feed you."

Hunter snatched a bit of veggie from the plate, dipped it and held it an inch from Gray's mouth. "Open," he said.

"I could just put the plate down and do it myself."

"Nonsense," Hunter said. "Let's have some fun. You like fun, don't you?"

Gray wasn't sure. What if someone saw? L'aura? Or Breeze? But he had to play along or give himself away. He closed his eyes and opened his mouth, ever so slightly.

Hunter touched the broccoli to Gray's lips. Gray pulled away and the hors d'oeuvre dropped and ricocheted off the toe of his shoe, rolling merrily out to the middle of the floor and leaving an accusing arrow of ranch dressing along the way.

Now everyone in a twenty-foot radius saw. Hunter seemed unbothered. He had another tuft ready to go.

Finally Randy caught up with them. "You bad boy," he said. "I was wondering where you'd snuck off to."

"This is my…boyfriend, Randy," Gray said. He watched both men's eyebrows rise.

"Randy what?"

He'd never bothered to ask for the last name and couldn't now.

"Knight," Randy said.

"I've met you before, haven't I?" Hunter said.

"Anything's possible."

Hunter pulled a business card from his pocket and handed it to Gray. "There are shows opening in the region almost every day," he said, backing away. "I get to review them. Restaurants too. Let me know if you're ever interested."

"Bold," Gray said when Hunter was out of range.

"Or maybe he could tell we weren't really together."

"Then what would make him think that I—" Gray stopped before he insulted Randy again. The more he experienced, the more confused he became. He was on the other side of the city, in it for the first time, among the alternative he'd dissed as its fringe. Gray had driven through these streets on his way to campaign business, but had never stopped; had once imagined visiting for a drink and a respite from Bob and Patsy's insanity but could not find the nerve. Some residents of the city scorned this area, blamed it for Grand River's troubles; Fox and Zinger and their cronies did not even acknowledge it. Before tonight, he'd been like them, believing it populated by people who didn't count, rarely voted and had little say in the decision-making process, and was therefore not worth considering seriously in his work for candidates. An entire zone of outsiders. They all looked like voters now; like people now. And there stood Reason, surrounded by maybe fifty of them.

"Do you think you can get close to him?" Gray asked.

"The big boy with the hair?" Randy said. "Let me at him."

Randy moved to the edge of the pulsing mass of bodies and turned sideways, easing into the imperceptible spaces between Reason's groupies. To Gray, he resembled an electron, fully charged, making progress no matter the impediment, pure energy. He moved halfway toward Reason in just a few seconds, and then slowed as he got closer to the nucleus of the group.

Gray strained to see. He moved closer and gripped the camera tighter, fingering the lens cover, ready to move into a position where Reason's face might reveal its connection to the undead.

Someone tapped his shoulder. Not Hunter again. Didn't the man know when to give up? But the voice that accompanied the touch was not a man's. It was familiar, but a little dreamy, almost echo-like. "This is my ex-husband," L'aura said.

He spun around. Her orange hair consumed her head like flames, the strands licking the shoulders of a silky black blouse, which, with matching pants, made her look like a pasty sort of ninja. He took a moment to take her in. She held hands with a thin man in black jeans, a skin-tight black pullover shirt and black vest, and three-days of facial hair, also black.

The man turned to her. "Really?" he said. "I would never have guessed you could be so boring."

"It was another life," she said. "So long ago."

Her initial comment finally registered with Gray. "What do you mean, 'ex?'"

"Our divorce is final."

"What divorce? I never got any papers."

"The Reverend Hand made the sacrifice and spoke the words of asunder."

"That doesn't count," Gray said.

"I am free from you. I am free to do great things for this city."

She sounded like Reason. Gray took a step back and assessed her escort. "And you?" he asked.

"I am Tristan," the man said. "The owner of Tryst." His voice had the same, distant, empty sound. "We're all working for Reason now, and if you were smart, you would too."

"I guess I'm not that smart," Gray said.

L'aura began to laugh, but stifled it with a hand over her mouth.

Gray ignored the insult and asked, "What's he going to do for Grand River?"

"Well, great things, of course," Tristan said.

"Like what?"

"The details aren't important. But he will turn this city around."

There was no sense in arguing.

Then from behind, Gray heard a sickening, unforgettable bellow: "My friend! So glad you could be here for me. And what is your name?"

The crowd quieted just enough so they, and Gray, could hear the answer: "Randy Knight."

No! What had he done? He had no idea if Randy could resist

Reason's spell or not. Maybe he could get over there before it was too late. He left L'aura and Tristan and made for the throng Randy had penetrated so easily, but his every attempt to part the sea of flesh was met with resistance, as though the crowd knew he was immune to Reason's power and acted to keep him from their idol. Gray grabbed shoulders and pulled on elbows, but no one let him pass. He jumped as though trying to vault the mob, and when he landed, Randy's camera came tumbling from his grasp, rattling along the floor.

He went to his hands and knees and chased the recorder as it slid along the hardwood. When he retrieved it, he was met by low-cut boots and yet another pair of the ubiquitous black jeans. Security? Muscle for Reason? He looked up.

This time it was Randy.

"You okay?"

"Never mind me," Gray said. "How do you feel?"

"Feel? I feel like having a margarita."

"And Reason? Anything to say about him?"

"He's really big… but kind of an idiot. He smells a little too."

Phew.

"Sorry. I was worried. Sometimes he has this weird effect on people."

"Worried," Randy said. "How sweet."

Randy helped Gray to his feet. He checked the camera, which still worked, and Gray tucked it back under his jacket.

"Did you get decent footage?" Randy asked.

"I got a little sidetracked. L'aura and some guy. I'm thinking they delayed me on purpose. Some kind of mind control—"

"So you didn't get anything."

Gray looked back toward the crowd, but they, and Reason, had left, ducked out through a back door. L'aura and Tristan must have gone with them. That Hunter fellow was absent too, not that Gray was looking for him. In fact, besides themselves, only three others remained to look at L'aura's art.

"Next time," Randy said.

They started for the Honda, but Gray stopped. "Randy Knight. You were kidding, right?"

"It had a nice ring." He laughed. "And no way was I going to give him my real name."

"Which is?"

"Fingers."

Gray took a step away from him before walking away. He felt he might never know when Randy was putting him on.

With the gallery almost empty and the show virtually over, it seemed strange that someone should be arriving. A woman entered, partially obscured in the shadows. She looked hurried, disheveled, as though she'd rushed to get there, but Gray knew her immediately. She looked around and then went toward the back, as though searching for someone.

Gray handed the keys to Randy. "Wait for me in the car," he said.

Napoleon and Cleopatra

Eventually, he would have to change his pose, remove the hand from under his jacket and expose the video camera—about which she would no doubt have questions—but for now he enjoyed the stance, his Napoleon facing off with her Cleopatra, two giants of history, and history in the making, confronting each other one last time before all-out hostilities.

"Yes?" she said.

Breeze stared through those wide, enticing eyes. She did not, however, focus on his face as she had before, not on the eyes, or mouth, or even the beak that was his nose, or on the bulge below his waist. She looked past him into the void of the gallery, as oblivious to Gray as if he were a stranger. Her refusal to acknowledge him, this retreat from their previous connection, unnerved him. She was still as beautiful as before, in a clingy number that might have rekindled his imagination had he not been so disenchanted. He stared before he spoke, seeing the fringe of her hair lift as if blown by a puff of wind. But they were indoors now. Was he imagining it? Was the idea of Breeze more powerful than reality?

She remained distant. She held her mouth open slightly, as if waiting to be kissed, but her eyes had a vapid look, like a Victoria's

Secret catalog model—all that arousal flattened to the page, just there to sell something.

In the last two weeks, she had seduced him out of the depression in the wall that had been his life, offered him the 3-D of imagination, and then pulled it away. And as anxious as he'd been over her disappearance, as much as he convinced himself he would berate her for vanishing, he felt ready to forget the insult, give her another chance, and go back to that puppy-dog state of devotion to which unrequited hope leads. He despised himself for it.

"Where have you been?" he asked.

"With Reason," she said.

And the way she said it, without emotion, and with only that simple preposition to define it, made him realize there were two possibilities regarding her absence: yes, she might have become part of his campaign, working in the office, churning out marketing pieces and coordinating appearances; but the word "with," by itself, could mean something else, and she had left its meaning open so he could fill in the blank. In bed, of course, was the obvious conclusion. In Reason's dead, tree limb arms, which only she could bring back to life. And what other parts had she rejuvenated? He cringed at the idea. The monster's power had been underestimated. Breeze had won the battle, but Reason had won the war.

Napoleon was exiled, the foyer at Tryst now his Elba of embarrassment.

Gray let the camera tumble to the floor. The lens cap popped off and another piece of plastic skittered in the opposite direction. He knew he'd have to pay to repair or replace it. The fall must have somehow started it recording, the lens angled toward him. He stared at the red diode, which stared back with the brain-dead prurience of reality TV. He saw his misery digitized for posterity. But he no longer cared.

"You didn't return my messages," he said. "You could have told me. I thought we were…a team." He'd wanted to say "couple."

"I am for Reason." She hadn't even noticed the camera crash. "There is no other way."

She seemed haunted. More so than L'aura and Tristan, who were programmed to follow the giant. Breeze spoke in a B-movie monotone. How could Reason—or was it Hand—have manipulated her so thoroughly? He had seen no weaknesses in her, but then, he hadn't wanted to.

"Don't you remember what we found? How we snuck into the mansion and learned his secret? How can you be on his side now?"

He took a chance and grabbed her by the shoulders. His fingers touched the skin below the sleeves of her dress and made him clamp down harder, until he could see the blood rush away from the points of contact, the indentations becoming paler. How he'd wanted to do that from the first moment at Bob's house, to take her in a rush of lust and not care how she might respond. But he'd been reserved, a gentleman—the necessary rationalizations needed to control his urges and keep him coming back for more. He looked around. The gallery now, as far as he could tell, was empty save for them. Perhaps this was the Monterey Jack moment. He could push her, force her into a back room, take her the way Reason must have and bring her back to his world.

But he couldn't. He thought of her, of what she might want. The Gray universe held no attraction for her. Its physics predicted so many limits. No wonder L'aura had booted him to live on her own planet.

But at least he could kiss her. Her lips remained parted; all he had to do was lean forward, open his mouth, and aim.

Instead he shook her, gently. And then he let her go.

As a man he was a coward; he knew it. An also-ran. He did not need Monterey Jack to tell him.

"They've all gone," he said. "Everyone left a few minutes ago. Probably back to his mansion for a post-party celebration."

Breeze pulled on her dress to straighten it. She turned and made for the front door. As she opened it she looked back at him, and for a fleeting second, Gray saw her eyes engage his, the way they had at Frenchy's when he got her to relate her past, the way they had when she escaped the scrum of lotharios at the yacht club to talk to him.

"Thank you," she said, and raced toward the parking lot.

Busted Loose

The numbers looked better for Bob, depending on how one looked. According to the Journal poll, Gray's candidate had pulled into a dead heat with Vega—for second place. More accurately, Vega's poll numbers had plummeted back to where Bob's had yet to budge. The giant held a commanding lead, and Reason's seventy percent of the respondents meant he had more followers than the other two combined.

But wait a minute—it was the *Journal* poll, and they had listed only percentages, not counts, and now that he'd met Homer Hunter, Gray suspected the man who claimed to wear many hats had donned another, maybe a shady accountant's visor. Without raw data to support the results, Gray surmised Hunter had probably only buttonholed a dozen or so passersby to conduct his so-called survey. From the figures presented, no one could say how many people the *Journal* had questioned, or whether they had even registered to vote. But Bob and Patsy viewed the report as though it had been carved onto a stone tablet and delivered from on high. "It took some time, but we're on our way," Patsy said, as she sat on her big ball in Bob's living room. She had bounced in that spot for so long she'd created a three-foot-wide depression in Bob's carpet, so it was nice to know she finally felt like moving.

Gray decided to look at it as good news too. He had to, since he'd received a gut punch an hour before, when he'd logged on, once again, to his bank account to see if the old boys' funds had cleared. The check had bounced. Fox and Zinger had screwed him and probably planned to screw him all along. The conniving old buzzards were fakes. They were probably writing bad checks all over town to keep up the façade of their wealth.

"Thanks to you, Gray," Bob said. "Without your input I don't know what I would have said at the debate."

Gray should have acted embarrassed, as he usually did, but instead he listened, impassive.

"Really. Those ideas were great. They got people talking. Not that I can actually do those things if I get elected, but they sure generated interest."

"I'll admit, Gray," Patsy said. "My seven years of training you have finally paid off."

What, exactly, was she admitting?

"And we could use more of those ideas," Bob said.

More? He had a million of them, stored up from his college days and incubated throughout his career on the councilwoman's staff, at the newspaper, and in the seven years he'd been with Patsy. He had so much figured out, yet no one had bothered to ask. Never mind that Bob had no intention of putting any of his brainstorms into practice. His man still had no chance in the race, but the opportunity to throw new views into the public arena was, perhaps, enough.

"Give me a few days, and I'll write them down for you," he said. "Then we can go over them together."

Patsy shook her head, which caused her body to sway, almost upsetting her balance, making the ball break wind again. "No need to be so formal, Gray. Give us a few of the good ones. We can discuss them now."

Even Patsy had developed respect for him? Hmm. Maybe that wind was one of change.

"I don't know..."

"Come on," she said. "What do you think about...oh, let's say the homeless problem?"

Gray clutched his chin in his hand to appear thoughtful, even though he'd had the answer for years. "What's the real problem with the homeless?" he asked. Bob and Patsy remained mute.

"Is it that people are honestly concerned? No. It's that they just don't want to see the homeless. You see a guy in rags on a park bench and you steer clear. A homeless guy on a street corner? You start thinking the neighborhood's going to hell. But what if he didn't look so bad? What if the guy wore a suit and tie? Or just a knit shirt and khakis? He could sit on that bench, or stand on that corner all week and no one would care."

Bob didn't see it yet. "But where does he get the clothes?"

"We give them to him. And not the usual throwaways that come from Goodwill. Real clothes, from the city's clothing stores. Decent stuff. A dozen outfits a month from each shop. Call it a thread tax. Doesn't even cost that much. And then we still have homeless, but they look good. People aren't afraid of them. If anything, they become advertisements for the city—best dressed bums on the coast."

Patsy nodded. She appeared to think it over.

Bob liked it, too. "And maybe some of them will feel good about themselves and go get jobs," he said.

"How about the environment?" Patsy asked. "I've heard some people are a little concerned."

The airborne particulate from the coal storage facility upwind had defiled the city's air for decades.

"Umm, why don't they just cover the dust piles?"

"You think that would work?" Bob asked.

"Either that or give out free cigarettes to people so they get more used to breathing poisonous air." He grinned at his joke.

But Patsy rocked the ball in excitement. "Now that I like."

"Traffic," Bob barked.

"Staggered work schedules."

"Zoning disputes."

"Citizens' panel. Let them work out their own compromises."

"Corruption at City Hall."

"Ethics commission. Fully empowered." He wished he had a cigar so he could sit back and take a victory toke.

Bob sat back on the couch, the pace of the session proving too much for his metabolism, as well as his intellect. "Wow," he said. "That's really a lot. I never thought about those things before."

Gray fought the urge to slap the man, partly for his failure to devote any real thought to the future of the city, but in part, because he so readily bought into what Gray was selling. There should at least be some debate, some tweaking to appeal to a wider audience, some concern over who might be opposed. There were special interests to consider, the very groups that had kept common sense from being employed in the first place. Now, the fact that Bob liked what he'd presented got Gray thinking maybe they weren't such good ideas after all.

"Listen," he said, "There's still a long way to go if we're going to overtake Reason. He's like a cult. Almost everyone who meets him becomes a convert." He couldn't get the images of L'aura and Breeze at Tryst out of his mind—how they were now zealots for the monster. Randy hadn't been affected, but maybe it was just a matter of time.

The same might eventually happen to him. He'd shaken the giant's hand, stood right next to him, smelled him. His head had hovered just inches from the creature's zipper and his no doubt kielbasa-sized...ugh, he couldn't stomach the thought. What if he woke up tomorrow babbling about how wonderful the beast was, how he would do great things for the city? God! That was Reason's line. It was happening already.

"Maybe we should debate him again," Bob said. "With these great new ideas, we could make him look bad."

But just seeing the giant, even from a distance, proved enough to mesmerize some people. If Hand insisted the next debate be televised, Reason could influence thousands of voters.

And he thought of other factors, which Bob and Patsy clearly hadn't considered. "We can't count out Vega either. He can throw money at the race, and if he throws enough of it, people will believe his bullshit. So we need to be able get our message out too."

He had to slow down before he got carried away. The excitement of having the opportunity, finally, to promote his ideas and strategy almost started him thinking the campaign had a shot, and if he thought that, then he'd be in the same intellectual boat—okay, ship of fools—as Bob and Patsy. He didn't want to deceive himself about Bob's chances. He didn't want to be responsible for the inevitable election debacle. He'd always felt safer deferring to Patsy's so-called experience, letting her decide the direction of the campaign, knowing that it wouldn't work, and avoiding blame for their failures.

It had always worked as a trade off. He didn't make much money from Bob and the few other clients they'd served over the past seven years. He didn't expect to, considering their lack of success, but it kept him going. Maybe that's what being a neutron was all about: tradeoffs, comfort zones. It wasn't exciting, but it was stable. Neutrons were supposed to be stable.

Yeah, maybe that's why L'aura gave up on him and went with Reason. Breeze too. But dammit, what was wrong with stability? Why wasn't enough enough?

This time, however, it wasn't enough. The down payment for his services still hadn't happened. Bob's financial support, never quite sufficient to carry him through to a general election, had dwindled. The contributions from his remaining old friends, and from the well-meaning seniors who slipped him five- and ten-dollar bills at his Boren Backyard Barbecues, barely covered filing and other official costs. And Gray knew Bob had run out of personal options—he'd drained his savings and sold off his mall cop portfolio. His home had two mortgages, and the bank probably hung up on him when he called.

Gray had always felt a little guilty about taking the man's money, but he wouldn't this time. With the check from Fox and Zinger gone NSF, his balance had shrunk to double digits. If Bob wanted to risk the security of his future, time and time again, that was his decision. For Gray, the campaign had become a matter of survival.

"Speaking of money, Bob, how are we doing with the fundraising?"

"That was one of the other things we wanted to talk to you about," Patsy said.

"That bad, eh? Well, I have to tell you, I could really use a check right now. I've had some unforeseen expenses—"

"Listen, Gray," Bob said. "I don't want to drag this out and make it more painful, but we have to let you go."

A vein in Bob's neck throbbed. He wiped sweat from his forehead. Gray paused to make sure of what he'd heard. It took a full minute before the meaning became clear, before he realized he was being fired.

He wanted to scream at Bob for being such an idiot, for running in elections in which he didn't belong, for blowing what was probably his and his wife's retirement account on these pipe dreams, for listening to Patsy, ever. But he couldn't. Bob, in his pathetic, bovine way, was the gambler he'd never been. Stupid gambles, to be sure, but he'd be able to someday look back at these quixotic runs, from whatever hovel or cardboard box he and Mrs. Bob were eventually forced to inhabit, and he'd take some pride knowing he'd given politics—and life—his best shot. He, not Gray, was the Monterey Jack in this group.

Gray looked at Patsy, not that she'd be any help. "From the campaign?" he said. "But I thought we were on our way."

"Well, we are," Patsy said. "We just don't have any money."

"You said the poll numbers looked good." The *Journal's* lack of statistical validity hardly mattered now.

"Poll numbers aren't dollars and cents."

"Wait a minute," Gray said. "Are *you* being paid?"

"Of course," Patsy said. "I'm the consultant."

Gray looked back at Bob, but he'd trod into the kitchen and buried his head in the refrigerator. Bob's massive ass, the shadow of its crevice peering out between his polo shirt and slacks, offered the blank stare that typically came from his face.

Gray called across the room, "Well, of course you're going to pay me for the work I've already done. Right, Bob?"

His client—now his ex-client—didn't move, but kept searching the bottom of the fridge. His response echoed from the cold cuts bin: "Sure, Gray. As soon as I can. As soon as I get some contributions in."

In other words, not for a while. In other words, never.

"Unless you want to volunteer," Patsy offered.

They had set him up. They'd gotten him to spill his creative guts, to give them more ideas to make Bob seem more erudite. Then they would use them to scam the voters with titillating proposals that they had no intention of fulfilling. He'd been outsmarted by two people he'd figured had IQs that matched Bob's percentage in the polls. It had to be Patsy's doing. Bob came back into the living room with a plate of salami, crackers and cheese, and began to nosh, as unaware of the impact of his statement as if he'd asked Gray to pass him a napkin. The look on his face said he had merely followed her suggestion. Maybe the campaign really didn't have the money to afford him, but if so, they should share the burden. Maybe she wanted all the pay for herself. Most likely Patsy saw Gray finally coming of age as a consultant and couldn't handle the idea.

He saw her looking at him as he slid his notes into his briefcase and stood to go.

"Wait," she said.

Second thoughts. It was a joke, or a mistake. Of course.

Patsy pulled a sheaf of forms from a pile of papers.

"I need you to sign these," she said.

"What—?"

"Releases, disclaimers, non-disclosure forms. Just some legal documents to make sure the details of Bob's campaign aren't made public in any way. If you're not part of the team, we have to consider you a potential threat. We have to protect Bob's interests."

She held a pen out for him. He took it, clicked it open, and eyed the big red ball on which she wobbled. The polyvinyl must be pretty thick to support her ego, but if he stabbed hard enough—

Instead he took the forms and without further protest, signed them. Exactly what a neutron would do. He grabbed his briefcase and made for the front door, but stopped when he got to Bob's gunroom. He looked inside. He'd never really assessed the firepower in this house.

He saw pieces from the 1800s: Winchesters and Colts and a Derringer that looked like it had been used for an assassination. World War II and Vietnam relics vied for supremacy on adjoining walls. The surface closest to the door must have served as the terrorist wall—all manner of automatic, and possibly illegal, weapons bristled. With enough supporters, Bob wouldn't have to run for office—he could take it by force.

Gray reassessed the man he'd known for so long. Bob had always been civil to him, even if he wasn't capable of carrying on a decent conversation. Perhaps the niceties had clouded his judgment and helped him ignore the latent malice that lived in this room, in this house. Even now Bob seemed as docile as the steer Gray had always thought him to be, munching his snack as idly as if he were chowing down on a bale of hay.

If these babies were loaded—and who could say they weren't—Gray might pull the matched revolvers from the door and go back out to Bob and Patsy. He'd point one at their bloated countenances and use the other to scratch his three-day stubble. Monterey Jack was all about intimidation; he could be all about revenge too.

Sure, he could go through with it. And he'd relish the feeling of power as he kicked at their bodies to make sure they were dead.

Then he would walk back to the gun room and pluck the most menacing piece of hardware from its perch. He'd turn it around, look the barrel in the eye, and finger the trigger. He'd pull on it a little. The neutron inside him would feel something then. And he would close his eyes, take a deep breath, and pull a little harder, go out without leaving a note, but definitely making a statement.

He shuffled to the front door and turned the knob. He should say something. They should. A thank you for seven years of hard work, at least. He opened the door, took a step outside, and placed his hand against the evil stucco that had ripped his suit. It had been trying to tell him to stay away, but he hadn't listened.

He turned back. "About what you suggested," he said. "About volunteering."

Their eyes widened in unison. Patsy almost smiled.

"Go to hell!" He had to let it out. But it would have been so much more satisfying had his voice not squeaked.

The Interior Universe

The chaos of the Pollock walls would comfort him right now. Their eddies and swirls had communicated to him at last through L'aura's exhibit, and in his despair he believed they might provide solace. If he could go back to the condo now, he would. But it remained forbidden while he floated in the outer limits of the Star, and the barren canvas of the room's empty walls would surely magnify the isolation he felt. So he sat in the Civic outside Randy's unit, engine off, laptop on, picking up just enough of the manager's Wi-Fi to surf. The little car felt cozy, and that was what he needed—that and a connection to some kind of human activity, specifically, sex.

Who would see at two a.m.? He shielded the glow of the monitor with his hunched torso. Damn Randy for not wiring the individual rooms for the net.

Perhaps he could have maneuvered better if he'd moved to the passenger side, but it was too late for that. He clicked through images on hump.com, with the computer jammed against the steering wheel, and the seat slid back as far as it would go, just enough to allow his pecker access to the grimy night air between the edge of the keyboard and his belt buckle, and through the fangs of the zipper that threatened to take a chomp if he wasn't careful.

He needed this, a release from the cruel world, a statement that said he didn't care anymore who thought what about him—an act of defiance, of depravity, of gluttonous self-indulgence. Lean back, Gray. Don't hide it. Wank it in their faces and let them see you paint the dashboard with angst.

But his cock refused to cooperate. It ignored the tits and ass and pubic pixels and acknowledged the fact it had come out in public, where it had never been before, and it approached the new experience with the same trepidation its so-called master would, had he encountered a similar situation.

After ten minutes of jerking and massaging, he was still as flaccid as an uncooked churro. Half the pictures reminded him of Breeze, or L'aura, and instead of arousal, he felt dick-shrinking bitterness.

The ambient noises didn't help. Doors slammed and laughter echoed. A car engine gunned. Don't the people around here ever go to bed? But why should they? They lived their lives in little rebellions against a system they were convinced was dedicated to keeping them on the fringes. So they stayed up all night just to annoy the establishment, to make the haves ask how the have-nots could live so opposed to their own well-being. Dammit, he should be like that. He *would* be like that.

But not at the moment. He zipped up, shut the clamshell, and went to his room. It had been a long night, made longer by his post-Bob's-house wanderings.

He'd driven to the beach and stared at waves pushing garbage back toward the shore, as though fighting the land over the city's mess. He parked near an overpass, sat on the warm hood of his Honda and watched traffic on the freeway above ignore him. Had he not been nearly out of gas, he would have driven further, maybe out of the city, but instead he pulled into a pink shoebox of a bodega that sold liquor and lotto and spent the bulk of his last forty dollars on a box of Ho-Hos and a Bordeaux whose name he couldn't pronounce. He still had half the bottle, and since he couldn't beat his sorrows away, he would drown them in style, although with the markup in that place, it probably wasn't worth half the price.

He'd forgotten to buy a corkscrew, of course, and rather than hunting one down at that hour, he resorted to driving the cork inward with a pen and the heel of his shoe, and he couldn't help thinking the ink that had exploded into the wine just as he popped it through was fouling the dark-toned nose of black currant, cool stone, tobacco leaf, leather, and bits of flint around the edges that made for immediate consumption, according to the label. Or maybe the ink improved the taste. After two bathroom glasses of the stuff, he still couldn't tell the difference from the eight-dollar supermarket red he usually quaffed. In the wee of the morning, that made sense—he'd never been able to tell his life from a real one either.

The bottle, and the infomercials he watched to provide at least a pretense at companionship, lasted until three. He finished the wine, because that was the only way he would be able to sleep. But four hours of unconsciousness did little to rejuvenate his body or his spirits. In the morning, he sat on the unmade bed, not quite hung over because he was still drunk. He had nowhere left to go, no gas or money to get there. Maybe Randy would pick up the telepathy of his misery and come by. Two hours later, though—two hours of almost comatose self-pity, during which he did not move even so much as a finger, he laid there, still alone.

If he hadn't had to pee again, he might not have moved for days, or ever. But once up, he could at least muster the energy to think of how he might end the wretchedness. There was nothing in the room that looked useful—no gas stove, no knives, no cords. The storage closet had mops and brooms, but nothing of a chemical, and possibly poisonous, nature. Anything potentially self-inflicting had likely been removed long ago, for who but the most depressed of outcasts would rent here for more than a day or two? He could go back to Bob's and ask to borrow a cannon or something he could use to off himself, but even the steer would be suspicious of such a request. Besides, if he were going to go, he wanted his suicide to be as spectacular as his life was not. Perhaps he had enough gas to coax the Civic to the bridge connecting the city to that fabulous Shangri-La to the north. He'd drive halfway across the span and yank the wheel, and if he had enough momentum and the retaining wall had a weak spot, he'd give Grand River an adieu to remember.

Better yet, a dive from the top of City Hall, maybe even off that stupid billboard on the roof. He could take his time about it, walk up to each floor, saying hello and meaning goodbye to the people he'd met in his years at the paper and in politics. If death offered any kind of influence, any possibility of ghostly visits upon the wicked, he'd be sure to remember who said "hi" back and who blew him off.

But such dramatics entailed effort and stealth, planning on a scale he'd never attempted in life. It would be so much easier if he could only spread his arms and let the wind swallow him, as he had seen in the movies. His body would simply dissipate into the air, his spirit set free to wander the earth or even the cosmos. If he abandoned himself completely, maybe he could pass into another dimension, cross the mathematical divide that separates coexistent membranes of space-time, and come out whole into one of them, a place where he would be permanently removed from L'aura and Breeze and Reason and Bob and all the things that conspired to frustrate his every effort and destroy his self-esteem. What he really needed was a passing black hole—it would suck him away from his problems, compress him down to a point as close to nothing as quantum mechanics could predict, and then wormhole him to a fresh start where he would be recreated in a little bang of brilliant expansion. Spectacular indeed.

That new world beckoned. It would be clean and simple, and no one there would know who he was or what he had done, or hadn't done, and they wouldn't care anyway because they'd be all about what a person could do, not what they could keep him from doing. It might even be a mirror to this reality, a place where everything worked in reverse, where left was right, and Gray was liked and respected, successful in business and matters of romance, where women would be attracted to him and wouldn't L'aura have a time dealing with that? It would be a universe where he didn't even have to try and things naturally worked out. All would be backward, even the names. Arua'l would be his devoted spouse. Agev would be a man of honesty and erudition. Nosaer would be a midget who could make eye contact. And Bob… well some things are resistant to change.

Gray realized he was still drunk.

He closed his eyes and let his head spin, like a neutron enduring the pull of electrons speeding around him. A creeping nausea began to seep up his esophagus and forced him to blink open, grab the sides of the bed, and steady himself. He couldn't even get blitzed right. Breakfast remained out of the question.

Gray sat staring, one hand on his stomach, unmoving for another twenty minutes, but ready to vault into the bathroom if the wine and ink blend threatened to regurgitate. And he waited. For…what? No black hole was on the way. If other universes existed, they would remain distant, even though, if the theorists are correct, they could occupy the same physical space as the one Gray knew. There might even be an entire universe inside him, with its own set of physical laws unrelated to those of the oppressive and vulgar reality around it.

Often from despair comes resolve. Whether it came from Gray's mind, or from that little universe within his core as a transmission to his mind, an impulse congealed into a thought. Perhaps it originated from some other Gray, a scientist let's say, on a planet no larger than an atom in that tiny cosmos in Gray's innards. And that Ph.D. Gray beamed a signal in search of alien life, saying simply, "We are here. Come find us." The message traveled across the vastness of this little space, until, at the edge of that universe, it encountered Gray's gray matter and was received as an idea. It's not impossible.

Whatever the source, Gray sat up straight at the recognition that the answers he sought lay not so far away as to be inaccessible. Reason was the black hole into which everything was drawn. His gravity overwhelmed the pull of any other body. Some objects were distant enough that he did not initially lure them in, but as more and more mass collected, the attraction became ever greater, ever more irresistible. In time, all things would spiral down to his center. This is what had happened to L'aura, and eventually, Breeze. It would happen to Randy and even himself if he didn't find a way to stop it.

The answer, Gray realized, was within.

Switching Teams

The Civic got him only three-fourths of the way there. When it coughed to a gas-parched stop, Gray found himself in an enclave of the working poor, which in Grand River could have meant anywhere other than Island Retreat, but in this case was a shady street of post-World War II shoebox houses within smelling distance of the river and the abandoned landfill. A bedroom community, the elite liked to call it, perhaps because the only fun these folks could afford was in there.

He parked in front of someone's home as though dropping by for a visit—nothing he could do about that—and walked the last two miles to Reason's, breathing the funk and debating whether today's odor wafted in from the water or the trash heaps. Not that it mattered, since either scent by itself assaulted his exquisitely sensitive olfactory. The smell had a greasy sheen to it, interlaced with methane and spiced with a hint of rotting produce. Funny that he couldn't discern a fine wine from a bottle of home-stomped and fermented grapes, but was able to parse the subtleties that divided genres of garbage. He voted for the dump.

At least he didn't worry about being mugged in this strange neighborhood. He'd found a crushed pair of jeans and a sweatshirt at the bottom of the L'aura-packed suitcase, into which he'd finally delved a couple of days ago or face reusing underwear, since in his financial malaise he'd cut back on non-essentials, like laundry. It gave him a down-and-out look that fit with these surroundings, and would make him sympathetic when he got to the giant's door. If he'd found a pair of sneakers, the outfit would be complete, but the list of things L'aura had neglected grew longer every day. The brown dress shoes—the right one now lower and more wobbly than the left, thanks to last night's corkscrew debacle—would have to suffice again. No matter where Gray went and what he wore, those wingtips were out of place, and he could no longer remember why he ever bought them. But he was so broke now he couldn't replace them. He had no hope of collecting from Fox and Zinger, and L'aura had drained the remainder of their checking account since he'd been booted, maybe to help finance Reason's campaign. Whatever they paid her (assuming she'd told the truth about wages) must have been deposited in a new account she'd set up to keep the money from him. So the decision as to how to spend the last four bucks on his debit card was between food and fuel, and Denny's was closer than Mobil, and his stomach made more noise than his engine, so it seemed, at the time, an easy choice. He'd felt a little guilty as he shoveled his hash browns and scramble, and now felt stupid, because if he'd passed on the extra egg, he'd have had a dollar for gas, and it might have made the difference.

Oh well. He stood, back at the gate to the manse, a touch sweatier than he'd planned, but maybe that would help convince Reverend Hand he was serious about joining their ranks.

He rang the bell, wondering who might answer. But Castle Wilder stayed as silent as the crypt Gray knew it was. He rang again. He pounded on the thick door and heard his knocks echo within. No one came. This was the way it had always been for him—ringing the bell of opportunity with politeness, and when that didn't work, knocking to be noticed and still being ignored, and then giving up and going away, promising himself he'd do better next time. Where would next time come from now?

He backed off the front steps and surveyed. The first-floor windows looked like old, single-paned affairs. If he broke the glass near the frame with a carefully thrown stone he could probably reach through, unlatch the window, and let himself in. Not the best way to introduce himself to the team he hoped to join, but it wasn't like he had a choice, apart from continuing on to that bridge he'd considered last night, or finding a nice overpass and settling under it for the next ten years.

If he could have found a rock big enough to do the job, he would have used it, but a search of Reason's grounds turned up only a handful of pebbles. The hell with that. He pushed through the hedges in front of the window closest to the door, spread his legs as far as the brambly shrub would allow, rolled up his sleeve, made a fist, and braced. A tinge of salt air as though from the ocean carried over the stenches of the landfill, and the river, and the house, and he breathed it in. He lifted his chin with a newfound confidence, and Gray sensed the stubble of his beard as his skin pulled taut—was it three-day stubble?

He punched at the glass. His knuckles bounced off and the window laughed in at him B-flat.

He punched, harder. The pane at least vibrated this time.

Again, with everything he had… and in a second, he was up to his shoulder in broken glass. He froze, making sure he hadn't sliced a tendon somewhere, but apart from a trickle of blood on his hand, he remained intact. Even the sweatshirt had come through clean.

Gray brushed a few threatening shards away and reached around the center post to find the latch. But as he did, he heard the rumble of a garage door and tires squealing on cement. Gently he extracted himself from the incriminating pose, wiped his hand inside his pants pocket, and went back to the entrance.

Once there, he turned to see L'aura and Tristan examine the broken window. She leaned to get a closer look, and Gray noticed she'd colored her hair ocean blue this time, and styled it in—of course—a permanent wave. Reverend Hand appeared next, took a look and then cast his gaze skyward, as if to ask who might have desecrated his temple of Reason. He heard other voices too, and decided he could wait no longer. He pounded on the door.

At last it opened. Tristan put up a hand to keep Gray outside. "What do you wish?"

Gray looked into the dim foyer. They were all here, together. Reason stood in the back of the group, looking at him over the tops of their heads. Breeze stood next to the giant, close, the way a lover might.

"Mr. Jack Gray!" The monster's voice sounded as though projected through a feedback loop.

"I chased him off," Gray said. "A prowler. He was trying to break in through the window. He would have made it if I hadn't come along."

"I see," Reverend Hand said. He licked his lips as if seeing made him hungry.

"Who knows what he would have gotten away with."

"What did he look like?"

"Umm... Average height. A little pudgy. Slicked-back hair. Funny mustache."

"Why didn't you call the police instead? Taking on a strange trespasser could have been dangerous."

Gray considered saying he didn't need the help, but they would never believe him. "There was no time," he said. "He was almost inside."

"And you just happened to be on our street."

"Nothing suspicious about that," Gray said. He stood at attention and fixed on Reason. "I am ready... ready to do great things for this city."

"What are you talking about?" L'aura said. "You've never been ready—"

"I am now. I wish to join you."

"You are ready to commit yourself to our cause?" Hand said.

"What a great leader he will make."

L'aura stepped forward. "No. It's a trick. He is my ex-husband. He works for that Boren, our opponent. Our enemy."

"True," Tristan said. "He is no competition for Reason, but still, we cannot allow him here."

The fist he'd used to break the window still hurt, but Gray balled it again, considering Tristan's jaw as its next target. But he had to stay under control. "I have left the Boren campaign," he said. "I have seen the damage they will do to the city. I only want to serve the city. To serve Reason."

They all looked at Breeze. What had she told them about him?

"I don't know if we can trust him," she said.

Her word, he assumed, was law, second perhaps only to the reverend's, and even then the lip-licker was at least partially under her sway and might listen to her counsel. Tristan and L'aura came closer to him, the look in their eyes like angry, vapid villagers determined to cast him out.

But to their disbelief as much as Gray's, Reason took a thunderous step forward and rested a paver-sized hand on each of their shoulders, holding them fast. Gray caught a whiff of the odor the man had laid down at the debate.

"No," he whined. "Mr. Jack Gray is a good man. He will be our friend."

"Reason..." Breeze said. "I don't think you know what you're doing. This man—"

"I have decided." The monster seemed insulted by her comment. "We welcome him."

Who was in charge here? Gray wouldn't have believed the giant thought independently. He shot a look at Hand, whom he figured controlled Reason via some form of telepathy. But the reverend merely observed while his tongue slowly, almost erotically, traced the contours of his lips. The brains of this group had to reside somewhere in this room, but the locus of its intellect posed a mystery.

"Thank you," Gray said. "Let's get to work. I have many ideas."

Reverend Hand crooked a finger at him. "Then come with me." He started for the dark hallway.

Of the tribe, Hand was the last person he'd hoped to work with. He wanted Reason, a chance to examine the beast up close. Or Breeze, to see if he could learn about her defection. Even L'aura would be better, no doubt eventually cluing him in as to the purpose behind this cabal.

He walked past them to follow into the narrowing gloom, the same passage from which he and Breeze had run just a few days ago. He was cautious of this white-haired witch doctor, wary of where he might be taking him. The movie archives of his life played a clip of an unsuspecting victim, taking a never-to-return trip into a similar corridor, and he almost turned back. He'd seen that little room, that vat of green. What other tortures did Hand have back there?

Part way down the hall, Hand turned left, into an uncharted passage, which contorted until Gray became thoroughly disoriented. Near its end opened a door to reveal a small office, adequately lit by a window overlooking the mansion's backyard. It contained a desk and a computer and a file cabinet and a not uncomfortable-looking chair, and no instruments of menace that Gray could see, except for… No! The wall where he would work had been Pollocked. He would have to stare at L'aura's handiwork while he typed whatever it was they would want him to type, and be reminded of the condo, the art show, that ex-life, that past humility.

"You may have this space," Hand said. "What is it that you do?"

Do, or believed he should do? Should he relate only the contributions Bob and Patsy had allowed from him in the past seven years, or what jobs and authorities he believed were rightfully his? No time to be reticent.

"Ideas," he said. "I'm an idea man. The kind that changes lives and campaigns—"

Hand cut him off. "We do not need that. Reason has a plan and it is working."

"But I—"

"You shall write press releases. Keep the media informed about where he will be appearing. Update our web site. Perhaps you can write a short speech. He has to visit the Rotary Club next week..." An orb of drool formed at the corner of Hand's mouth, and he licked it away.

"I was hoping—"

"Here," Hand said. "His calendar." He slid a Xeroxed sheet closer to the keyboard. "Take these events and write a paragraph on each one. I will get you a list of media contacts."

Some change. It was as though there were a sign hanging from his neck that he wore everywhere he went, one that described a set of skills so limited as to preclude anyone giving him a chance to show what he could truly achieve. "This is all I can do," was the headline, and underneath it listed the menial bullet points to which he'd always been relegated:

Write mundane blather.

Look things up on Google.

Avoid conflict.

Subordinate to authority, no matter how dimwitted it may be.

But for the moment, he had to play along. "I have my own list of contacts. I will bring it tomorrow," Gray said. "Maybe there's a few people I can add to yours."

"Good," Hand said. "Tomorrow we will show you the kitchen and the rest of the house. You shall be properly indoctrinated then."

He left, and Gray paused for a few moments to look out the window and away from the turmoil of the walls surrounding him. He noticed a weedy lawn, backed by a row of trees and brush thick enough to keep neighbors from prying. A pair of black, industrial-gauge wires ran along the ground, from the house to a tiny shed in the far corner of the property. Tomorrow he would start to get the lay of the manse and figure ways to investigate when no one watched.

Gray scanned Reason's calendar for details. An office supply store opening, a visit to the senior center, lunch with the Local 494 pipefitters.

Sure.

He started typing absentmindedly, the words like an ancient river, meandering and muddy, on their way to nowhere.

He took a deep breath and blew it out deliberately. That wasn't why he was here anyway.

Two Guys in a Hot Tub

Randy insisted on pouring him another glass of wine, and Gray, enjoying the relaxation of alcohol and conversation, and the hot tub in which they were offered, eventually stopped refusing.

"Tomorrow," Randy said, "we'll pick up a can of gas and rescue your car. Then I won't have to drive you eight miles to and from work." He lifted his glass clear of the water to toast. "And congratulations on finding a way to infiltrate the big boy's house. Inspired."

Gray clinked his glass with his host's. "I don't know how long I can do it," he said. "I don't even know how I can pay you back for the gas."

"Who said anything about paying me back?"

"I can't let you do that."

"Why not?"

"It's not right."

"Who cares about right?"

"And something else..." Gray squirmed. The trunks he'd borrowed from Randy would have been tight even if they were the proper size, but being at least two inches too small, they pinched his waist and shrink-wrapped his privates into an obscene 3-D sculpture, a vacuum-sealed still life of the male anatomy. He sat close to the bubbly jets of air piped in to hide his embarrassment and hoped that no other borders decided to join them.

Randy sipped on his chardonnay as though he hadn't heard. "This really is an exquisite bottle," he said. "More?"

"I'm paid up here until Thursday, and then I'll have to go. L'aura got hold of the bank accounts, and—" Gray's mind drifted—how cold did it get under those overpasses?

"Oh, you're not going anywhere," Randy said.

"What?"

"I'm letting you stay. Free. Room, and if necessary, board."

"But you can't do that."

"I own this place, right? I can do whatever the fuck I want. So, you stay."

Gray looked almost disappointed that Randy wasn't planning to kick him out. "Why are you doing all this?" he asked.

"Can't you just accept the help? Is it because you feel you don't deserve it? Or there'll be strings attached?"

Gray had to think for a minute. "Yes," he said. "To all."

"Poor Gray." Randy reached behind him for the bottle of wine. "Poor, poor Gray. You know, the world is getting a little tired of your 'I'm not worthy' sermons." He topped off his glass and took another sip. "Tough to keep it cold in the hot tub," he said.

Gray held out his glass for more. If he had to receive a lecture it would help if he were at least buzzed. "Maybe we should be drinking red."

"Mmm, no. Red doesn't go with chlorine."

"Listen. I know you're right," Gray said. "About accepting help, I mean. It's never been easy."

"You've been in politics too long. No wonder you don't trust anyone."

"Yeah, I think it's been longer than that."

Randy pointed to a garden hose that sat coiled next to the tub. "Would you mind?" he asked. "The leak. I promise to find it someday."

Gray put the open end into the tub and reached back to turn the spigot.

"So you're cool?" Randy asked. "Like they say, 'Don't look a gift horse—'"

Gray found it hard to answer. All those people he'd known and worked with and lived with for so long who demanded he give and give and give a little more, and now this man, this near total stranger, wanted nothing in return. He raised his wine glass to salute his landlord.

"So what's your plan for Reason? Did you have a chance to explore yet? I'll give you my video camera again. Sneak into that secret lab and get some footage of big boy taking his bath. Film at eleven!"

"It's not that easy," Gray said. "There's too many of them. The only one who seems to trust me is Reason, and who the hell knows why. The rest of them would rather ditch me in the landfill."

"So we need a diversion. Something to get them all out of the house while you stay behind. Then you can snoop to your little heart's desire."

"Yeah, good luck there. It's like L'aura and Breeze and that gallery guy have all been programmed. They catch me spying and you may never hear from me again."

Gray stood and looked in the distance at a reddening sky as the sun dipped behind the abandoned factories lining the river's edge. The city had tried for years to lure a developer to at least tear the old buildings down. Planners and council members proposed elaborate schemes to infuse this part of the riverfront with luxury condos and retail centers, mixed-use meccas to pave over decades of errors and neglect. Still, the teetering brick structures remained, untouched, tombstones in Grand River's cemetery of dreams. He thought of how he had trusted Breeze, for a little while. And L'aura too. Maybe he trusted Bob and Patsy once as well. But relationships changed, always. Allegiances shifted. Throughout history, cities and states made allies, signed treaties, broke them, made enemies. People did too.

Randy pressed the switch on the side of the tub to extinguish the jets. He picked up his glass and the empty bottle in one hand and started to get out, without flinching from the abrupt change in temperature from the water to the air.

Gray rolled himself out of the tub, the vise of the trunks precluding him from bending at the hips. "I can't believe you're doing all this," he said as he maneuvered himself upright and followed Randy back into the manager's office.

"Hey," Randy said. "I want to do great things for my city too."

The Real Reason

Around every corner in the mansion lurked the promise of bowel-clenching fright. Gray dreaded finding L'aura in bed with the gallery owner, or Breeze in bed with—oh, God—the monster; or he wouldn't find her, exactly, since she'd be hidden under that monolith of flesh, and he would only hear her muffled squeals of panic and ecstasy in counterpoint to the rhythm of the distressed box spring, their dueling vowel sounds taunting him: ohhh, eeee, ohhh, eeee, ohhh, eeee.

He pressed on, driven, initially, by his plan to expose Reason, but now pushed as much by the need for self-abasement. Gray would force himself to look on what he had let get away: the life and loves of a successful, unafraid man. He was still having trouble walking, thanks to Randy's eighteen-hour support trunks, and took halting, old-man steps through the corridors as he went from room to room, listening.

Muted voices echoed, but he could not tell from where. Hand kept the house dark, and the inner hallways had the feel of an abandoned coal mine. He didn't know how he'd stumbled into this newest labyrinth. He'd only tried to find the office to which the reverend had relegated him, but seconds after Hand pointed the way he became lost, reduced to sliding along walls, feeling for non-existent light switches. But no one watched, so he would put the mistake to his advantage and explore; maybe find the room with the vat, which he felt sure contained Reason's magic elixir, the green plasma that kept him alive. Maybe something even more incriminating. He patted Randy's video camera, secured in a backpack. Whatever he found, this time he'd get the visual proof.

Another two turns and finally the voices became louder. They were coming from behind a closed door in the middle of this latest hallway. Someone directed. A chorus responded.

"What are we?"

"We are the future of Grand River."

"Who can stop us?"

"No one."

It had to be Hand. The other voices must belong to L'aura and Tristan and...Breeze? Gray would never have believed anyone could hypnotize her like this, but he detected her lilt as it mixed among the others, as much a droid to the reverend as they.

The voices paused, as though the group had merely been warming up before the real agenda. After a minute, Hand spoke again: "He needs education. Who will volunteer to give him the lesson?"

"I will." It sounded like Breeze.

"Teach him about power. Make him understand what we can do."

"It will be a pleasure," she said.

They were coming for him. No wonder they'd let him join. Reason's powers hadn't worked on Gray, so they would brainwash him to make him like the rest. But would their hypnosis be enough? If he were truly immune to the voodoo, they might have to resort to more visceral tactics. He fantasized his shoulders and feet pinned to a metal table while Hand administered Phenobarbital, or worse yet, prepared to perform a lobotomy. A chunk of his brain sliced away, leaving him dim and passive, unable to control his thoughts and open to any suggestion. He and Reason would be equals then.

Gray didn't stick around to listen to more. He was sure that somewhere within the mansion lurked a medieval torture chamber, complete with rack, stocks and an iron mask, and that he'd wind up there if he hesitated. He took to spelunking again, figuring if he explored enough hallways he would eventually find a way out.

He picked up his pace, knocked into walls as he negotiated the dark. Never mind the racket—he had to get back to the light before they caught up. As he glided—okay, stumbled—Gray listened for footsteps, for the clomps of the giant. He negotiated corner after corner without finding his bearings. How could the house have this many passageways? When he heard the voices again, he realized he must have somehow doubled back, traversing the same spaces, not recognizing them because of the dark. Damn. If he didn't find the way to the front door, he might be trapped in here forever, a mouse in a little maze of his own making, unable to locate the cheese.

Cheese?

Gray stopped and sniffed the air. His nose had often been a nuisance. It noticed scents others missed, forced him to endure bad air the rest of the world had long since become used to. He had to explain its size, apologize for its intrusiveness, deal with the distractions it presented. But once in a while, his schnoz proved useful.

The odor of the river and the landfill had a different quality outside the house—less B.O., more trash and methane. His nose, and possibly his alone, could discern that difference. It could decipher the nuances between the atmosphere of imprisonment here and relative freedom out there.

He would smell his way out.

He inhaled, and quarts of air rushed past his olfactory, imparting their hidden clues. The landfill remained prominent today, offering a whiff of alley-behind-a-restaurant stench strong enough for him to follow. Left here, then right, then left—no, right—now straight. A hint of rubber added to the mix, as though someone had discarded a set of retreads. Now, a note of pine, perhaps from a pallet or a crate. The unmistakable perfume of coal dust. Why he couldn't sense differences in wine was a mystery he'd have to explore. But later—he felt close to escape. The hallway lightened. At the far end of the corridor, he saw the glow of freedom. Just a few more steps—

But another smell overpowered his senses. It was a sharp, tidepool mix of brine and seaweed and primitive life. Decaying flesh, moist dirt, the unmistakable notes of a graveyard. The hallway went dark again, the light at the end eclipsed by a massive object that filled the space before him, floor to ceiling and wall to wall, and which, when its skull bumped against the door frame, produced a thump and a shudder, as though a boulder had been placed to seal him off.

"My friend Mr. Jack Gray!" The beast's voice changed pitch with almost every syllable. "You appear to be lost."

"Oh. Reason. I was just trying to find my room—"

"Your office is right here." Reason pushed open a door. The light from the back window washed into the hallway, illuminating the giant's features from the side, casting his shadow like that of an enormous gargoyle against the wall.

Gray slithered into the room and sat at the desk. "I guess I'll get to work," he said. "I have some press releases to write for Reverend Hand."

"Let me join you. I need a speech for the Rotary luncheon next week. You can write it for me and I will help you." Reason pulled a chair alongside and sat, his mass bending the frame to the breaking point.

Gray turned the computer on, and the two of them sat in silence as it booted up. The giant loomed over him like a condemned building, and Gray prepared to bolt at the first sign of danger. He heard the monster's breath whistling through his nostrils; he smelled the ooze that had attached to his skin and triggered his body odor. And then he felt it, what L'aura and Breeze and Tristan and the rest must have felt: the power, the pull of the magic that throbbed deep inside the man, and which radiated outward, past the crumbling flesh and butchered features. And in that moment, Reason became beautiful to him; no longer mere exhumed parts stitched into the figure of an enormous golem, but a human being. More than a human being, in fact, because he comprised the souls of perhaps a dozen human beings, and more than that even, more than anything human, he represented the ideas and hopes of all those people when they were alive and all the people who were still alive and had chosen to follow him. Those dreams coalesced and emanated from the giant, enveloping Gray, and their force was like a tsunami, like an earthquake, like gravity…like love. Gray felt his focus begin to wander, his resolve draining away, and experienced an urge to wrap his arms as far as they would go around the monster, proclaiming his devotion. No hypnosis administered; no lobotomy need be performed. The power of the magic overwhelmed resistance.

Shake it. Shake it off. Fight it. Stay composed, man. Stay apart. Remember who you are, Gray: the neutron, the chargeless, unbonding particle to which no element is attracted. Only you can resist the forces that must drive the beast. If you allow yourself to be captured by Reason, the city will be doomed.

Ah, but all his life Gray had only wanted people to like him. He had played the friend, the crony, the fool, in the forlorn hope that others would, at some point, return the favor, grant him access, buy him a beer, let him be part of the group. It had rarely happened, and he knew he could not let it happen now. Maybe the people didn't realize the danger Reason and Hand represented; maybe he was the only one who did. The others had succumbed, but he could not, as much as he now wanted to give himself over to it. He took a deep breath. Eyes closed, he revisited the feeling of a young man turned away, ridiculed, shunned. He embraced it as his role, his responsibility. And instead of giving in, he sat there, in the giant's presence, holding back from hugging the colossus, holding back a tear, because he felt he might never have this opportunity again.

The giant did not perceive any of this, and Gray composed

himself. When the computer blinked ready, he clicked a file on the desktop, the one he'd worked on yesterday. As it opened, he remembered what he had written and tried to cover the screen. But too late. Reason stared at the frustrations Gray had tapped out.

Maybe the giant couldn't read. Maybe he was merely enthralled with the symbols on the monitor. But, no.

"What is this?" Reason said. He read from the text, although the words seemed difficult for him: "Candidates should not be allowed to run for office...unless they can prove they are at least as smart...as the people they wish to represent."

"I was just daydreaming—"

"Grand River will elect another...clown to lead its circus."

The beast put a hand on his shoulder. This was it. Gray had crossed the line and infuriated the monster. Reason would crumple him like a sheet of paper. He would toss his body like litter into the wastebasket, and that would be the end of him and his stupid dreams of glory, and of the lifetime of rationalizations that kept him from acting on any of them.

"I agree with you," Reason said. "It is true. I am not a smart man."

"I didn't really mean it."

"Yes, you did. And it is fine. I am trying to learn, but it is difficult."

Gray rolled his chair back a few inches and took a fresh look at Reason. Instead of the patchwork smile he'd seen that first time at the fundraiser, he saw a man struggling to make sense of his world. The eyes were still cockeyed and darting, the mouth still a sliver of confusion, but now the beast's countenance did not appear evil, but empty, and begging to be filled with knowledge that would liberate the ideas inside. Disengaged from the others he might become his own man and not merely a tool. Although he couldn't allow himself to idolize the giant, Gray felt something that was, perhaps, stronger, and better.

"What must you learn?" Gray asked.

"Everything. There is so much."

"Everything?"

"I must learn government and how to run the city. I must learn economics and business and politics. And I must learn how to be with people. How to understand them." He sounded like a child thrust into a party for adults, trying to sound more intelligent than he was capable.

"It's a lot," Gray said.

"And I must do it all so fast. Before I am elected mayor. Reverend Hand demands it."

Gray had to ask, "Do you have some kind of... disability?"

The titan shook his head. Gray watched his tresses sweep around his skull like the strands of a mop. He had said the wrong thing again.

"How long have you been studying?"

"A year, I think. I do not remember what came before."

Gray brightened. "What do you remember?" he asked.

Reason squinted as though thinking hard. "I remember the room," he said. "I remember the Reverend Hand standing over me. He gives me what I need."

"And before that?"

"Only shadows."

His theory nearly proved! Gray had to push for more. More evidence. He reached for the backpack.

"Do you know who you are?" he asked.

"I am Reason," the giant said. His eyes had gone glassy, as though he were imagining himself somewhere else.

"Who is Reason? Are you...a man?"

"I am men. I am not of this world."

"What does that mean?"

"I do not belong here. I belong in the place of those who do not live."

"Who told you this? Was it Hand?"

"I only know this myself."

Gray had the camera in his hand, ready to record the giant's testimony.

"Think again," Gray said. "Was there a time before you knew the Reverend? Maybe it would seem like another life—"

Before the monster could answer, Gray heard the little hammers of high-heeled shoes against the hardwood in the hall. Breeze's voice carried into the room.

"Reason! Are you in there?" she called.

"Quickly, man. Answer me!"

Reason only stared at the computer screen, which had dimmed.

"I have to know," Gray said. "Are you undead?"

Breeze called again. "I'm looking for you. Where are you?"

It snapped the giant out of his hallucination. He returned to the present, to the original conversation. "It is important that we do well at the luncheon. The Rotary will be good supporters." His eyes opened and he smiled—as much of a smile as his brutal face could form. "Together we will do great things for this city," he said.

"Fuck," Gray said.

Reason rocked back in his chair and produced a shrieking hee-haw sound that reverberated down the hallway. Gray froze, assuring himself it was only laughter and not some primal war cry before an attack.

"I hear you, Reason. I'm coming."

Breeze. She was almost at the door. Gray stuffed the camera into the backpack and zipped it.

Breeze stopped at the office doorway, and Reason turned to look at her. "It is time for me to have my lesson," he said.

All that anxiety for nothing. They had been talking about Reason. The education was his. Hand and the others were programming him for the job of mayor, training him to carry out some purpose. Maybe Gray's ideas about that would turn out to be right, too. But maybe not. Reason wasn't the blank slate he'd assumed. Something more lay just beyond the stupid slogans and oddball statements he'd spouted at the debate and throughout the campaign. And Gray had been so close to tapping into it.

"There you are," Breeze said. "You've been hiding."

How an eight-foot-tall being managed to hide was a stretch. But Gray ignored her comment to focus on the woman he had idolized until a few days ago. Her blouse flared open to the third button. Her hip-hugging skirt clung an inch shorter than most women would dare. Even in the most mundane circumstances, she remained as sensual as ever, and Gray's disappointment and disdain for her fought with his desires. He felt a droplet of saliva at the corner of his mouth and thought of Hand. He checked to make sure his tongue stayed in place.

Breeze looked at Reason and spoke as though Gray wasn't there. "Time for your class in government. Come. We have much to teach you."

The giant rose and followed her, looking like a man just found guilty, and headed off with the bailiff. Once in the hallway, he turned back and said, "Thank you, Mr. Jack Gray."

Gray poked his head around the doorjamb and watched them go, Breeze's curves shifting sideways, Reason's slab of a body lurching forward and back. The taps of her heels interspersed with his size twenty-three clomps. As they turned the corner Gray, whispered, "It's Gray, by the way, not Jack. Gray Davenport."

Comparing Notes

A campaign headquarters, even in Grand River, should qualify as one of the hottest spots in town: dozens of phones ringing like a handbell choir, a bank of computers staffed by eager volunteers, printouts, piles of mail, people coming and going, talking, arguing, and laughing, and in the middle of the room, a huge whiteboard with the campaign logo and graphs showing how the candidate is kicking ass in the polls, precinct by precinct, interest group by interest group. But no hubbub here. When Gray heard the phone down the hall, he realized it was the first time since he'd been at Reason's so-called HQ that any contact between the staff and the outside world had occurred. The scene was too quiet for an elections office; too quiet for almost any kind of office, except perhaps a funeral home. Any more comatose and it might pass for Bob Boren's campaign central. Yet out there, in the particulate-riddled air of Grand River voter land, Reason attracted followers like ants, drawing them to his cause with the same instinct, the same lack of thought as scent-crazed drones, and the same willingness to be pacified by a leader's ruling aura.

It had to be the Reverend's doing. Gray now believed Hand maintained a level of control over the population, an offshoot of the science that had created the monster, lining eligible voters up like cows to an abattoir, herded in the same direction but not really knowing their destination.

Hand held even tighter control inside the organization. A look at Reason's calendar showed every event and appearance planned out weeks or months in advance. The Reverend made every decision. The campaign cleared each statement through him. So Gray was surprised when Tristan appeared at his office door with an announcement.

"You have to leave now," the man in black said.

"A bomb scare?" That some local whack job wanted to off them all would at least lend an air of legitimacy to the campaign.

"Reason has been invited to a meeting with the Citizens for Inclusion. We're all going."

"Let me get my—"

"Not you. You go home."

"You don't want me here, do you?" Gray asked. Their mutual dislike would come to a boil sooner or later, why not now?

"I don't see what you're bringing to the campaign. If Reason hadn't insisted, you wouldn't be here, and we wouldn't have to watch you."

"So you don't trust me."

"None of us do. Why should we?"

"Why not? I trust you."

"You do?"

Gray was pleased he'd won this round even before he delivered the big punch. "Sure," he said. "You're screwing my wife. It's no secret. You have nothing left to hide, so why shouldn't I trust you?"

"Maybe there's more to it than that."

He looked the gallery owner up and down. The black clothes couldn't conceal his twiggy frame. If there were anyone Gray could take if it came to blows, it would be Tristan. "I doubt it," he said.

Tristan turned to leave, but stopped and looked back. "Did you notice L'aura's new hair color?"

"Yeah, I saw it. It's blue."

"That's the hair on her head," Tristan said. "But do you know what color her hair is... down there?"

Gray leaped out of his chair and balled his fists. Tristan recoiled.

Still, he couldn't bring himself to swing. He seethed, but rationalized that punching the gallery owner out would be his ticket to the street, before he could continue to snoop.

Or, maybe he was still a coward, still a neutron.

Tristan smiled at having called Gray's bluff. "Go home, dude," he said.

Gray packed his briefcase and followed Tristan out, lest he have to rely on his sense of smell again to find the front door. The Citizens for Inclusion. It sounded made up. In his work for Bob, he'd dealt with just about every special interest group Grand River had to offer, but he'd never heard of these people. Must be a new organization. It would probably last as long as most of the others—maybe a few months or a year, tops. But a candidate couldn't leave any gathering unrecognized during an election.

As he arranged himself in the Civic, Gray noticed a car exiting the garage and turning out of the driveway. Big and black. A hearse. A Cadillac doctored to transport coffins, and—yeah—whatever body parts one might load up at the local cemetery. Reverend Hand drove. Reason sat shotgun, his head tilted to avoid the headliner. The rest of the windows were blacked out, but Gray assumed the others sat in the back row. The car whipped onto the street, tires squealing to make up for lost time.

Gray grasped the key to start his engine when it hit him—this was the perfect time, maybe the only time, he would have to investigate Hand's operation. He probably had two hours before they returned. The window he'd broken the day before hadn't been repaired yet, protected only by a sheet of plywood. When the hearse disappeared around a corner, he got out of the car and slung the backpack with the camera over his shoulder. If he could get inside without anyone seeing, he'd have a good chunk of time to explore. A car motored down the street, but as soon as it passed, he'd make his move.

But the car slowed, as if on patrol for Neighborhood Watch. Who would want to watch this house?

It eased to the curb behind the Honda, and Gray knew—Randy.

His landlord almost jumped out of his car. "Citizens for Inclusion, at your service."

"You?"

"The entire organization, right here in this compact little body. President, Vice-President, Secretary, Treasurer, and Member-at-Large…and I do mean large." Randy laughed at his joke. Gray tried not to, but let out a snort.

"So *you* made the phone call," Gray said.

"You needed a diversion. Well, you got one. Let's get inside."

They ran toward the damaged window. Gray had to ask. "Where did you send them?"

"The VFW hall on the other side of the city. I told them we'd provide free lunch for anyone who wanted to attend."

"But that place has been vacant for almost two years."

"Yeah," Randy said. "They'll figure it out in an hour or so."

They sized up the plywood and pushed. It had been secured with only a few nails and gave without much effort. A quick look around to ensure there were no witnesses and they stepped inside, propping the wood back against the opening to cover their move.

"By the way," Gray asked. "What does Citizens for Inclusion do?"

"We include, baby. When we party, everyone's invited. Now, which way to big boy's room?"

"This way," Gray said, heading back to the hall. "And it's not just him we're after. It's the Reverend Hand, too. He's behind all this. If we find something on him, we bring the whole operation down."

"Lead the way."

Gray paused. "I'm not sure…" His nose might have been able to lead him out of the house, but could it get him back inside? He concentrated on Reason's primordial stink, which had left a permanent impression in his memory. Like a bloodhound who'd been given a scrap of clothing to process, he concentrated and sniffed the air, hoping to pick up a trace of the scent.

"If we can get back to the laboratory, Hand's office should be somewhere nearby," he said.

"I just want to see that vat of goo."

Gray took off down the hallway. "This way," he said. "I'm on to it."

"Go get 'em, boy," Randy encouraged.

As before, no lights to illuminate the way, so they felt along the stairwells and walls until they encountered a doorway. Each room revealed some piece of the Reason puzzle: piles of books, some of them looking centuries old, with strange authors like Cornelius Agrippa and Albertus Magnus; discarded newspapers and glassware; empty cardboard boxes. Gray did not know what to make of them. The real goal, he sensed, lay farther down the corridor, and as if to confirm his feeling, the scent he tracked became stronger as they went in deeper.

A few more turns and the reek, magnified by his determination to find it, became overpowering. "Here," Gray said. "Behind this door."

But it was locked. "Should we break it down?" Randy asked.

"Can't take the chance. If I'm wrong, I won't be able to stay here and look again."

Randy said, "Let me try this."

He pulled a credit card from his wallet. Doorjambs didn't protrude over latches in a house this old, and locks jimmied open with ease. In a moment the door came free, revealing the Reason-sized tub, still brimming with slime and secrets, still smelling like a prehistoric swamp.

"Eureka," Gray said.

No kidding.

"Now that's what I call a Jacuzzi," Randy said. He took the camera from Gray's backpack and started recording. "A few minutes in that stuff and I'd be as loose as petroleum jelly."

"Don't get any ideas," Gray said. "Now that we've come this far, we've got to search the offices nearby. I want to know the truth about Hand as well as Reason. I want his records, his science, how he did it. How he uses Reason to control the minds of voters. I know it's all here."

"Yes, it is."

Gray pirouetted in surprise. Breeze stood, one shoulder against the doorframe, holding a thick folder pregnant with documents. "Everything we need is in here," she said, tapping the manila.

Randy started recording her. Gray thought to stop him, but why cancel what might someday be the only visual record he would have to remember her by? As the camera digitized her, Gray noticed how relaxed she seemed, flirtatious, how aware she was of her surroundings. The way she'd been when he first—

"You're you again," he said.

"In the flesh."

Did she have to put it that way?

"I thought you'd gone over to Reason's side," Gray said.

"Pretty good acting, don't you think?" She seemed relieved at not having to keep up the pretense any longer. "I've been gathering the evidence a little bit at a time, piling it up, waiting for an opportunity like this when I could get into Reverend Hand's office. Whoever called to invite them to that luncheon today is my hero. It gave me a chance to uncover the mother lode."

Randy beamed from behind the camera. He moved around the room until he focused on Gray's face.

"Why don't you put that down now?" Gray said, turning from the lens.

Randy complied. "Mission accomplished?" he asked.

"We've still got to make this information public," Breeze said.

Gray held out his hands to ask for the documents, but Breeze wasn't ready to let them go. "All right," he said. "What have you got?"

"It's big," she said. "Turns out Reverend Hand is a doctor, too. Trained in Germany. Someplace called Ingolstadt. Studied anatomy, biosciences."

"I should have known. What's he doing in the states?"

"Kicked out for going too far with his experiments. He tried to implant bonobo genes into his girlfriend and then had sex with her, hoping it would produce some kind of cross-breed."

"What?"

"He said he was trying to create an inter-species being."

"The bastard. That should be enough to finish him."

"Wait," she said. "There's more." Breeze laid the folder on a steel table and opened it. She leafed through the pages and extracted one. "When he came to the states, he couldn't get work in his field. He wandered around for a couple of years and then started a church in Georgia."

"That explains the reverend part," Randy said.

"The Church of the Sacred Hand. But he never got his tax-exempt status. The feds were investigating."

"Indicted?" Gray asked.

"They never had enough evidence to charge him."

"Innuendo is enough for us," Gray said. "This is sure to drive him and Reason from the election."

"And here," she said, pulling another sheaf of paper free, "are records of cemetery plots from around the region—names, dates of death..."

"Like who?"

"Politicians," she said. "Dead politicians. Democrats, Republicans, left-wing, right-wing, independents, Peace and Freedom, a communist, and even a John Bircher."

"I see it now," Gray said. "It's all making sense."

"What about the brain?" Randy asked. "Big boy's not the

smartest student in class, but he must have something upstairs. Where did Hand get the noggin?"

Breeze slipped another form from the pile, holding it up. "That part's sketchy. Like he didn't want anyone to know where it came from. The only record that's unaccounted for is this one."

She handed it to Gray. A ledger from a cemetery in Georgia, probably near where he'd run his church.

"Farmers, laborers…the rural poor, looks like," Gray said, scanning the records. "Why wouldn't Hand pick someone more academic, like from a university? Someone easier to educate?"

"Maybe someone less willing to oppose him," Randy offered.

"All I've been able to figure is that Hand thought if he could create a human life, he'd be honored as a genius. Every scientist who'd ever dismissed him would have to kneel down in homage. Apart from the head, everything else is here—lists of body parts, anatomical diagrams, even a schedule for the surgical procedures he planned to put everything together."

Gray said, "There's something else I want to know." Now she gave him the folder, and he leafed through, stopping when he came to a set of pages stained in green. "Ten gallons of swamp water, one quart of mixed amino acids, a cup of bile, essential oils, tincture of bone marrow… Yeah! This is the formula for the liquid in that tub."

"Gray, you were right," Breeze said. "Reason is a monster—a Frankenstein's monster."

Gray nodded. Being right and getting credit for it was a new feeling. Now they could turn the city against Hand and Reason. The FBI would investigate. The public would demand Hand's head. They'd be so busy defending themselves they wouldn't have time to run their campaign. And the other charges would be sure to scare the rest of the voters away. "You're incredible," he said to Breeze. "No wonder you left Bob's campaign."

He looked directly into her eyes. They were citrine gems. She looked back at him.

Randy put the brakes on this mutual, if momentary seduction.

"Hold on, kids," he said. "If the doctor reverend brought big boy to life, why didn't he just announce it and make a splash? He would have had his glory right there."

"This is all there is," Breeze said, pointing to the documents. "Maybe he had something else to prove."

"He did," Gray said. "The accomplishment wasn't enough. Respect wasn't enough. Hand wants power. He wants the world to come crawling. He puts Reason in the mayor's office and Grand River has to deal with him. Then, after he's sucked patronage from everyone in the city, they move on to the state, and maybe the national level." Being right had gone to his head. Gray believed he could explain anything now.

Breeze crossed her arms in thought, pushing her breasts up until they were nearly bubbling out of her blouse. She shifted a hip to the side, absent-mindedly, but still sensual. The sight broke Gray's concentration and stopped his ramble. Her open neckline, the open folder on the table—it was all too suggestive.

"What do we do next?" she asked.

He had an answer, but didn't want to say it in front of Randy.

She'd come back to his side. Mysterious as ever, more alluring than before. Reason and Hand and the others would return soon. Maybe, if they'd caught on to Randy's ruse, in just a few minutes. But there was something about being in this room that turned him on, something more than just Breeze's sexuality. The severity of the steel surfaces. The clean, hard lines of the scientific equipment. The primitive aroma of life in the vat. He looked at her and she became the porn star in the triple-X shop. Randy started the video camera again.

Gray fought his baser urge. His rational mind did not want to deal with this ridiculous carnal yearning again. He would embarrass himself, this time in front of his friend. But his senses had been overcome by the raw, organic nature of the surroundings. This room held the origin of life, the desire to exist, and more—to propagate, to proclaim, perhaps to evolve, or maybe devolve. He could sense it in his medulla; feel it in his loins, and down deeper, much deeper—at the subatomic level. His neutrons pulsed as though they had been charged with sexual energy, and he felt himself lose touch with civility and enter a state of pure lust.

The others seemed not to be affected, or maybe they could hide their feelings better than he. Gray breathed deeply, hoping he could clear this nonsense from his head. But breathing the heavy air only made the urge stronger. Denying Reason's pull was child's play compared to this.

For a fleeting instant, an image of L'aura—no, not L'aura, but Laura, his wife, his real wife—danced through his consciousness. But now under the influence of the primordial vapor, he blinked her away. There was Randy to consider too, and he did. He'd never participated in a threesome before, and had always imagined it as girl-girl-boy, but what the hell—

"Give me that camera," Gray said. "Let's make a movie."

"A movie?" she asked. "You mean like a documentary? I think it's a little soon for that. We still have to get this information out."

"Something more revealing than a documentary," he said. She was hiding her urge, but he felt sure it was there, just under the surface, ready to surrender to his. Gray moved toward her, reached for her hand. "Don't tell me you haven't done this before."

"Done what before?"

"A handsome research scientist, the beautiful assistant, a mysterious laboratory… It's a natural setting."

"For what? I don't follow."

Randy put the lens cap on the recorder and slipped it into the backpack. "Gray, you need to calm down. There's already a big boy who lives here, and you aren't him."

"You start that camera again and we'll see who the real big boy is."

"I don't know what idea you've got," Breeze said, "but I'm sure it's the wrong one."

"Oh, really," he said. "You think I couldn't figure out who you really are from what happened in the triple-X shop?"

"Gray, come on," Randy said. "You're out of control."

Breeze put her hands on her hips. "Triple-X shop? All right. Who am I?"

He'd never found the proof, but this was no time to back down. And now he felt anger too, his unrequited lust morphing into a desire to hurt her. "Star of stage, screen, bedroom and casting couch. Shagging dudes in all fifty states and half of Europe, and taking it in every way along the way. Ladies and gentlemen, I give you Breeze Wellington, porn actress extraordinaire."

She should have been mortified, or at least insulted. Or at least pretended to have been insulted. Instead she glared at him. "So what if I am?"

Had he been right? Again?

Breeze retreated into the hallway. Gray followed. Randy put a hand on his shoulder to hold him back, but he flung it away and charged toward her.

But as soon as he crossed the threshold into the corridor and its less potent air, the feeling drained from him, and he found himself apologizing. "Something came over me, like getting totally drunk in just a few seconds. It was that room, the air, that green soup. Breeze, I—"

"Enough," she said. "So you think you know."

She didn't seem angry, just perturbed. If he refocused on their mission, she might even let it slide.

"Why don't we take this evidence to the newspapers?" he said. "I'll bet they'd kill to get their hands on this."

"I'll take it to the News-Press," she said. "You can meet me there."

Fair enough. If he were she, he wouldn't want to share a ride with him either. Still, he had to smile just a little—the fumes in the lab had pushed him past his usual barriers, had allowed him to defeat his inhibitions and make the move on Breeze he'd imagined from that first moment. And the fact he didn't take it any farther than just talk—or wasn't permitted to, thanks to Randy—didn't matter. This time, in there, he would have done it.

Sure.

Yellowed Journalism

The staff at the News-Press—technically the Grand River News-Press-Enterprise-Courier and Daily Tattler, reflecting the last four corporate takeovers—made him wait, as usual. He'd never managed to catch their arrogant attentions when he flogged for Bob, and now that Gray didn't even have cred, he might not get in to see someone until after the current issue deadlined, sometime after midnight. And to think he had worked here for five years a decade ago.

But as soon as Breeze stepped off the elevator and joined him, still clutching the folder of evidence against her chest, three of the male reporters raced over to welcome them. Her magic radiated as powerfully as ever.

The staff led them to a desk and offered her the guest chair, but forced Gray to stand behind the two men who had jumped their colleague's claim.

"We have some evidence that incriminates the Reverend Inchoate Hand," Breeze said.

"What hand?"

"Inchoate."

"Who?"

"The man behind Reason."

"The giant?"

"His creator." Gray tried to squeeze in among the reporters.

They ignored him and she went on. "These documents follow a trail of perversion and corruption that's logged nearly ten thousand miles. From Germany to Georgia to Grand River, it threatens the race for the mayor's office in June."

She opened the folder and let them browse. "From Reverend Hand's personal files."

"How did you get these?" the sitting reporter asked.

"I worked there for a while," she said.

"Me too," said Gray, still ignored.

"I began to have suspicions right away. Contributions weren't making it into the bank account. Personal expenses were charged to the campaign."

Man, she was practiced at this. And she laid it on thick. If the staff bought it, this would warrant all caps on the front page. Gray had the headline: "Hand Dips into Own Till." Damn, he should never have left his job here.

The reporters perused the folder's contents, as Breeze showed them the most damaging papers.

"Hold a slot in section one and dial up the Wilder campaign," said one of them. "Let's get some comment from the candidate and see if we can reach this Hand."

Gray remembered the phones at the manse. Reason's crew would be loathe to answer after being duped, and incensed once they found out what Breeze and he had stolen. They would come after them, and who knew what mayhem they'd bring? He imagined his neck in Reason's hydraulic press hands. Yet he didn't fear Reason so much as L'aura. She might look at his actions as vengeance for what she did to him and seek to escalate.

And they'd come after Breeze, too. She'd betrayed Reason and the campaign to a much greater degree than he, and she was the one who lifted the damaging files. Gray felt protective toward her, this woman who seemed so independent, so unafraid of consequences. He couldn't let anything happen to her.

But as long as they were spilling the beans about the Wilder campaign, they might as well go all the way. "There's something else, "Gray said. "Something that's even more amazing."

The reporters disregarded him to pepper Breeze with questions about how she'd infiltrated the campaign office and gained the confidence of Reason and Hand.

"Really guys," Gray continued, "This is pretty important. Hand is not just a crook and a fake. He's a mad scientist."

Breeze talked over him, relating to the reporters how she'd played up to each man's insecurities. The giant needed a mother figure, she said, and the reverend was just looking for sex, not that he ever got any, of course, but she admitted she led him on to gain access. "Drop a few compliments, do a little shake, and a good-looking woman can get whatever she wants," she said. "Right, guys?"

The reporters didn't argue, pressing closer to her.

The scenario she related, however, sounded familiar to Gray. That first encounter in Bob's living room, her low-cut dress, the way she moved to make sure he got a good look…

"Reason's a creature," Gray tried again. "He's all parts. An experiment—"

They continued not to listen.

"He's a monster!"

"Yeah, we know that from the evidence," the first reporter said, finally looking. "But leave the opinions out of it. This is journalism, you know. We don't editorialize except on the editorial page."

The reporter on the phone got through and received the official "no comment." The three of them huddled around his monitor and began to compose the story. They did not attempt to corroborate the evidence, as Gray would have in his journalistic days. This was the *News-Press*, after all, not the *Times* or the *Post*, and this was Grand River, not New York or Washington, and people here, the reporters included, did not appreciate the difference.

Oh well. The cause was just, so what was a little lack of integrity if it would ensure the right outcome?

Gray and Breeze watched as they cobbled the story together. They left words misspelled and sentences ungrammatical, and Gray tried to correct them, but he remained lost in the noise of the newsroom and their collaboration. The copy editor would have to catch the mistakes.

They finished in just a few minutes. The men thanked Breeze for being an involved citizen, a local hero; and one asked if she would consider having a profile written for the features section, and could he have her phone number to follow up? She could probably have said no, and they would still have gone with the story, but she didn't disappoint. Gray waited for her by the elevator as she let them blubber over her—her nature, he knew. She'd used it when it suited her, and it had made her successful, but now she seemed a little too comfortable in that role—manipulative, from his perspective. And as she finally walked over to join him, he felt a twinge of sympathy for the giant. Reason had no chance when she showed up at his door.

Twisting Homer

Fairness. Integrity. Unbiased reportage. Commitment to the truth. Gray should have known better.

The headline on the front page of the *News-Press* the next day trumpeted the arrest of a local man for running a bestiality site on the Internet. Below that, a feature on a colorful homeless woman who had built a huge nest to share with pigeons. In the sidebar column, a report on the high school basketball team's chances in the county playoffs. Below that, an ad for great deals at a furniture store clearance.

Gray checked inside. Movie reviews, weather, comics, community calendar. He went to Randy's and tried the paper's website; maybe they'd opted to break the scandal there first. But instead, more local fluff, more weather, more sports, more ads—in other words, nothing about Reverend Hand and the Wilder campaign.

Maybe the staff had opted to do some actual legwork after all. Maybe they'd initiated a thorough investigation and contacted the state election authorities. Maybe they would run the story when they had more complete and damning information. Of course. Gray applauded the reporters in absentia for continuing the grand journalistic tradition in which he'd once participated.

But Randy had other ideas. "I smell a cop out," he said. "You should call them and make sure they're going to follow through."

All right, he would. But before he could punch the paper's number on his cell, Breeze called him. When he saw her name on the caller ID, it reminded him to set aside some time later for more "research" on her past life. She hadn't quite admitted anything about a porn career, but neither had she denied it.

"Gray, I'm in trouble." For the first time since he'd known her, she sounded scared, not in control of her situation. He would never admit it to her, but he liked hearing the fear in her voice.

"What's wrong? Did something happen?"

"I got a call from Reverend Hand. He knows we stole the documents."

"It's too late for him," Gray said. "The copies are already with the reporters at the *News-Press*."

"That's just it. Hand called the publisher. He got him to kill the story. There's not going to be an exposé. He said he's going to prosecute, and that he's going to take care of us."

Would Hand dare send the monster to do his dirty work and jeopardize the campaign? Would he dispatch his twin zombies, L'aura and Tristan, or do the job himself?

"I think he means to kill us," Breeze said.

Gray's thought process, typically the consistency of wet cement in critical situations, became strangely lucid. Options flashed through his mind. The city had no radio station, no TV outlet, no bloggers who mattered, and the media in the bigger cities up and down the coast had never bothered to cover Grand River stories, and wouldn't now, no matter how significant the issue. He had to think of another way to get the news out. "Not if we take care of him first," he said. "Meet me at the office of the *Journal*."

"We can't go there. They can't help us now."

"Not the *News-Press*; the other paper. The weekly."

"That sleazy throwaway?"

"That's the one. Bring the folder. I'll message you the address."

Gray turned to Randy. "Still want to do a great thing for this city?"

Apparently, the *Journal* staff was so inept, they'd printed the newspaper's address incorrectly on its masthead. Gray and Randy drove past twice, but could find no offices in this neighborhood a block from where the ocean met the river, just a line of California bungalows in dire need of repair. But as they approached for a final look, they saw Breeze's Benz parked out front, and, peering closer, Gray saw the hand-lettered *Journal* sign over the front door.

The house presented two stories of salt air-blasted wood that hadn't seen fresh paint in decades. The trim along the windows and roof had rotted. A pair of wires, one red, one black, protruded from the wall where a porch light should have hung. It may once have been stately, but now, had Grand River actually enforced building codes, this residence might have found itself on a list for demolition.

The newspaper, from the glance or two he'd given it in the last ten years, wasn't any more impressive, from his journalistic perspective. His staff mates at the *News-Press* regularly ridiculed the weekly and its stories about the history of a park bench, a senior's beer bottle collection, beachcombing for grunion and other such trivialities. But the readers loved it, as evidenced by the *News-Press's* own trivialities now moved to page one to compete. And the fact that, every once in a while, a disgruntled source with some juicy gossip came to them first meant the *Journal* occasionally scooped the daily, making it a perpetual thorn in the *News-Press* staff's side. Now Gray would give them a chance to be so again.

He knocked, and a man in a faded-blue terrycloth, Goodwill-quality bathrobe, with a striped tabby piggybacked on his shoulder, answered.

"Sorry," Gray said. "We thought this was the newspaper—"

"Come in, gentlemen. Are you here to see Homer too?"

He led them along a carpet dirtied with footprints into a grim living room. The beamed and smoke-stained ceiling came to a peak twenty feet up and invoked a cathedral during the Dark Ages. Homer Hunter sat at a desk off to one side, typing on the keyboard of what appeared to be a Mac Plus, a computer so old its files had to be transferred by floppy disk. Breeze and her folder stood alongside, even though two director's chairs sat empty, waiting for him to finish whatever news brief had engrossed him.

"I'm Zen. Zen Boudreaux," the bathrobe wearer said. "I'm Homer's uncle and the advertising manager for the *Journal.*"

"Do you both live here?" Randy asked.

"Sure. We own this house."

"And work here too?"

"Why pay for an office?" When the man smiled he revealed a set of tobacco-stained teeth. "We do interviews in here and hold our staff meetings in the kitchen. Upstairs is the production department, in the spare bedroom."

Surely Accounting was located in the toilet, but Gray resisted the easy joke. He and Randy joined Breeze in her vigil, and Gray lightly, but intentionally kicked the desk to break Homer's concentration. The filth that covered the chairs explained why she'd been standing.

The editor looked up. "What do we have here?"

"You remember us from the gallery show?"

"Of course. Mr. and Mrs. Aesthete," he said. "Only which is which I can't tell."

Randy squinted at him, his displeasure rekindled. "Uh-huh. Then maybe one of us should write the arts reviews for you. That way you can stick to what you do best. What was it? Writing the horoscopes?"

Gray stepped in to make peace. "Obviously Mr. Hunter has many journalistic talents. It isn't easy for one man to write politics, sports, business, and a woman's advice column in the same issue."

"It's nice to know you appreciate our coverage," Hunter said. "So what brings the cast of 'Gays and Dolls' to my humble abode?"

Now it was Breeze's turn to squint. Gray raised his hand as a signal for her to ignore the remark.

"We have an opportunity for you," he said.

"Hmm. That means you want something."

Gray turned back to Breeze and glided his palm like an emcee to introduce her presentation. She balanced the thick folder in one hand while she sorted through the papers.

Sit, honey, why don't you?" Hunter insisted.

Breeze looked again at the chairs. Ruining her dress apparently was not worth the comfort. "No thanks," she said. "I'd feel awkward sitting while they stand."

She ran through the allegations against Hand and the evidence they'd pilfered. Gray acted as her personal assistant/bookshelf, letting her lay the pages she had finished in his hands. He did his best to embellish the impact of her words with head nods and low whistles as though in surprise. When she finished, Gray placed the spent pages back on top of the others and Breeze closed the folder as though she had just finished reading them a fairy tale. In a way, she had. She looked for a relatively clean space on the corner of Hunter's desk, and laid the evidence there.

"We're giving this to you," Gray said. "You can beat the *News-Press* on this one."

"That's a big story," Hunter said. "Lots of accusations."

"And it's all yours."

"Big job writing all that up."

"But what a splash it will make throughout the city. Everyone will want to read it," Gray said.

"I suppose," Hunter said. "But there's a problem."

Gray tried to anticipate. "You don't have to worry about repercussions. We'll handle the heat."

"The newspaper is going on hiatus."

"Why?" Randy asked. "Run out of news? Or readers?"

Gray nudged an elbow into his friend's side.

"I'm taking six months off to write my memoir," Hunter said.

Gray scanned the surroundings. Memoir of what? Thirty years of living in filth? Of covering city council meetings? The international intrigue associated with printing ship arrivals? He looked around the room to see framed copies of old *Journals* behind fogged glass, depicting the city's better days, when commerce here rivaled the region's richer neighbors, when an old amusement park served as an entertainment hub, when Grand River mattered. On a stand in a corner sat leatherette-bound volumes with covers imprinted in gold leaf, spanning the last three decades, no doubt containing copies of issues going back to Homer's inheritance of the paper. Homer's memoir, Gray understood, would consist of thirty years watching other people live their lives. The thought froze him for a second.

He noticed Uncle Zen in the kitchen feeding his cat. As the old man bent down to lay the food dish on the floor, his robe came open, and Gray could see he was naked underneath. Yeah, this was an existence worth chronicling.

While he was trying not to ogle the uncle's privates, Breeze decided at last to sit. But she disdained the chair in favor of another corner of Hunter's desk. A quick brush with her hand to dust it and she slid a hip into a practiced, suggestive pose that Hunter could not miss. She leaned her cleavage close to the editor's face. "Isn't there anything I can do to persuade you?" she asked.

"Not that," Randy said. "We'd have a better chance if I tried."

"Oh," said Breeze, quickly hopping off and patting the dirt from her dress. "I wish you guys had told me."

"What if I write the story?" Gray blurted.

"What do you mean?"

"I used to work at a newspaper. Wouldn't be that hard for me to put the article together, and then all you'd have to do is print one more issue before you get into your book."

"A special edition," Zen called from the kitchen. "Give me a chance to book a few extra ads, Homer. We sure could use that."

"An exposé might do some good, image-wise," Hunter said.

"A win-win," Gray said. "So it's a deal?"

Breeze brushed his shoulder as Hunter nodded yes.

Another Visit to Sodom

One of the marble tiles at the base of the stairs had chipped. A panel of wainscoting hinted its readiness to dislodge from the wall. With every visit to Island Retreat's private yacht club, Gray saw more clearly how decayed the place was becoming. True, the gates to the enclave had reprised their wrought iron sneer of exclusivity when he approached, but the twenty borrowed dollars Gray laid on the guard took care of that pretense, and the security dude's corruptibility reinforced his observation. The façade of the club appeared as impressive as before—he noticed a team of gardeners carefully tending the flora as he marched past—but of course, the yacht clubbers were all about appearances. They would never let the outside world see the malignancy that festered inside.

He took the stairs two at a time. If his crusade against Reason had been just, this sortie was more so. After further reflection, his altruism had faded enough to let cold, hard financial reality take hold again. They had promised him pay for his efforts, he had come through, and they had screwed him. The bounced check meant typical rich man's usury—promises of urgently needed cash, and as important, inclusion in that padded world—but only made in jest to deceive him. Fox and Zinger must have always known how to get something for nothing, or else they wouldn't be sitting in that leathery, smoky nirvana right now. They'd probably planned the whole scam, writing him a bogus payment only part of the ploy.

Gray glided past the few patrons hunched over the bar and went straight to the old men's lair. He did not bother to knock, but swung the door open to announce his "Aha!" moment.

Aha, indeed.

Breeze sat on Zinger's lap, her hands laced behind the back of the buzzard's head, which Gray could not see because it was buried in her cleavage. Her spaghetti strap was off her shoulder, her dress pulled down at the side. He heard a sucking noise. She was breast-feeding him! Fox sat across the room, puffing on a Cuban, entranced, and probably next.

That magnificent tit in the gargoyle's mouth! The demon sucking the milk, the very life, out of the one who had the most life to offer.

He reached for his stomach to stem the budding nausea. What he'd slobbered over in his imagination from his first encounter with Breeze was now so close and yet farther from him than ever. How much had Zinger paid her for this? Gray maneuvered to see her face. Instead of the fear and disgust he expected Breeze to express at being forced into this, he saw a look of vapid contentedness.

He looked around the room for a cane, a candelabra, something he could use to smash in Zinger's vulgar and ancient skull, but found nothing. No matter. He would choke the life out of him with his bare hands.

"Mr. Davenport..."

It was Fox, his stupor broken when Gray began to move toward his associate.

"Have a seat. We'll be with you in a few minutes."

"You expect me to just sit here and watch this?"

"Well, you can participate if you like, if Mr. Zinger doesn't mind."

Gray gave the old man his most sour look. He would have to

take the both of them out anyway, to eliminate the witness. "And what about Breeze?" he asked. "What about what she wants?"

Zinger extracted his spotty head from the pillow of Breeze's breast and wiped his mouth on his sleeve. "How do you know what she wants?" he asked.

"Excuse me?"

"Gray, don't." Breeze slipped her dress back into place and stood to face him. "I'm not being forced."

The fight drained from Gray in an instant, and he unclenched his fists. "You can't tell me you're doing this because you want to."

"Charles and I have been together now for several months."

"You do it in front of him?" Gray pointed to Fox, who was still puffing away, enjoying the circus.

"I don't care who sees," Breeze said. "I want to be here. I'll do whatever Charles asks."

Gray couldn't stand still, and began pacing in a tiny square near the door. "So that whole time at Bob's campaign, when you were letting me pursue you, that was, what, a big tease?"

"It was necessary, my boy," Zinger said.

Breeze looked embarrassed that she'd fooled him, which Gray found strange since he'd just caught her semi-nude and engaged in sex with an eighty-something-year-old man and she hadn't flinched over that. Her porn-hardened psyche allowed her to do just about anything in public.

"Go ahead. Tell him," Zinger said.

"Gray, you're a nice guy," she said.

Ah, the cliché so many women had used before they'd cut him loose.

"I hated to hurt you." She paused for a few seconds to consider her next line, and Gray used the moment to imagine she meant what she'd said.

"I wasn't interested in Bob's campaign…at least not in helping it."

"I don't get it," Gray said.

"I was spying."

"On Bob? For goodness sake, why?"

"A mistake in our planning," Fox said. "We thought he would be our greatest competition."

"It was you," Breeze said.

"Huh?"

"I did go to the debate that night, like I told you. When I reported how well Bob had done, Charles and Sylvester decided I should try to infiltrate the campaign."

"We actually thought Mr. Boren had a chance," Fox said.

Breeze continued, "And later I found out you had written everything he said. You were the voice behind the man."

Behind the dummy, Gray corrected silently.

"So it was really you who were the competition."

"Which is why we recruited you when you attended the mixer," Zinger said.

"You planned that too?"

Fox rose from his seat, went to the mini-bar and pulled a bottle and some glasses from below. He poured what looked like an expensive brandy for each of them and brought the glasses around. He had a nineteenth-century finesse in his manner, an Old World sensibility that dictated proper behavior, even toward interlopers.

"Completely spur of the moment," Fox said. "We do enjoy the changing dynamics of a political campaign. Always presents interesting challenges. We thought if we could lure you away from Boren and have you investigate Wilder, we could damage both campaigns. A master stroke, don't you think?"

Zinger held his glass up, as if to toast. "Thank you for making it so much fun for us," he said.

Duped again. As always. By Breeze, by these old, crafty goats. Seven years in the business and he hadn't even begun to understand the minds and motives of the people involved.

Gray stared at Breeze. "And so with Reason—"

"Simply more of the same," Fox said, downing his drink in a

gulp and pouring another. "It worked so well the first time. And this girl is a natural Mata Hari. Everyone wants her and everyone trusts her."

"And how far did you go with Reason to get him to trust you?" Gray asked her.

"I did what I had to do…just like with you. Just like with every man." she said. "It's what I do, what I am."

Gray wanted to spit the ugly word. It edged along his tongue, pushed its way between his teeth. He fought the rage, the urge to say she hadn't changed at all from her pornographic days. She would take it from any guy, at any angle, to get what she wanted.

Zinger said it for him. "A whore is what she's trying to say. I think we can all be honest about that."

She looked betrayed. But who was she kidding? The old man was right.

Now Gray guzzled the last of his brandy. "The hell with that," he said. "I didn't come to talk about Breeze. I came to collect the money you owe me. You offered ten thousand to get the dirt on Reason's campaign, and we got it. When the story comes out in the media, Reason will be history. But your check, as you no doubt know, bounced."

"For that we apologize. We have so many accounts we're never quite sure where, exactly, the money is," Zinger said. "An oversight, I assure you. Let me write you another."

"And how do I know this one will be good? Maybe you're just scamming me again."

"Dear boy," Zinger said. "Take a look at this stunning example of womanhood." He gestured toward Breeze, still sulking by the fireplace. "Would she, in your wildest imagination—in my wildest imagination—stay with me if I didn't have money? We're good for it."

Without rising from his leather cocoon, Zinger contorted himself and pulled his mobile from his pants pocket. He punched a button, and then chatted quietly for a minute. Gray heard the magic number repeated. When he finished, Zinger asked if Gray could stay for the twenty minutes it would take to have a cashier's check delivered.

"Yes," he said. "But I'd prefer to wait outside."

"As you wish," Zinger said. "Order whatever you'd like from the bar and charge it to our account. Consider it interest on our late payment."

Gray went out to the main area and chose a seat at the bar as far away from anyone else as possible. He squinted out to the ocean and saw some kind of freighter plying the corrosion-colored waters near the entrance to the river channel, belching a contribution of thick smoke to Grand River's noxious air. Anything he wanted, Zinger had said. He looked over the menu of elite wines and specialty cocktails that the bartender slid in front of him. The members and their guests probably enjoyed Courvoisier and Opus One. He slid the menu back at the bartender and ordered a Coors.

He was still waiting for the foam to settle when he heard voices raised in the back room. Breeze was yelling, bordering on screaming, but Gray couldn't make out the words. Even the imperturbable Zinger raised his decibel level. A few minutes of that and the inevitable door slam, and Breeze's heels ticked against the marble tiles, coming toward him. But he wouldn't turn to acknowledge her. Let her walk past and out of his life. It was best that way. Yeah, he felt used by her, and by everyone—even L'aura—even, for God's sake, Bob and Patsy. But he didn't have to like it. Maybe the first step toward self-respect was to not try to get along in every situation.

She stopped, however, and slid onto the seat next to him. When the bartender hustled over, she ordered a beer, too. "Whatever the gentleman is having," she said.

Gentleman? He didn't feel like one. In a few minutes, he'd have his money and could start getting his life back, but he knew he hadn't achieved anything, at least nothing he initially set out to do. The payment would get him back to where he'd been financially before the campaign started, but the rest of his life still resembled a shambles. Still the neutron, the loser, by his reckoning.

"Don't hate me," she said, like a child.

"He shouldn't have called you that," he said without looking at her.

"Isn't it what you were thinking, too?"

"No man has the right to say that," Gray said.

"Well, he won't—at least not in my presence."

"What do you mean?"

"I dumped the old fart," she said.

The bartender appeared to eavesdrop while drying a shot glass. Gray gave a look to get the man to stop, and he caught Breeze in his periphery. Her mascara had smeared—could the rough talk have penetrated her emotional shell? Was there a soft core inside Ms. Hardcore?

"So what now?" he asked. "You go back to your marketing business and teasing fat executives?"

"There's no business," she said. "That was a front Charles invented. Something to give me credibility. It doesn't take much in this town."

He took a sip of beer and let the foam linger on his upper lip before dabbing it away. He looked out the window again and noticed the freighter had sailed on, although its smoke trail remained, dissipating slowly over the reddish sea. "So who are you then?"

"I'm the maid's bastard daughter. I'm whatever you want me to be," she said, and inhaled audibly as though realizing how pathetic it sounded. He'd hoped since the first they had something in common, and now he knew what it was.

"I'm almost done writing the article for the *Journal,*" he said. "I'm putting everything in, even the accusations we're not sure of. I doubt Homer will edit them out."

"Hand could sue, you know. He could say it's intentional."

"I don't care. Maybe I'll use a pseudonym. That could buy a little time."

She looked at the bartender to signal for another beer. "You're really a pretty smart guy," she said. "How come you're not sitting in that room, telling other people what to do?"

He didn't want to go down that road again. "With a little luck, maybe a bigger media outlet will pick up the story," he said.

"That still scares me," she said. "When word gets out… I'll have to get out of the condo Charles let me use. I really don't have anywhere to go now."

"Can't you stay in a hotel somewhere?"

"I wish I could afford to. I couldn't even get to one now. Charles made me give him back the keys to his car, too. "

"And you have no money?"

"He gave me whatever I needed."

So the Benz wasn't hers. Nothing was hers, he bet—the condo, the clothes, her entire lifestyle had been fronted.

"I suppose I could sell some of my jewelry before he asks for it back. But I'm not sure about a hotel. Someone would notice. Hand would find out."

"So where will you stay?" he asked.

She didn't answer. The courier Zinger had called bounded up the stairs and came directly over to Gray. He handed him the check and had him sign a receipt. Gray read every word on the clipboard before releasing his signature. As the man turned to go, Gray asked, "How did you know it was me?"

"I was told to look for the man with the biggest nose in the club," the courier said, smiling. "No contest."

Gray held the check under that nose—so powerful it was that it might pick up the smell of the money it represented. "I should get to the bank," he said. "There are some bills that need to be paid. I've been borrowing from a friend for a while, too."

"I'm glad for you," Breeze said.

He stood to leave and looked down at his feet. Those damn brown shoes peeked out from his pant cuffs like a pair of Fox's stogies. His first stop after the bank would be a shoe store. Then maybe a clothing store. He might come back here after he'd been renovated just to show these people he had taste after all.

"Good luck with the article," she said. "Let me know if you need anything else to finish it."

"Breeze," he said. "There's a place I know you can stay. No one would find you there. No one would even look."

The Relationship Killer

At least Zinger gave them access to get her clothes and things from the condo before he kicked her out. And after she decided not to keep any of his gifts, Gray had only one suitcase to carry to the Honda.

Breeze wore sweats and minimal makeup as she rummaged through the condo. They stood in the elevator on the way down from the penthouse without acknowledging each other. After all the glamorous façades she'd constructed for him while she spied, it was disarming, a little, to see this other side, not knowing if this informality represented the real Breeze, or yet another pretense. Gray entertained a vision of her someday replacing L'aura as his wife. He imagined, for a few seconds, sincerity, friendship, honesty—but the dream bubble burst before they got to the ground floor, replaced by the nightmarish memory of seeing her on the old buzzard's lap. No, she could never change her lifestyle so radically as to settle into the middle class conformity he promised. Not after basking in Zinger's largess. But screw the overthinking—he would enjoy whatever this was while it lasted. He watched her as she watched the floors count down on the display above the buttons.

He walked beside her to the street, his anxiousness over her discovering what kind of car he drove now gone, and Breeze slid onto the torn vinyl without commenting.

Instead of driving directly to the Star, Gray detoured. Since Breeze had no idea of their destination, she didn't complain that they had passed out of Grand River and into one of the trendy beach towns to the south, and headed to a shopping mall. He would fix a few things first.

"I can't go in there like this," Breeze said, when he approached the center's high-end annex. "I'll just wait for you in the car."

"It's not how you're going in," he said, "but how you're coming out. This trip isn't about me."

"You are still buying shoes, right?" Breeze smiled for the first time he could remember since before they'd crashed Reason's mansion together.

"And I thought you hadn't noticed."

"Gray, everyone noticed. The waiter at Frenchy's suggested I dump you before dessert. I had to ask some people at the club to keep their laughter to themselves so I could keep playing you."

Until an hour ago her comment would have hurt him. Now she could tell the embarrassing truth and he shared in the humor. He drove up to the valet—the first time he'd ever opted to use that service in the old Civic—and ran around to the passenger side before the college kid could hold the car door open for her.

He would have bypassed the men's shoes in deference to her needs, but as they came near the store's entrance, Breeze put both hands on his shoulder and pushed him inside. "Black shoes!" she called to the saleswoman. "And make it fast." Gray could not stop laughing for several minutes, until his schoolgirl giggles brought the stares of other customers.

He bought her jeans and dresses, blouses and shoes, and she liked what he'd helped pick so much she left the sweats behind in a dressing room and wore one of his choices out. They walked from shop to shop, weighed down with bright bags of goodies, but he felt lightened. He might have blown the entire ten grand if she hadn't made him stop. "You have bills to take care of and people to pay back, remember? It's not like you're really rich."

She could have left the reference to his sorry financials in the parking lot and let him enjoy this brief illusion. Of course, she hadn't meant to insult, and that was the problem—it hinted at what she really thought about him, and how much money mattered to her. Even if his fantasy somehow became real, she'd always have his account balance in mind. He let her get a step ahead of him as they walked and watched her swing a Max Mara bag in rhythm with her gait. The contented look she wore told him she had already forgotten what she'd said.

At lunch, in the high-end restaurant in the high-end annex, the waitress treated them like a couple—not necessarily married, but one that had been together for long enough to get over any sexual pressures. Gray decided to play that role, at least for the duration of the meal, maybe longer. It might even be worth learning about her, the real her—her life, her likes and dislikes, her evolving goals. If only he could think of her as a person first, and a voluptuous piece of ass second, they might be heading back to his place right after the meal for an afternoon romp...

Damn, this maturity thing was going to take some work.

The need for sex screwed everything up for people. Apart from the occasional perpetuation of the species—an outcome on which the jury continued to debate the merits, as far as Gray was concerned—it caused much more harm than good. Insults and mistrust, the phoniness, the façades and the constant conniving and sneaking around. Damage to egos and sometimes to bodies. Ruined dreams and furniture—and that was just *his* marriage. Even abstinence translated to sex for Gray, because the effort it took to keep one's hands off other people (or oneself) eventually became so great the carnal pressure had to be released somehow. Sex caused fights. It caused wars. It made men go off to the sea in ships and made them come back again. It made them take jobs as bartenders and male strippers, instead of pursuing ambitions of becoming doctors and physicists and others who could possibly help the world. It made young men into old fools and old men into tragedies. It sent Monterey Jack stumbling off into the Sierras, descending when his urge for a woman became greater than that for silver. And Gray could do without it—would do without it. Hell, he'd already gone months. He would learn to accept Breeze as nothing more than a friend, and then, at least, he would appreciate her company, which was still far better than never seeing her again. That right there sounded to him like an improvement.

Zinger's check made another improvement possible too, but there was no way now he would move out of the Star. Gray paid Randy for the back rent, despite his friend's protests, and laid out two week's worth for Breeze, which should have been long enough for any fallout from the Reason story to resolve. Randy obligingly found her a room next door to Gray's, but one with hot water, precluding the possibility of them all having to shower at the landlord's.

The crepe paper walls added to Gray's challenge. Sure, he'd determined to forego lustful advances, but having to listen to Breeze's every movement on the other side of a barrier he could probably punch his way through was simply not fair. Give her a room at the other end of the building, where he didn't have to listen to her gyrations and sensuous exhalations. Gray let those simple sounds trigger primal responses. He imagined hearing the zipper on her jeans sizzle open; feel the release of her bra clasp as it popped undone. The pipes in her shower squealed their delight over her entrance, and he had to pull away from their common wall, and put the bathroom glass he'd used to eavesdrop back on the sink, to make himself stop listening, stop lusting. The icy waters of his room's shower beckoned, and he plunged in, standing and shivering long enough to put his libido to rest.

He'd promised to deliver the exposé to Homer by morning, but had yet to write a word despite what he'd told anyone. He opened the laptop, but his concentration was shot. Too much going on, so many issues and feelings swimming inside—

Start writing and everything would be all right—the focus necessary for the article would pull him back into the world of callousness, the world he'd known throughout his political career. He typed:

...by Gray Davenport. Return, return. Then a minute, two minutes, while the cursor blinked its impatience.

The screen dimmed.

What a time for writer's block.

He decided to mosey down to Randy's. Perhaps his friend had another Chilean wine they could sample. It might loosen his knotted brain and then at least he could get something down on the computer tonight, and fix it in the morning. But first he had to traverse the gauntlet of conflicting emotions that were Breeze's threshold. Simple enough. Just point himself toward Randy's. Take a step, then another. Refuse to look to the side. Ignore what sounds might emanate from within her room.

On a witness stand someday, he would not be able to recollect the motions needed to place him at her door. He simply stood there as the sun set and the sky darkened, for who knew how many minutes, as though transported by that wormhole he'd prayed for during his despair. He imagined himself transported to the dimension that promised reversal of fortune. How would one say "Breeze" backward?

He had not knocked, yet the door opened. Breeze had changed again, having done her hair and makeup the way he remembered first seeing it. But now it didn't turn him on. She had placed her suitcase near the entrance to her room. It looked repacked and ready to go.

"What are you doing here?" she said.

"Where are you going?" he rejoined.

"Don't tell me you were going to hit on me again, Gray."

"I don't think I was," he said. "Not this time."

"Are you sure?"

He pondered for a moment. How to get out of this moment, whatever it was...

"You couldn't have given me one night?" he said.

"What?"

"You played your part, but you didn't take it all the way. That's not a very good acting job. Besides, what difference would it have made for someone like you?"

She pulled back and slapped him, hard, across his face. "You're such a boy," she said.

She didn't mean he was an innocent yet arousing youth, and certainly not one of the red-faced, HGH-drenched costars she was forced (he hoped) to have sex with in her porn days. She meant a clueless child, a sexual and romantic amateur. He rubbed the sore spot.

"I want something more in a man than pickup lines and naïveté," she said. "I want, I don't know, sophistication."

"Like that old man?"

"Yes, Charles is a sophisticated man."

The image of the spotty relic suckling like a baby didn't quite reconcile with that.

"It's the money, isn't it?"

"You know," she said, "I knew you would think that."

"Because that says a lot about childishness, being so wrapped up in money and image that people don't matter."

She shook her head at him like a disappointed teacher. "Charles's wealth is an outgrowth of his experience and drive. But you wouldn't see that."

"He's a greedy old fossil who cheats and uses everyone he can. You might have noticed *that* by now."

"He does what he must to ensure his security and the security of those around him."

"You dumped him, remember? Does this look like security?"

"Go back to your room, Gray," she said. "Go right now. Write your story and get it to Homer, and let's finish the job we started out to do. Forget about me and think about what you're doing for Grand River. That's what a man would do."

She didn't have to add that last sentence.

He gave up the idea of visiting Randy and did what he was told, but not, this time, because he'd been told. He closed the door and pulled the shades, and sat on the edge of the bed, in the dark, the laptop still closed, for what seemed like hours, thinking about the conversation, and the story he still had to write, and so many other things from the past few weeks, letting the tides of his frustrations swell and ebb until he felt nothing except the pull of sleep.

He began to get into bed. He thought: no one is born a porn star. How did Breeze go from the tony suburbs of Chicago, from the best schools and all her financial advantages to a life of such unfeeling depravity, willing to prostitute herself for the attentions of the perverts—himself and Zinger and who knew how many thousands, millions of Internet creepers included—who abused her, whether in real life or fantasy? Then he remembered: Mom was the maid. Guilty Daddy sent her away so she'd be out of sight. What kind of family life must that have been? He realized there was a hole in her psyche, maybe as big as the one he now felt sucking his innards toward oblivion. Terminal gravity. Not even light can escape.

Who she'd called remained a mystery, but then she probably knew dozens of men of sufficient masculinity who would abandon their evening comforts to rocket into this deep space and rescue her. A car pulled up to the Star in the middle of the night. Gray heard Breeze's door open, her steps on the sidewalk, the car door slam, and by the time he roused himself from bed and to the window, she was in a sportscar shuttling back to civilization. Three a.m. The disorientation of the hour kept him from making a final judgment about their relationship—if it had been a relationship—instead swinging his thoughts like a pendulum between guilt and blame.

It *was* about the money, no sense in her denying it. There was no way she could prefer that scarecrow over him. A boy… Just a trick to get rid of him.

He'd have no trouble writing the exposé now. No trouble at all.

He left the room lights off, and the glow from the laptop's monitor became a comforting pulsar as he tapped away. Gray layered everything he'd learned about Reason and Hand into the story, and as he rambled on, the narrative became less journalism and more fiction, but if they could get away with it in government, then why not in print? He guessed Homer wouldn't care, being more concerned with making a public splash than preserving accuracy.

The words came easily. Just draw conclusions in the form of questions. *Is Reason real? Could he possibly be a collection of reanimated spare body parts? Here are the facts; let the reader decide... A trail of corruption has followed Reason Wilder's campaign chief for the last several years, and casts doubt on the legitimacy of the mayoral candidate's organization. Other questions, just as critical, probe the origins of the candidate himself, who may not be what he claims.*

Call to Action

By eight he was done, dressed and ready to deliver. But now his sense of purpose was drifting away. He went to an office supply store to print some copies, and then motored toward the Journal, but decided to stop for breakfast and reflection at a cheap diner. The sense of altruism he'd entertained over this cause had left in the night, crammed into the sportscar with that woman. He'd lost his zeal for politics. It no longer mattered who won the election—as long as it wasn't Bob. Why go through with this little crusade except to keep Fox and Zinger off his case? Breeze had the evidence; let her make it public. Frankly, what would he get out of it apart from a little satisfaction and a lot of criticism? He'd be hounded by the giant's supporters and cast into the role of villain. There was that vague threat from the reverend to consider, as well.

And yet, he didn't care. If the voters wanted Reason, they could have him and whatever shady intentions Hand had in mind.

That settled it. He would go back to what he always did and stand in the back, away from the fray, and let the world decide its course without him.

But as he drove through downtown back toward the Star, he found Pisces Way blocked by a throng of what had to be hundreds of people—maybe thousands. Gray steered the Civic to port, but the next street was blocked too, jammed with bodies all seemingly headed toward City Hall. As was the next. And when he cranked his window down to ask someone what the gathering was about, he got a sonic boom of Reason, coming through a tinny loudspeaker, like a Muslim call to prayer on steroids, the shriek of his voice testing the limits of the device and Gray's eardrums.

"Great things," Reason bleated. "Great things for the city. Together. Come now and hear them."

Gray parked the car in a fire zone and joined the pilgrimage. As he walked, he noticed none of the people around him spoke. He heard no excited chatter about the event, no anticipation of any kind, just men, women and children walking, jogging, bicycling, a few in wheelchairs or on skates, summoned and obeying. Reason's ability to perform mass hypnosis had multiplied. A virus infected these people—maybe something brought back from the grave and spread through Reason's handshakes and backslaps. Or Hand had concocted this malady in his lab and pumped it into the air wherever his creation went.

Gray settled in at the back of the crowd. He was more than a hundred yards from where Reason stood on a balcony in the building next to the seat of government. The giant wore a shroud-like garment that draped his huge torso and extended past the top of the parapet. His staff: Hand, L'aura and Tristan, but no Breeze, thank God, surrounded him as he continued to entice citizens to attend.

And as they did, the people filling in behind Gray pushed forward to get closer. He became trapped in the sea of flesh, stuck now in the center of the mob, unable to move of his own accord and subject to the swirls and eddies of their movements. The crowd forced him to take three steps to the left, then four to the right—either that or fall down and risk a trampling. A surge from the rear plastered him into the back of a heavy woman, burying his nose in her hair, which smelled of sticky hairspray. He could suffocate in there, but Reason called out, "Now, listen," which calmed the throng and allowed Gray to take a half step back.

From where he stood he could not make out many details of the group on the balcony, but it looked as though Hand had his palm against Reason's back, like a ventriloquist manipulating his puppet.

"Great measures are necessary to save this city," the candidate said through the speaker.

L'aura and Tristan applauded and waved at the crowd to join in, which they did.

"Only we can do the saving. Together."

The people cheered again.

A chant of "We want Reason" began, but the giant raised his arms to quiet it.

"Who doesn't want Reason?" he bellowed, and threw his head back as though struck by his wordplay. People screamed and squealed in approval. A group managed to create a small clearing within the mass of bodies and began to dance: men and women, men with men, women by themselves, the combinations irrelevant as they praised their god. Gray got the pun too, but apparently was the only person in Grand River who didn't appreciate it.

The monster signaled his followers again to quiet. "It is important to tell your friends to vote for me," he said. "Have them register to vote if they have not. Insist on it. Remind them to vote for me on Election Day."

More cheering, more dancing. L'aura and Tristan embraced to one side and started their own routine, which included her jumping up and wrapping her thighs around his hips. Reason dropped the loudspeaker to his side for a few moments and nodded his approval. Hand, however, remained motionless, his palm still glued to his protégé's back.

"It is important," Reason said at last, "that I do not endure a runoff election. I must win in June so I can get to work right away."

Before anyone could respond or question, Reason and his entourage turned and hurried into the building. He'd said nothing. Nothing remotely controversial, nothing even resembling a platform, not even an acknowledgement of the city's problems. Just more of the same pabulum he'd been spouting since the campaign started. And yet the crowd called for him to come back and give them more. It was some form of mass hysteria, a mob with a single-mindedness for their leader's goal, whatever it might be. A rally transported through time from Nuremburg, for all Gray knew.

He knew as well that he couldn't just kill the story for the *Journal.* Not even he could be so inert as to shirk this responsibility. Another half hour passed before the crowd thinned enough for him to get back to his car—which had been ticketed, of course, but thankfully not towed—and he headed immediately for Homer's.

He would handle the fallout from the bomb he prepared to drop. He would just buck up and do it, come out from life's wall and stand center stage, no Breeze at his side, no L'aura, not even the fantasy of Monterey Jack to back him. Besides, he'd spent a chunk of the payola Fox and Zinger had laid down, and despite Breeze, they might send their goons if he didn't follow through with their wishes. He'd be pursued no matter what he chose to do, so why not make it the right thing?

Still, what was right was relative. If this story somehow succeeded, the upshot would mean Vega elected as mayor. But his kind of corruption the city was used to.

He raced past Uncle Zen, still in his bathrobe and cat, to hand Homer the printout.

"Couldn't you put this on a disk?" the editor asked.

"They don't make floppy disks anymore," Gray said.

"But that means I'll have to retype it."

Which meant mistakes and possibly editing.

"Never mind," Gray said, pulling up a filthy chair and sliding in next to Homer and his keyboard. "I'll do it for you. Wouldn't want you to go to any trouble."

Homer moved over to make room and looked at his watch.

"Type fast. I've got this special edition scheduled at the printer's for this afternoon. We'll be just in time."

Yes, they would.

Media Penetration

By the fourth coffee shop, Gray was wired, but at last he'd found a stack of Journals with his exposé blaring from page one. The weekly's boast of "news that can't be questioned" was essentially true, since if people couldn't find the damn thing, they couldn't debate its veracity. But here it was, and Gray sipped another cup of joe as he prepared to watch the birth of public outrage over the improprieties and astonishments he'd uncovered. Yes, Homer could have done a better job of communicating the import of the story—his headline of "Campaign Shenanigans" sounded so fifties, and might have meant anything about any candidate—but once people started to read they would understand the seriousness of the allegations against Reason and Hand.

If they would only do so.

He sat at a table by the pile for over an hour, yet no one paused to glance at the weekly, never mind pick one up and peruse. Another cup of coffee to assuage his guilt over occupying a seat and then he would give up. How did Homer stay in business if the public ignored his product?

A couple, probably in their twenties, came in and of course, walked past the display. Those kids never read anything anyway. But when two old men ignored the story to set up a game of chess,

Gray finished that third cup of Guatemala Antigua, made his third trip to the men's room, and then approached them.

"Gentlemen," he said. "Sorry to interrupt."

"Then why do it?" The man had a walrus mustache that had swept up bits of the scone he was eating. He cocked his head and stared at Gray as if to accuse him of lunacy.

"Easy, Chet. He looks like a decent guy. Let's hear why he would need to break our concentration." The friend mimicked Chet's look, with a touch more concern.

"I was wondering if you'd seen the story in the *Journal.*" Gray held up the front page for them to see, but they kept staring at his face—his nose, actually. "Big exposé on the Wilder campaign. Lots of dirt."

"Don't read that rag," Chet said. "Get all my news from the Internet."

"Same here, son. Tell 'em to put it online, maybe I'll take a look."

Homer was at least ten years from that level of technology. If only the staff at the *News-Press* had exhibited integrity. With the paper's web capabilities, the story would be all over town already and might even have made network TV.

Three women—they looked like moms who'd dropped the kids at soccer/ballet/violin practice and had decided to take a break before picking them up—had a table by the window and chatted nonstop, laughing occasionally. Perfect mainstream voters.

"Ladies, have you heard the latest about Reason Wilder?"

"Yes, we have," one said.

"You've seen the story?" He held it up again.

"Story? What story? We went to the rally yesterday. We love Reason."

"He'll do great things for this city," said another.

The third pointed at the newspaper. "Hey, I guess the *Journal* decided to endorse him too. It's about time."

The young couple overheard them and leaned in. "Reason? Dude's awesome!" the guy said.

"He's got our vote," said his girlfriend.

Gray thanked them all, walked back to the stack of papers, and put his copy on top, taking a moment to align it with the others, nice and neat. He walked out toward the Civic, but stopped and went back in.

An employee noticed him and asked, "One for the road?" She tried, unsuccessfully, to stifle a giggle.

"No thanks." Gray waited until she went back to the counter, and then grabbed the stack of *Journals* and took them to the street, where he dropped them in the nearest trashcan.

Let the people indulge their fantasies. If no one cared to know the truth about the man, about the monster—if no one cared to know that the city and the voters were being played for fools—well, then he would stop trying to tell them. He was more upset that he'd wasted all the time and effort writing the article and trying to get it published, and then believed a throwaway tabloid would be sufficient to convey the message to the masses. After a lifetime of preferring not to, he'd finally tried, and still achieved the same result as if he'd stayed in his room at the Star and watched ESPN. He was no longer merely inadequate, which he was used to, but verifiably ineffective.

He had to admit it did feel a little different, though. A strange sense attached to what he'd done—one of statement, of meaning, one that he might call pride if he didn't know better. But he couldn't take pride from such a miserable loss. As failures went, this one tasted of vintage disappointment.

Back at the Star, he slipped quietly into his room, taking care that Randy didn't hear him return. Commiseration and alcohol could come later, but for now, he wanted only to be alone, to have an opportunity to think about what might come next. This road had dead-ended. The politics was over—he couldn't see himself latching on with another campaign, and he wouldn't go back to Bob even if he could. It seemed as though no more options remained, no future beckoned, and yet, strangely, he found that thought comforting. Now he could relax and be like most people, like the people who'd made themselves zealots for Reason. He no longer had to know anything about politics to decide for whom to vote. He could base his opinions about government and war and religion and sex on what he saw on TV or heard at his local tavern. Or he could throw the candidates' names in the air and vote for the one who landed upright. His vote would count just as much. He could get a job—a regular job—just some nine to five straitjacket to pay the rent and pass the time of day. He could get out of the Star and into a decent apartment, and then he could contact a lawyer and get divorce paperwork started. And when that was done, he could embrace complacency and never again try to be something he wasn't. Or maybe he didn't even need to do that much. Life at the Star didn't rival a suite in Monte Carlo, but then it wasn't stressful either. Gray slid the latch to lock the door and hit the remote. The sitcom that tuned in on the portable was a little fuzzy, but watchable.

Two Guys in a Hot Tub, Part Two

In the week that followed, Gray made exactly no trips into downtown Grand River or to Island Retreat or to the waterfront or to Reason's mansion. He made no cell phone calls and received none and did not use his laptop to send email or access the Internet, except, well okay, one time in a last, fruitless search for photos of Breeze in her pornoramic glory. Randy took him out to dinner a couple of times, and he returned the favor, and they spent late evenings in the leaky hot tub with his landlord's good Carmenère and Cab, talking about sitcoms and documentaries they'd watched.

At the rate he was spending, or not spending, the ten grand would last as long as six months if he stayed at the Star, so he felt no urgency in his situation, although the first stirrings of dread over a life permanently on this margin did not pass unnoticed. Randy was pouring a Pinot Grigio through the hot tub steam and picking winners on a reality show they planned to watch the next day, when the image struck Gray: he and his host, twenty years older and wrinkled from more than the tepid water, still discussing whether to try to locate the leak in the tub. But Gray said nothing and let the moment pass.

He leaned back while the alcohol and vapors massaged his

psyche. They had finished two bottles and were considering popping a third, and Gray knew the hot, moist air in the tub would amplify the wine's effect. Let it.

"You know, Randy," he said, "I don't think I've ever thanked you for everything you've done for me. Or anything you've done, actually."

"Don't feel any obligation. I never asked for that."

"That's why I should do it. You never expected anything in return for your kindness."

"That's not exactly true," Randy said.

"No?"

"I'd hoped for some company. And now I have it."

Whose foot slid along the tub's bottom to contact the other's Gray was too drunk to know. But Randy's toes had already danced up to Gray's ankle and were intent on staying there, their gentle flesh both igniting and easing his never-ending anxiety. To look at his friend's face, floating just above the water, there was nothing going on; Randy appeared as impassive as his conversation.

Gray should have said something. A simple, "Hey man, watch your foot," would be the friend's way out of the discomfort; treat it like an accident and no one need be embarrassed. Randy would withdraw his trespass, Gray would move a little further into the corner, and they would act as if nothing had occurred. A drunken slip, a clumsy moment, and no more.

But Gray did not move. For the past few days, he had worked to convince himself he was better off alone—for his own good and certainly for the benefit of others. But now the feeling of skin on skin, any skin against his, was what he craved. Contact. Amperage. The transfer of electrons from one body to another in that greatest of conductors, good old H_2O. He avoided thinking where this sensation might lead. Surely there was no way he would wind up in Randy's room for the night, and so he didn't want to encourage his friend, but the touch right now might be the elixir he needed to return to a state of caring about his life, and he let it go on for a couple of minutes.

Gray's mobile, sitting on the little deck that surrounded the tub, vibrated like a beetle knocked onto its back. Why he'd even brought it with him puzzled, considering the dearth of calls, but now it offered the perfect out. He drew his legs away from Randy and tucked them under as he swiveled to answer.

"It's Zen Boudreaux. Remember me?"

How could he forget?

"Someone is looking for you."

Shit. "You didn't tell them that you knew me, did you?" All Gray needed was for Uncle Zen to help Hand and Reason find him, and he'd be history.

"Why sure I did," Zen said. "Man called all the way from Athens, Georgia trying to find you."

"I don't know anyone there."

"He doesn't know you either. But he knows his cousin in Grand River. And his cousin read your story to him, because he knew he'd be interested. The man is from The Church of the Sacred Hand."

Gray stood in the tub, his torso slapped awake by the cold air. "What does he want?"

"Let me quote: 'Only to find that son-of-a-bitch-Reverend Hand who bilked our congregation out of all its funds.' You want his number?"

There was no way to write it down out here, and Gray didn't trust his short-term memory—considering all the wine he'd consumed—to just have Zen say it. He threw Randy a look of panic, hopped out of the tub, and ran back to his room to find a pen and paper. He would get the green shag, and the bed, and his briefcase a little wet. But what was a little water when it came to catching a big fish?

Filing the Fantasy Away

Gray wanted to see it in high-def, in the splendor of liquid crystal display, and the half-hour drive down the coast to the big-box store full of flat screens was more than worth it for the twenty-second clip of Reverend Hand denying all accusations on the local news broadcast. Gray had to convince the salesman of his intent to buy, and cajole through more popular news like sports, weather and anchorperson banter to keep the guy from switching the channel, but finally, there sat the ghoulish lip-licker, spraying a bank of microphones with saliva and flanked by his entourage, which included a vulturine-looking man in a black suit who had to be his lawyer—or an undertaker who'd helped unearth Reason.

"These charges are groundless," Hand said, which as any political observer knew, equated to an admission of guilt. Just look at the faces—downcast, angry—they all knew the Reason ride was coming to a close. L'aura, dressed in full Goth, flaunted her emotions on a moon-pale face. Her hair and clothing matched in midnight black, and seemed on the screen to meld into a dark armor with only her sickly visage showing. Tristan's scruff of beard had graduated to wolfman whiskers, and he had dark circles under his eyes, as though he'd been unable to sleep since the charges against his boss were made public.

Only Reason appeared unchanged. He stood behind the other four, framing them with his wooly locks, sporting the same crooked smile he always did, which may have pointed to the inflexibility of his once-dead skin. Despite that, the news report said nothing about Gray's allegations of his origins. Nor did it mention how he had broken the story in the *Journal*, although that was no big surprise. Big media never mentioned their tipsters, so Gray's call connecting the Georgia man to real journalists would remain anonymous.

Hand played the requisite role necessary to deflect guilt. "Obviously a smear campaign," he said, "started by those who don't want to see a minority in the mayor's office."

Gray replayed that last line in his head. What minority? Mentally-challenged undead hippie freak show refugees? Somehow in America, things always went down that road. His thoughts turned to Vega, who despite his arrogance, was a bonafide minority, whether one considered his Latino heritage or his status as token toady to Fox, Zinger and the yacht club clan. Bob, too, could be thought of as a member of an oppressed group: poster boy for the clueless. But Reason?

He focused on Reason, standing behind the macabre campaign team, the slash of his smile unwavering. What did the giant think of all this, or did he think of it? Gray had talked to him only for a few minutes at the manse, but the wretch's frustrations and pain had been obvious. Perhaps there'd been more to Reason than Gray had realized. Standing among the electronics, with the salesman now explaining payment options for the sixty-incher that would impress the neighbors and make his den a real man-cave, he could only think of going back to the mansion and talking to Reason one more time. He suspected that dead skin covered more than harvested, reanimated organs.

But not so fast. Before Gray could escape the salesman and get out of the big box, Breeze called him on his cell. He almost didn't answer, but realized if he did, it would get the sales guy to back off.

A reporter for the Associated Press had contacted her. The guy wanted an interview about how she'd investigated the Reason campaign and turned up the damaging info. "I was going to meet him," she said, "but I couldn't do it alone. You were as much a part of that as I was."

How the reporter knew to call her was another of Breeze's mysteries, since Gray hadn't mentioned her in his story. He'd done it to spite her, and now felt bad, but she didn't seem to care. "You sure you want me there?" he asked.

"This thing will go national. You deserve the credit too."

National. The country's media spotlight would shine on Grand River. It would finish the charlatan Hand and maybe, with a little luck, help break the psychic grip that held the voting public like zombies in Reason worship. Gray could push it further. With a news agency of that magnitude, he could bring up the city's list of ills: the corruption, the pollution, all of it, maybe even implicate Fox and Zinger's political machine, turning the story into a critique on how the city had failed its residents, and how this election and its Three Stooges candidates for mayor held no hope for change. And there was the other aspect she'd mentioned—credit. His fifteen seconds of fame would make him look pretty good to her, and to the dozens of Grand River players and power brokers who'd not so secretly laughed at his antics through the years.

He would go. He would be a spokesman for Grand River and its future. A pro. He would answer his share of the questions and defer others to Breeze; treat her as a colleague, a comrade in espionage, and when the interview ended, he wouldn't allow himself to get the wrong idea, wouldn't harangue her for a drink or dinner in celebration.

But wait.

Gray stopped in the automatic doorway of the store, momentarily blocking a family of five and the monster HDTV they'd purchased. As they butted him out of their way with the shopping cart and an expletive, he remembered how things had gone with the media a week before.

Just like at the *News-Press*, the reporter would dwell on Breeze and ignore him. If he did get a few words in, and tried to speak truth about the city and its crumbling institutions, he would come across as rambling and irrelevant, and ultimately no one would care. The old frat boys and sorority gals would have the last laugh on him, as they always did. Besides, he didn't trust himself around her. She'd smile, she'd touch, and he'd misread it as he always did. She'd hurt him and would do it again if he gave her the chance.

He would not fall into that trap again.

"No," he told Breeze.

Hand Waves Goodbye

They wouldn't have the Reverend Inchoate Hand to kick around anymore.

Without word or sign or excessive salivating, Reason's creator had pulled out every remaining cent from the campaign account, slipped into his hearse, and headed who knew where, on his way to another place, another scam, and the next community of suckers. All he'd left behind was the house and lab equipment, a few old books, and—oh yeah—the people who'd trusted him.

The news at last went big time. It made dozens of websites and blogs. The major news bureaus all sent teams to Grand River to get the story. Gray had his chance to take part in the circus, but after he turned Breeze down, she didn't bother to invite him to subsequent interviews. Instead, Homer joined her in the spotlight. The man appeared useless on camera, but Breeze carried him. She looked not only as radiant as Gray had ever seen, she came across as approachable—at least in an on-screen way—so it was no wonder when he checked the news site again that she'd been offered her own daytime talk show on a network affiliate. Gray did not foresee himself on the show's upcoming guest list. She would have to be content with aging soap stars and self-help gurus.

Randy tried to console him by saying it would be her loss. Sure.

Each time Gray replayed the videos on YouTube, he imagined himself at the mic, the James Bond of municipal intrigue, wowing viewers with his spy tale. The scene included him in tuxedo and Breeze in evening gown and pearls, martinis at the interview table and flashbulbs popping, and the fantasy finally became too absurd to continue. He cut it short and switched to the *News-Press* site, the other party in this saga that had opted to let the train leave the station unboarded. The staff hadn't followed up the *Journal's* article and was blindsided by the national media blitz. "Background" stories since then about Tristan's gallery and the history of the old mansion hadn't helped the paper's reputation. They dispatched a couple of reporters in a futile attempt to track down Hand before the various law enforcement agencies and private detectives could, and the pair dutifully filed daily articles from the road as though the paper had covered the situation all along, but as the trail grew colder their stories became ruminations on bad motels and greasy spoons. Hell, Gray could have written those, too. At least he took some solace in shared ineptitude.

But the shutdown of the Wilder campaign, the goal he'd pursued for so long, didn't prove as satisfying. Reason's official withdrawal was expected, but not announced, although Gray assumed there was no way the beast could clomp on without his handler. In fact, L'aura tried to paper over the campaign's distress by churning out daily media updates, claiming the Rev had left to attend to family matters, then turned his trip into a fact-finding mission, then a fundraiser, and eventually decided to take a short sabbatical to recharge his electoral batteries.

After a few days, even the *News-Press* had figured out the real situation, and they conducted a poll showing that without the giant in the race, voters overwhelmingly opted for a return to the sleaze of Elvis Vega, over the incompetence of Bob. Maybe Reason's spell had finally broken, and they were coming to their senses at last.

But not everyone. Gray was in a supermarket of all places, when the sound of polyvinyl on ceramic tile came from the next aisle over. He recognized it, and rather than drop his groceries and run for the nearest exit, he made one more bad decision and nosed around the corner.

Patsy wasn't just dragging the ball along with her, she was bouncing on it, like a child on a hobby horse, coming out of an aisle, forcing old women and moms with kids to plaster themselves against shelves of canned vegetables as she headed for the Cheeses of the World display. Bob followed, pushing her cart.

She traveled about two feet per bounce, not a bad rate considering her size and condition, and stopped in front of Gray just as he prepared to leap to safety.

"They let you do this in here?" he had to ask. A couple of the women who'd been sideswiped were talking to an assistant manager.

"This is great for my back," she said, her head still bobbing a little from the ball's abrupt stop. "Really works the lumbar."

"Seems like you might be inconveniencing some of the other shoppers—"

"I haven't heard one person complain," she said.

True, if shrieks of panic didn't count. Gray turned and eyed the Express Lane, and did a mental count of the items in his hand basket. He could still escape this conversation if he left right then.

But Bob rolled up beside her. He looked distracted, haggard. Gray felt compelled to broach the obvious.

"How goes the campaign?"

Bob nosed the cart toward a row of Gouda, but shook himself free of its spell and turned toward Patsy. "Tell him what we decided."

"We're suing you," she said, smiling.

"Suing?"

"For a million, or whatever it would have taken to finance Bob's campaign in the runoff election. Better get yourself a lawyer."

"Wait a minute," Gray said. "What is it I'm supposed to have done?"

"You wrote that article, didn't you?"

"In the *Journal?* Sure."

"You saw the latest poll results?"

"Yeah, I saw them."

"Well," she said, "put two and two together."

And get what, seventeen? "I don't follow your logic," Gray said.

For the first time Gray could remember, the jolly loser looked angry. "Your story made Reason quit the race."

Thank God, someone had finally noticed.

"When he was in there, I had a shot," Bob said. "Now...well, you saw the numbers. All Reason's support is going to Vega."

"I have nothing to do with what the voters decide." He stopped for a moment. How was that any different from when he worked in politics? Never mind, he'd save that for later. "I still don't see what you're getting at."

"Reason's in, it's a three-way race," Patsy said. "Might go to a runoff, and Bob has a pretty good chance to make that. But against Vega alone, we'll lose in June."

"So?"

"And it's all your fault."

"No, it isn't."

"Is too," Bob said.

"Listen," Gray said. "You fired me. After that I could do anything I wanted."

"Aha!" Patsy said. "So you admit it. Get this down, Bob."

Gray's former client pulled out a pen and fumbled for paper, but produced only a candy bar wrapper. He tried to write on it without success.

"I admit nothing. The charges are groundless," Gray said. Where had he heard that before?

"We're suing anyway. If Bob's in the runoff election, then funds still come in and we could still win."

"But they haven't even held the first vote yet. You can't predict how it will turn out. Not for sure." Gray noticed a group of men in blue shirts at the end of the aisle, who were huddling and pointing at them, as though debating a strategy.

Patsy adjusted her position on the ball. "We have the poll for proof, but we can wait," she said. "The day after the primary, if Bob is out, so are you."

Insanity, pure and simple. The pressure of all those losses they'd suffered together had eaten away what little sense they had left. But as crazy as this was, he would probably have to hire an attorney, at least until the case was thrown out of court, and possibly for a longer term, because who knew what a judge might allow. Gray saw the rest of his ten thousand climb onto an open windowsill, look back at him and wave, and get ready to plunge. The small comfort that his actions really might have changed the course of the election had already jumped.

"I'll fight this," Gray said. "Maybe I'll counter sue for wrongful termination." They were sucking him back into that vortex of lunacy he once believed was a career. This was their way of saying they needed him to be part of their co-dependency of dunces.

He couldn't look at them any longer and turned toward the display case. There, among the cheddars and Gruyeres, he spotted a reminder of his fantasy other—the hombre, the guy so tough that trouble like this not only didn't come calling, it didn't even drive through the neighborhood. He picked up a small brick of it and looked closer. Wrapped in thick, vacuum-sealed plastic, with jalapeño added, for extra menace. But pretending to be Monterey Jack had never solved anything. He tossed the package in his basket. Maybe a Mexican cerveza would go well with it.

The supermarket staff approached at last. "Ma'am, I'm the manager," the tallest among them said to Patsy. "I'm afraid you can't go around the store like that. There's been some complaints."

"But it's for my back."

"If you're handicapped in some way we have motorized carts you can ride in. I can have one of my boys bring one around."

She stood. "A lot of good that would do me. That hard seat would put me in traction for sure."

Gray and Bob looked at each other in a moment of solidarity. Gray was sure neither had seen her standing for years. She picked up the ball by its handle and rested it on the top of the shopping cart's cage. "Come on, Bob," she said. "We can do our shopping elsewhere."

Patsy shuffled and stumbled, like the rich paraplegic trying to catch the last spaceship off a doomed earth. While she and Bob headed for the exit, Gray took his basket toward the opposite end of the store. That beer was sounding better with every minute.

Still a month to go before Election Day. He'd hoped it would be without the usual pressures he felt while working with candidates to prepare last-minute statements and marketing ploys. This one was going to be pure entertainment, watching the Wilder campaign fall apart, and Vega and Bob scramble to woo the giant's supporters to their causes. But now Gray felt the weight of potential legal action bearing down on him. First thing when he got back from the store would be to see if Randy knew a good lawyer.

Or maybe second. There was still a little time for that. Instead he would go to the mansion. He could witness L'aura freak out over the developments of the past few days and watch Tristan draw a blank as to a solution. And what about the giant? How would he handle the loss of his mentor, his controller? Perhaps it was the last place Gray should go, considering Reason might be angry enough with him to inflict harm, but he'd had a strange feeling about the beast ever since they had their heart-to-transplanted-heart. Something like respect, or camaraderie. A feeling. Not much to go on, considering they'd only talked for a minute, but when he got in the Honda, Gray followed his nose and headed for the dump and the manse.

Monster and Me

Amid overcast skies Gray drove back to Reason's. The door to the mansion sat slightly open, more of an oversight it seemed, than an invitation. Or Gray could have gone in through the still unrepaired window. The big screen TV in the main room hung crooked; the furniture had been shoved into an awkward configuration. In the kitchen and offices, he found cabinets and drawers rifled, papers and books cast harshly to the floor—evidence of investigators, some perhaps from law enforcement, others snooping for private clients. The air in the house bore a whiff of desertion too, as though the inhabitants had cleared out quickly. Once Hand vanished, the rest must have realized that to stay would incriminate them.

"Hello!" Gray called. "I'm looking for Reason." He was not here to sneak, and wanted anyone about to know of his presence before weapons could be brandished.

But no response. He tried again, this time calling L'aura's name, which felt odd. It was a question more than a shout: "L'aura?" They hadn't spoken as a couple now for weeks—okay, months if one counted pre-separation angst. Even now the hiccup in her new name bothered him, so he tried once more, deliberately saying it the old way: "Laura!"

She and Tristan must be pumping out those press releases from some other location—the gallery or even the condo. And Reason? Where could the hulk go and not be noticed?

Gray threw switches, but the electricity had been disconnected, and any room without a window loomed as dark as the hallways. He found a candle in the kitchen, lighting it at the gas stove. After checking a few rooms and navigating the stairs and maze of corridors to the lab, he began to believe the monster had not stayed either. Could be L'aura and Tristan had taken him and he stretched out each night on Gray's old bed, eclipsing it. Or worse, he might be wandering around downtown, camping out in alleyways and melding—as best he could—into the city's homeless population. Reason might not even realize what had happened to him—how quickly his campaign for mayor had come apart as soon as his handler left. Without Hand's magic, Reason might regress to his primal state, a massive jangle of stitched body parts that scared people rather than seduced them. The wretch would roam the netherworld of Grand River, a pathetic beggar who instilled terror in those he encountered, eventually inciting a posse to hunt him down. A barely coherent monster lurking in the city's gloom? The cops might have him in a chokehold already. How radical is the public's ability to shift perception.

Satisfied the mansion was empty, Gray reversed his path. But as he turned, the candle extinguished. Now he felt not so alone. The coal mine darkness of the hallways bred its own sounds. Every footfall caused the floorboards to shriek. Each brush against a wall produced a hiss. He heard breathing too, the heavy kind, from behind one of the doors.

Damn! Gray felt his way along, trying to find the aperture through which he'd arrived into this part of the house, but the floor had become a maze, and in his blindness, every surface a barrier. He would have to locate whoever breathed that sense of dread into him, and hope it revealed a friendly spirit, one willing to lead him back to the light.

He tapped the first door he encountered. No response. The sound he heard, when he stilled long enough to triangulate, came from farther down the hall. Gray slid closer, hoping despite the possibility of rescue that the noise would stop and let him flounder alone. Confrontation, as he knew, was not all it was cracked up to be, and this one portended more than hurt feelings. But he had few other options—he could try smelling his way out again, or hunker down in a corner and wait for the next day's sunrise to infiltrate the space, but he had his doubts whether light or stink could reach this deeply into the labyrinth.

A few more steps and the breathing amplified, a slow and steady rhythm, perhaps someone asleep. He did not knock, but turned the knob and eased the door open. The room had a window, covered by a thick curtain, which allowed just enough light in to reveal shapes.

That body slumped in the chair, that monolith of reincarnated flesh, could be no other.

"Reason?"

The giant exhaled, but did not speak. Even in the dark, he appeared weak and immobile.

Gray made for the window and pulled the curtain back, raising the level of light in the room to that of an overcast evening. From behind, he saw the giant's head tilt to one side, his hair cascading over his face like a net thrown to capture him.

"Are you all right?"

The stupid questions one asks of another so obviously in distress. If Reason had heard it, he did not let on. Gray moved to face him.

"Can you talk? I'll go get help…if I can find my way out of this place."

Reason raised his chin an inch from his chest. "No," he whispered. "Mr. Jack Gray, do not help."

The voice, so often a clap of thunder, a full on electrical storm, had become almost imperceptible.

Gray leaned over the beast. He saw no signs of abuse, self-inflicted or otherwise, just the awkward visage Reason always wore. "What happened?"

"They leave me."

"They all abandoned you, just like that? Didn't anyone consider your welfare?"

Reason closed his eyes.

"Well, I will."

"No. You leave me too."

From Bob and Patsy's roller coaster, to L'aura's boot, to Fox and Zinger's espionage, to Breeze's everything, Gray had pretty much always done what other people wanted. Not this time.

"I won't just leave you. There's nothing here, no food or anything. No way to survive. You might die," he said.

"I am dead," Reason said. "I wish not to live."

Gray leaned over next to the chair, so he could be at eye level with the monster. Now that he had him weak, defenseless—what he'd imagined for so long—he didn't like that he was the one responsible for it. "I wanted to destroy you," he said. "I knew what you were and it made me afraid. The others never realized. Or they didn't want to know. If they did, they would have been far more violent than me." He was not sure if Reason had heard.

Reason opened his eyes. "Your violence was enough."

Maybe. It just didn't feel as good as it was supposed to. "Would it help if I said I was sorry about how things turned out?"

"What is sorry?"

Oh. In all the lessons on politics and history, on crime and taxes and the minutiae of running for office, Hand and L'aura and even Breeze had never taught him that.

"It's nothing," Gray said.

"Why do you say it?"

"It's a thing people say to make themselves feel better."

"Then I am sorry too."

The giant moved his hand from the chair's armrest and

engulfed Gray's, from the fingers to halfway up the forearm. Gray's initial reaction was to pull away, but he fought the urge, not that it would have done much good. Reason's skin was cold and clammy, the way it might feel had it just been exhumed.

"Mr. Jack Gray—"

"Gray," he said. "Just Gray. No Jack."

"I cannot die again."

"I won't let you—"

"I want to die. But I cannot."

"I don't understand. If you're damaged, or if you don't eat. If your body stops functioning—"

"Those things do not matter."

"But what if you're shot? Or burned?"

"One cannot die who is not truly alive."

Then what would become of the wretch? In his present condition, he could spend eternity in this room, in this chair, wasting away but never expiring, reduced to a lump of flesh that imprisoned a dwindling consciousness still aware of its predicament.

Gray stood. That was Hand's real crime. He created this being, took the pieces of men who had achieved what they thought was their final rest, and made them suffer again in Reason. And what of the mind? Whose brain had he plucked from the beyond and thrust into the vortex of the here and now? And then he dragged this creature through the trials and setbacks of a life, compressed into what, a year? As far as Gray knew, Reason had experienced none of the joys of a normal existence, none of the rewards. Even if he had been elected mayor, it would have been Hand's triumph. Reason would have been sentenced to four or more years as a slave, a biological robot doing Hand's bidding, helping to build the reverend's fortune and receiving nothing in return.

Gray's head snapped up and he cast his eyes at the ceiling. Reason had not been able to recall anything about his past when they spoke before, but now, having been consigned to this solitary state…

"Reason, do you still see the shadows?"

"I see them."

"Do you know what they are?"

The giant took a breath and nodded.

"Tell me."

The giant's face contorted in agony.

"What is it, Reason?"

"The pain. You have brought back the pain that is life. I did not wish to remember."

"I shouldn't have—"

"No. I must know it. It is a part of me. What men do to men."

One cannot die who is not truly alive.

The words repeated in Gray's mind. They seemed now to have something in common, he and the monster.

Gray took his free hand and placed it on top of Reason's. The giant exhaled again, his great breath a squall of regret and resignation. Gray would have to go, eventually, but how could he leave him here, alone?

He began to move his trapped hand back and forth until it wrestled free of the giant's grip. "I don't want to abandon you, like the others," he said.

"You must," Reason said. "There is no other way. You have a life. You must live it."

If only. Gray considered staying longer to explain to the giant how his life seemed as fruitless, as futureless as the one that would remain in this room. But like an apology, it would only make *him* feel better.

He went to the door and looked back at the body sprawled in the chair. If he could somehow lift him free, he might carry him outside, stuff him into the Civic and bring him back to the world. He would tell the story to Grand River—the whole story—and they would have to accept Reason for what he was—not a mayor, not a man in the way people think—more than a man in some ways—different from them, but still deserving of acceptance. But how could he do it?

Gray entered the hallway again, using the dim light from Reason's room to see down to the next turn in the corridor. Past that, the hallway stayed as dark as before, and for a moment, Gray braced himself against the wall and inhaled deeply to prime his olfactory, preparing for the arduous trip down to the front of the manse.

Outside the mansion, a rumble. The rain that had threatened was starting. Gray imagined a gentle shower, a blessing of sorts for the city, but instead of a light patter against the roof, the rain came down in torrents. The thunder intensified, shaking the walls of the old house. The lightning was so close he could hear it crackle in the atmosphere outside. He froze for a second, thinking a bolt might strike the manse and set the structure ablaze. But it gave him an idea.

He wouldn't need the nose this time. He encountered another doorjamb. This time he opened the door, unafraid of who or what might be inside. It was empty, but it, too, had a small window covered by a curtain, and when the fabric was pulled away, the lightning flashes created enough illumination to shine a path through the hallway and to the next room. Gray continued, one room at a time, for several minutes, looking for the stairwell. And instead of cringing at each bolt, he began to encourage them. He reveled in the storm, and urged it to continue. Bring it on! Light up the sky!

Soon he had confidence he would reach the front room without making a wrong turn and trapping himself in here forever. Forever, like Reason.

As he approached the lab, he smelled the vat of green ooze inside. Amino acids and essential oils to rejuvenate the giant like a spa bath. It had been his theory, and like the theories of many good scientists, the world had ignored it. He opened that door as well, requiring the light for the next leg of the trek. But the stench from the tub had gathered behind the door and assaulted him when he opened, almost knocking him to the floor. What a powerful solution.

Solution?

Gray turned around.

He ran back through the hallway, toward Reason, conking his head against the wall in the gloom, but making it to where the giant had retreated into his coma once again. He shook the beast to rouse him.

"Reason! Wake up! I have it!"

"What is it you have?" The voice was weaker than just a few minutes before.

"I know what to do. You must come with me."

"I cannot move. I am too weak."

"You can do it, and I will help you."

Before Reason could refuse, Gray had pulled him by the shoulders into something of a squatting position on the chair, forward enough so that if the giant leaned a little more and commanded his legs, he would be standing.

"Push," Gray said. "Stand." He grabbed Reason by the wrists and put everything he had into one effort, and the giant was up, all eight feet of him, slumping, but still towering over his rescuer. He leaned into Gray, who let him rest against his back. "Walk. Walk with me."

It had taken three of them to move the beast the last time, but now Gray handled the task on his own. The dead weight was more than he'd ever borne, and he staggered, but he refused to go down, taking tiny steps to make sure he could support Reason, who shuffled those size twenty-threes without lifting them from the floor, keeping his weight square against Gray's back. The storm pounded away overhead like a bass drum, driving him on.

It seemed to take ten minutes or more to negotiate the thirty feet to the lab. Gray felt his legs begin to give. His mind started to spin as his body threatened to shut down from the strain.

And when he could go no further, and resigned himself to giving up and letting both of them tumble to ground, where no doubt Reason's massive body would pin him for eternity too, the giant stopped and stood on his own. He let out a scream reminiscent of when he dominated the mayoral campaign and made the last few steps to the lab and the tub.

He did want to live.

Gray took a minute to gather his strength. Reason hung onto the side of the vat, leaning over the edge. This would be the easy part. Gray crouched down, and like a blitzing linebacker, body blocked the giant the rest of the way, over the side and into the green liquid. The splash stained Gray's shirt and pants, and the stink, to his ultra-sensitive nose, was almost unbearable. But the job was nearly done. All he had to do now was throw the switch and apply the charge.

Baptism

Gray Davenport had long entertained the idea that so-called reality was an illusion. He secretly hoped for the truth of it. How else to explain his failures and rejections, the illogic of effort unrewarded, of odds that never evened out? As on that lonely night at the Star, he'd searched his private cosmos often for wormholes that would take him to someplace else, some parallel universe that offered a more pleasant existence. After a while, after years of frustration, such dreams had replaced the ones of glory and success. They seemed, if it can be believed, more likely to come true, if only because unlike his real life, there was no evidence to refute the possibility. Those other dreams had helped sustain him once, but now he began to see just how foolish they'd been. Here was Reason, who maintained no illusions, no hopes of what might be, who understood in his muddled mind only what existed and accepted it, whether that meant ruling a city, living a life of inconsequence, or sitting alone in a darkened room for all time. Perhaps it was this innocence that Gray found so enticing, so worthy of saving. Everyone else he knew had an agenda, a secret plan, and too often that plan had included using him. Perhaps his own sense of guilt, that he as much as anyone focused solely on his own desires, had something to do with it too. Perhaps he saw an opportunity to make a small amends.

Gray looked into the wretch's jaundiced eyes. The giant's physicality derived from other people's limbs, stolen from their tombs, but Gray sensed that the great man's essence, the thing that made him Reason, was as individual as anyone else's. That man had lived a previous life, the evidence hinted, so meager as to make Gray's seem like a celebrity's, so filled with suffering that to be forced to live again was an abomination, an insult to humanity and science and God. And yet here he was, persisting, unable to return to his rest, wanting now to stay, fighting to claim his place as a human being.

The slime that had spattered from the tub seeped through Gray's clothing and tingled against his skin for a few moments before starting to burn. In seconds the effect became like a steam iron on his chest and leg, and he left Reason in the vat to douse himself with cold water from the lab's faucet.

"Ahh," he said, rubbing the still-heated part of his body. "How do you stand it?" Reason did not answer, but rested, eyes closed, within the steel enclosure, waiting for Gray to complete the process.

Gray reached beneath his shirt and pants to get at the enflamed areas, massaging them with his palms until the pain subsided. When he had rezipped and rebuttoned himself, he looked back at Reason, who had pulled in his arms and legs, and sunk his head below the surface of the goo, as though immersing himself to make the cruel world go away for a while.

Gray walked to the lever that controlled the current and gripped the rubber handle. He stopped.

The wormhole, right before his eyes. Escape from the illusion of reality. It dawned on him that all this time, the neutron had been the key. A lesson from high school physics, long forgotten, emerging again and reminding him of the latent power, the magic of this uncharged particle. The neutron was the catalyst, the igniter—it fired from an accelerator into a fragile lump of U238, striking an atom, splitting it, sending its bits flying in all directions until they, in turn, blasted other atoms. Then one after another after another, a chain reaction in a pulse of time, releasing the unimaginable energy of the strong nuclear force, of mass times light squared, growing in intensity until it could not be contained by a metal casing or a subterranean bunker or a man's years of self-doubt. And in the milliseconds that followed, annihilation of all that came before, a scouring of the land and the soul. If this putrid broth meant a renewal, an infusion of life for Reason, what would it mean for him?

He took off his shoes and socks. He undid his clothes again and slipped them to the tile, briefs and T-shirt as well. And when his pants hit the floor, out fell the wrapper from that cheese he'd bought under the duress of Patsy and Bob, and on which he'd snacked on the way over. The residue of the cheese it held coated the plastic. A little Monterey Jack in the mix? Why not? He tossed it into the goo and watched the liquid absorb it.

Gray hoisted his foot over the side of the tub and dipped it into the green. The feeling was warm and tingly, a little like carbonated body lotion, but in seconds, the temperature on his skin began to rise.

No time to think about this.

He hopped off the floor and swung his body in, stepping on Reason's leg, although the giant did not react. The tub was Reason-sized, but that was all. It could not hold both comfortably, and Gray's legs tangled with the big man's, causing him to lose his balance and dip his thighs and genitals into the brew. The heat turned to pain, which turned to agony. Another ridiculous mistake—and this one could prove fatal. He could lunge for the side and pull himself out, but he had to move now or he'd fall unconscious.

But really, wasn't going beyond the pain of life the point? Reason had tried to tell him. No more flailing, no complaining. Just take it, Gray.

He steadied himself, clenched his teeth, and looked down. Reason remained under the surface, barely visible from above. His clothes had been eaten away by the liquid, and he sat, naked, on the bottom.

The liquid seared him now, but Gray leaned out and took the handle on the switch once more. He felt the flesh on his legs begin to bubble, as though it were loosening from his bones. A quick look out at the laboratory—a snapshot of the last place he might see. And as he did, the lightning outside arced so brightly it flashed through the little window and lit the room like the sun. The thunder it engendered shook the vat, causing the green to slosh over the sides. The lightning rod! The power of the cosmos, added to the charge!

Now!

Gray pulled with both hands, as hard as he could, until the circuit was completed. It sizzled and crackled as electricity surged and fed the tub. It hit Gray like a sledgehammer, shorting his breathing and knocking him backward into the goo, into Reason's supine mass.

A tsunami of images washed over him as he submerged—every moment of hesitation in his life, every indecision compressed into a one-star biopic that played in the second it took for him to lose consciousness. The last thing he saw was the mossy surface of the ooze coming up over his eyeballs.

Who We Are, Who We Become

Gray's hands felt unusually heavy as he prepared to lift from the tub. Reason had left, having somehow extracted that big body from underneath without waking him, although he saw no trail of green drip leading from the room to indicate where the giant had gone. Yet Gray felt he was not alone. A voice in his head echoed like a TV in a room down the hallway, tuned to an annoying talk program. And he was still here in the lab, in the manse, with the same problems and issues waiting for him outside. It hadn't worked.

What hadn't? What, exactly, did he think would happen? Hope would happen? He'd acted, without overthinking, or even regular thinking—an outburst, impetuous, completely unplanned and unlike anything he'd ever done. He didn't have a specific outcome in mind. And with nothing changed, he wondered now if he had really done it. But he must have. The remnants of the slime had dried and stuck to his skin. The chemistry of the ooze had altered when the charge bonded it to his body, because now it smelled worse than ever—the same primordial funk he'd sniffed on Reason, but now fermented as though left out in the sun.

His clothes still lay in a pile on the floor. If he could find some soap, he'd wash the film off in the lab's sink, would dress and go, and pretend nothing had happened. Just another lunatic decision, but at least this time no one saw.

But as he stood in the tub, a strange duality struck him; everything seemed both familiar and unfamiliar at the same time—and he still couldn't shake that little voice. The view of the room looked much as it had before he pulled the switch, yet it appeared the fixtures had been lowered by a couple of feet. His body moved more slowly than usual—it seemed as dense and ponderous as a boulder—but part of him believed this was the way it had always felt.

He pulled his right foot from the few inches of ooze that remained at the bottom of the tub, and stepped over the rim, the green still clinging and covering it. Shit! That was not his foot. More like a circus clown's, without the funny shoe. It had to be more than twice as large as he remembered—at least, he guessed, size twenty-three.

A glimmer of recognition as his conscience assured him: it is our foot.

Our?

He nearly jumped out of the vat. The stainless steel cabinet on the other side of the lab might offer a decent reflection, and he staggered to it and stood in front. He had to bend down a little to see everything, and when he did, his mane of hair fell across his eyes, obscuring his view. He reached to brush it away—

Oh, God! Reason's body stood across from him in the mirror.

Mostly.

The massive frame, riddled with scars and stitches, filled the surface of the cabinet. The eyes still had a dull, yellow glow, but at least now, they worked in unison. The mouth sat straighter; the teeth still bleached a perfect white. The nose, though, had grown. This was largely Gray's nose, the mass of which could not be subsumed. In whatever had occurred during the chemical blaze, the Alp had survived. He surveyed the acres of skin, which presented a darker shade of Reason than he remembered, and definitely a lighter shade of Gray.

He looked lower, down below his waist... Well, not bad.

Their bodies had somehow melded. The one aspect of Hand's science that Gray hadn't deduced was that the giant form did more than refresh each time it submerged in the amino brew—it reorganized, reassembled, the power of the ooze breaking down the cells and then building them back up again. And this time, with that much more material in the mix, it simply incorporated Gray. Yeah, simple.

He braced himself against the wall. Not this, not this. To lose himself to the monolith... He'd only wanted some kind of way out, a transport to some other existence, some other Gray. But now to be trapped in this canvas of ancient flesh—it wasn't fair. It had never been fair.

He moved closer to the reflection. Was it reversible? If he followed the recipe for the goo could he fill the tub, switch the polarity of the charge, and undo this conglomerate? Instinct told him no. He of the strangest imaginations could induce no fantasy that would allow them to separate and go back to their original beings. The joining, he knew, was permanent. He would pass the remainder of his days inside this mammoth cage. There were indeed universes worse than the one he'd ached so badly to leave because he was in one now. Perhaps he could go back to the room where he had found Reason and park himself again in the chair. If he waited long enough, the power infused by the bath would wear off, as it had done with Reason alone. Then he would enter that catatonic state. He might not die, but at least he would not have to face this life.

He sensed that little voice again, fighting to get through the static of his thoughts. It had a high-pitched, echo-like, mysterious tone. It didn't come from any place in the house that he could tell, but seemed to emanate from within him. It couldn't be. The two of them sharing one skin, one heart, one cranium...one brain?

He spoke to confirm his identity. It came out, "We are Gray."

That didn't sound right.

"We are Reason."

Two consciousnesses.

The implications came in waves, threatening to ignite panic. Who would be in charge? How would they get around in this enormous body? The manse was barely big enough to accommodate the giant's stature, but the rest of the world presented challenges—the forehead still felt a bit sore from the last attempt at walking through a doorway of normal height. With two in that head, there'd be problems making even the smallest decisions. And how would they explain this to anyone—to the media, to Randy, to Breeze, and the old men? To L'aura? They had to get out of there.

They picked up Gray's shirt and held it at arm's length. It might cover a portion of the chest, more like a bib than a garment. They would have to find some of Reason's clothes before they could leave the house.

But at least now they knew where they were. The way to Reason's room was clear, as though they'd made the trip every day—which of course they had. Memory rendered darkened steps and hallways no obstacle, and in a half-hour, they had showered, dressed, and finished a Windsor knot—Gray's contribution—to go with one of Reason's suits—a sixty-six long, they noted proudly. The sleeves, however, hung a couple of inches short, as did the pant cuffs. The jacket felt tight. The body had grown even larger; apparently the process absorbed Gray's mass into Reason's, along with his consciousness.

They stood for a minute and stared into the bathroom mirror. The face that looked back was horrific yet familiar, sympathetic and conflicted.

They went back to the lab and fished Gray's mobile and car keys from his pants. Then, outside to the Civic and the way back to civilization. But once there, they discovered the car was useless—Reason's body couldn't fit behind the wheel. Even with the seat all the way back the knees jackknifed so high they blocked the view out the front window.

They tried to call Randy, but the buttons on Gray's tiny cell had morphed into an impossibility. They poked and pressed and misdialed every time, and initially became so frustrated they nearly flung the thing the half-mile to the dump. But a calming sentiment persuaded them to rest a minute before trying again. Whose side had recommended that?

They managed an 0 and held for an operator and at last, reached Gray's friend.

"Our car… It won't start. Can you come and get us?"

"You sound weird," Randy said. "It's all distorted like you're talking through a megaphone. What happened to your voice? Who's with you?"

"It must be a bad connection. Can you hurry?"

Randy said he'd leave right away, but it still gave them a few minutes alone. They went back inside and waited on one of the neon sofas. Sure enough, thoughts clashed. Part of them was content to sit and stare at the broken HD television, as though the blank screen could entertain. But another part insisted they make plans for later—things would change for both of them, and they'd better be prepared. At least find a paper and pen, and that way if an idea occurred they'd be able to write it down.

The best they could do was an empty page in the front of a book, and it sat open on their lap, the leaky pen resting in the binding, but nothing profound resolved, two heads, as it were, no better than one. Scary. Their minds might exist as far apart as galaxies. This body might become a shared purgatory. And catatonia wasn't oblivion. Reason had said he could not die—

Randy pulled up at the curb. They rushed out to meet him rather than sit any longer in each other's mental company, pondering a dismal future.

"Big boy! What have you done with Gray?"

"Randy! We're in here. In this body."

"Please. I may not be a genius, but I know that body, and that voice. It isn't Gray."

"We know you can't understand. We don't understand it ourselves. But we swear it is true."

"Listen, Reason," Randy said. "I don't know what you're up to with this charade, but I'm not buying it. Now where's my friend before I call the police?"

"We must think," they said. Yes, think. Better than talking because, God, this voice was annoying. The pitch occasionally skewed to that of an untuned violin. They'd have to find a way to modulate it.

Randy turned and started for his car.

"Wait!" They lowered their gaze to look at him. He really was way down there; it felt so good to be this high. They told him the story, leaving out the science neither of them could explain anyway. When he still didn't believe they told him again. They took him upstairs and showed him the lab: Gray's discarded clothes, the fried green tub. They described more of Gray's life, so much that Reason could not have known. But their friend continued to fight it.

"We know," they said. "What did you do last night?"

"Ha! Why don't you tell me?"

"Yes. You were in the hot tub with Gray."

"He could have told you that."

They took a breath and exhaled. "The two of you had too much to drink, and things went too far."

"Too far where?"

They looked away, but had to say it. "You played footsie underwater."

Randy's mouth fell open and he pushed his fingers up to shut it. "Gray?"

They offered a giant smile.

"Okay, but where's Gray's body?"

"Absorbed, we guess. Reason was the bigger presence."

Randy eyed them. "But it's Gray up there in the brain department?"

"Actually, it is both of us. Everything Gray ever knew is here:

the knowledge, the memories. But Reason is here as well. We are trying to make it work."

Randy seemed to still be debating whether he should believe all or any of this. "If you're not really Reason and not really Gray, then what should I call you?"

They hadn't begun to consider that, but it might be important. The part that was Gray had wanted to escape from the world, from the problems and responsibilities—and the ridiculous lawsuit Patsy and Bob threatened. He'd climbed into the vat with Reason not knowing what to expect, but hoping it would be different enough to allow him to change the path of his life. Why not fulfill that desire? And Reason was a way cooler name than Gray. The part that was Reason agreed. Common ground at last.

"Call us Reason," they said. "People will recognize us that way. But in private you can call us Gray, if you like."

"I like," Randy said. "Just hope I don't slip up."

He drove a full-size sedan, but even with the seat all the way back, Reason's knees folded to his chin. "There will be some things we'll just have to get used to," they said. "Some adjustments."

"Not the least of which is what you're going to do for a living," Randy said. "Obviously, jockey is out. You'll have to think about your abilities and limitations."

Yeah. Apart from a fallback position as a star in a freak show, they couldn't imagine much. As a consultant, they'd scare the wits out of most potential clients, and they'd have trouble finding a regular job that could accommodate this quarter ton of bulk.

"You are right," they said. "We will think about it."

"And are you going to keep referring to yourself in the first-person plural?"

"Sorry. We don't seem to be able to stop."

"Well then, you could follow through on the campaign," Randy said. "As long as you're going to sound pompous, you might as well stay in politics."

"Not a chance." The experience had been hell for Reason and had driven Gray to semi-suicide. They agreed completely on this.

"Then I guess Elvis Vega is our next mayor."

An evil that Grand River would have to live with; one, that in varying degrees, its people had endured for decades. With the Island Retreat cabal running local politics, Vega clones had dominated the council and mayor's office. The favors for cronies, and the deals and kickbacks that had kept the city on the brink of failure, would continue. Most people probably wouldn't notice four more years of corruption, at least not at first. Vega was a sleaze just by himself, capable of turning city accounts into his personal piggy bank, but add the avarice of Fox and Zinger directing his larceny, and the grand total might bleed the city dry this time. Maybe when his term ended, the voting public would demand a change.

"In fact, he's pretty much declared the race over, now that Reason's campaign has shut down."

"What about Bob?"

"Nobody's given him a chance. His percentage was down to four in the last poll. Another week and he could go negative. Next time he'll start in the hole and have to give votes back before he can run."

"What poll?"

"The one the *News-Press* did after Reverend Hand disappeared. Came out this morning. Didn't you see it?"

"We've been a little busy," they said.

"With you out of the picture, Vega has no competition. He's already started to name appointees."

Back at Randy's, they opted for a drink before considering their future. They knocked their head on the doorframe on the way into his office. Yes, it did hurt. Reason had never let it show, but now they couldn't help rubbing the spot.

"We'll need to get you set up," Randy said. "New clothes, new shoes...special order, I see. You'll have to find a car big enough so you can drive. Maybe an RV or a tour bus. You can stay here whether you have money or not, but eventually you'll have to get some kind of position."

He was right. They would have to do something; they couldn't spend the rest of their days soaking in Randy's hot tub and quaffing his wine, as attractive as that sounded. And the thought of Elvis Vega as mayor of Grand River, overseeing their existence, making laws that controlled them, cutting illicit deals and consolidating Island Retreat's hold over the rest of the city—that bothered both of them. Gray had always wanted to right a few wrongs. And Reason… Whatever happened to doing great things for this city?

While Randy poured the wine, they managed to extract Gray's cell from their pocket, almost breaking the thing in the process. They tried in vain to place a call. The buttons were simply too small for those pork sausage fingers. "Here," they said, thrusting the device at Randy. "You dial."

"Who're we calling?"

"The *News-Press.* We want to schedule a press conference. Reason is back in the race."

Togetherness

"Great things. Great things for this city." A few more seconds of practice before the media arrived.

They almost had the voice under control. No more death throes of laughter. Just the occasional slip into the old metal-on-metal screech, but otherwise, they would present a serious candidate, intelligent, speaking in sincere, measured tones about issues that mattered. Best of all, they'd washed off all of the green goo, and with it, the annoying smell, which Gray's intact nose appreciated immensely.

The magical attraction Reason had held for the voters would help too. No way of knowing if it still existed, or if it had been the result of Revered Hand's incantations and potions, but if the people still loved Reason, Reason would love them back. And now they would be more than Hand's catch phrases, more than vapid marketing. Time to get the people on their side once more.

"Come on. Let's hear the rest of it," Randy said.

"But to accomplish great things, we must all take part. Together. We will call upon neighborhood leaders and average citizens to participate in government. We will give them the authority to decide. We believe you care enough about Grand River to accept this challenge."

Together. Maybe it was dumb luck that Hand had included the word in the slogan he'd pounded into this head. Probably he meant only to play on the tired advertising ploy that insisted every person, and every person's opinion, mattered. But it had meaning now. The longer they considered what to say in the new campaign, the more they agreed this should be the theme. It had actually been fun to approach the problem from two minds; two minds that worked more as one as the issues came into focus.

"You sound good," Randy said. "You almost look good, too. Ever give any thought to cutting those locks?"

"No! Our hair must not be touched!"

Wow. If there had been any doubt Reason was still in there with Gray, Randy's suggestion removed it.

"That's okay. It makes kind of a statement of its own, anyway."

The media began filing into the ancient ballroom of the Continental and taking the seats that surrounded the stage. A crew from the local cable outlet had arrived too, and as their cameras rumbled across the floorboards, the vibration set the filmy chandelier above the dais in motion. It swayed above their head like a blunt, but just as deadly, sword of Damocles, ready to snuff out the campaign for good if the conference went badly.

The boys from the *News-Press* ran down front to make sure they got the best seats and continued the paper's effort to look relevant. A smug Homer and Uncle Zen sat a few rows behind them. How Zen had managed to sneak the cat past the hotel's security posed a mystery, however, and now the animal was digging its claws into the shoulder of a reporter from one of the big dailies up north. At least the editors at the media behemoth had finally deemed Grand River worth covering.

Not everyone in the crowd was credentialed, though. L'aura and Tristan had their heads bowed as they hid in the third row, behind the reporters, but rust-colored hair with glitter demands attention, and the photographers on duty did their warm-ups on her tresses. Gray and Reason each had memories of her, and together they watched as she pretended she wasn't the focal point of half the people in the room. And sitting in the last row near the door, wearing a blond wig and a long sweater meant to obscure the obvious—the unmistakable curves of Breeze. The urge to abandon the dais and clomp up to see her, to ask why she'd come, pulsed inside the awesome body, but the conference had begun. A spotlight from the cable crew flashed on, blinding them from seeing the back rows.

"Mr. Wilder!"

"Over here!"

"Take me first!"

The sheer size of the palm raised to the media quieted them.

"We would like to say how sorry we are for letting our supporters down. The news of Reverend Hand's misdeeds was as much of a surprise to us as to you. But now that he is gone, we wish to continue with our campaign…for the good of Grand River. Together…"

They didn't even have to say it. Nearly everyone in the room stood and applauded. Those who didn't could be excused for pausing to write down every utterance. A TV camera moved closer. Its operator brushed away a tear. The magic was unquestionably back. They fought the urge to bray.

The inquiries, once the proceedings calmed, were softballs. *Where will you appear next? Any rallies planned? Did you enjoy your time off from the campaign?*

An ovation punctuated every answer.

L'aura and Tristan came out from behind the bank of reporters and made their way to the stage, where they flanked their once and future hero. She went so far as to kneel and place her hands within that monstrous grip. Tristan crossed his arms in front of his chest, a stickman bodyguard. Nice to have them back too.

Since those two had crossed the boundary of the stage, many in the media could no longer restrain themselves and began climbing up there with them. They wanted to get close, to touch, maybe shake that giant hand. The cameraman left his post to join the celebration, saying it was all right, he'd left it on wide angle to capture the fullness of the scene.

They stood, head, shoulders, and half a torso above the worshippers. They extended their arms to encompass the good feelings.

Press conference over. Let the Reason fest begin.

But from behind the glare of the spotlight came a woman's voice, soft and lilting, like the mildest of zephyrs. The question it carried, however, bore a hurricane: "Where is Reverend Hand?"

They stood and shielded their eyes, but could not make out the source. But they knew it came from Breeze. "We do not know."

"He hasn't communicated with you since he left town?"

"We have heard nothing."

"Do you expect us to believe you had nothing to do with the crimes he's alleged to have committed?"

"We had hoped to discuss issues that are more important to the voters."

The group onstage, the ones that were supposed to be asking the tough questions, came to their defense. "Why are you attacking Reason?" one asked. "Leave him be. He'll do great things for this city."

But Breeze had a mission and would not be dissuaded. "What about the charges in the story that ran in the *Grand River Journal*, that you are something other than completely human?"

Homer sat up straighter and raised his chin as though he might be noticed. Many in the crowd laughed. Good. They had not taken that part of the article seriously. Someone yelled at her to keep quiet.

"That is a fabrication," they said.

"Then how do you explain the laboratory in your mansion? The steel tub big enough for someone your size?"

"We have to bathe somewhere—" More laughter. More applause. The crowd remained on their side, but the questions were bothersome. Why was she doing this?

Then a reporter still sitting in the first row turned to a colleague and mentioned they should call an editor to get someone over to the house and check out that lab, just in case. The spotlight from the unattended camera became brighter and hotter.

"And where is the man who wrote that article, Gray Davenport?"

"Who can say? Perhaps he has run away with Reverend Hand."

"You had nothing to do with *his* disappearance?"

They would have to get to Breeze and explain everything to her. Maybe she would understand why they had returned to the race. If only they'd done it before the press conference. Now some of the reporters might pick up this trail and magnify the issue. "We barely know the man. We have nothing against him."

"Where have you been the past week? The world heard no statements, had no access after the allegations against Reverend Hand came to light."

"Please," they said. "Trust us that we know nothing of these things."

"But you lived there with him. How could you not know?"

Their strength began to drain. They had to get away. A pleading look toward Randy and their friend knew what to do. "Sorry, everyone, but as you can see, our candidate is exhausted from his ordeal. Mr. Wilder will finish his campaign platform and send it to each of you via email. Thank you for attending the conference."

Still it took a half hour before they could persuade everyone to leave, and Randy had to schedule four "exclusive" interviews for Reason, plus one cable special, to make that happen. L'aura and Tristan stayed and promised to meet them at the mansion. They were ready again to dedicate themselves.

But Breeze had left. She'd planted a roadside bomb along this avenue of good feeling. And at least one of the news agencies had been interested in what she had to say.

Who Did What to Whom

The twin bed in Gray's room at the Star had been too small even before the melding. Now, the massive body lay spread eagle across the threadbare blanket, hands dangling to the carpet, knees bent at the edge of the mattress, size twenty-threes planted flat in the pea-colored shag. Comfort, though, was not the object. She'd come to the press conference, not to support their candidacy, but to assassinate it. One more confusing chapter in the Book of Breeze.

Gray's and Reason's memories of her competed in the shared consciousness: that first encounter when she seemed to float into Bob Boren's living room, the timid knock at the door to the manse when she asked to join the campaign, her apparent sincerity over drinks and dinner at Frenchy's, fucking Reason in his room at night—

What the—?

Gray commanded the monster's hands around the monster's throat. He would kill the bastard, even if it meant committing suicide. He did her?

No. She did him.

The wretch's recollections played like old videotapes—unedited, unbiased, sans comment. What he remembered only reenacted what he saw, unfettered by attempts to find hidden meaning. His mind then was still not sophisticated enough to interpret her actions, and when she came to him in the dim of the mansion, wearing a see-through negligee and navigating the hallway with a pen light, Reason only sat up in bed, unaware of any political or sexual motive. Her visit might have been a prelude to coercion, to get him to reveal campaign secrets the next day. It might have been pure lust, or a desire to test her Amazonian supremacy against his bionic manhood. But to him, she was just there.

Gray ditched his own memories and hit Reason's rewind button. The monster did not protest.

The door to the room had creaked a little when it opened. She brought a finger to her lips to shush him, no doubt to avoid the feedback loop of his voice if he started talking. She straddled Reason before he could move, and shed the flimsy nightie. Reason's eyes recorded every sumptuous curve, every inch of perfect skin. Gray watched, hypnotized. She was all there, all for him—but not for him. The ultimate tease. This body had had sex with her, and Gray's mind too, so many times. But never together. Never for real. And now, for sure, never again.

Gray tried to pause the video so that he might burn the image of her body permanently into his psyche, but Reason did not respond to his requests. He did to Breeze's, however. She had him hard in two seconds, and that was it for foreplay. She reached down, grabbed the resurrected member, and shoved it home. Her breasts and hips flapped and shook as she pounded him from above, yet her face remained as impassive as the monster's below. She was the consummate sexual pro. Gray watched the scene unfold for him as though he manned a POV camera from behind Reason's head, and he filled with passion and jealousy at once. He imagined what he would have done had he been in charge of the situation—grabbing, fondling, stroking, biting—but then, he would not have been in charge. Her porn star rut did not allow room for another's personal needs or emotions. She uttered no moans, real or otherwise, nor did Reason. This wasn't so much sex as biology; more like a task that needed to be completed than anything like human emotion. Reason, he could almost understand; the conjoined body simply reacted to stimuli. But Breeze… What to think of her now?

It was over in a minute, and as quickly as she had entered, Breeze dismounted, picked up her negligee, and strutted out, the diminishing light she'd left on the bed just barely illuminating her naked body as it taunted both of them.

At last he'd had her—sort of—yet Gray's frustration continued to grow. Reason's mind, still too confused to know the difference between this recollection and the real thing, demanded sleep. Gray insisted they stay awake to work this over, plan revenge, anything to keep from the realization that he belonged in this enormous body because only a fool as big as he could fit in here. Was this their future together inside the refurbished head? Would they fight over memories as well as decisions?

Come. Sleep.

Reason appealed to him once more.

The problems would not go away while they slept, but they might not seem as important in a few hours. Gray relented. They closed their eyes.

Re-summoned

Something definitely different at the yacht club, it seemed, although they could not deduce exactly what it was. A feeling. They clomped the marbled hallway toward the bar, on the way to meet those twin consuls of Grand River, those defenders of inequity, who had summoned them for a "friendly chat; a meeting of the architects of the city's future."

Future? These two were as old as ancient Rome. As the massive hand reached to turn the gold-plated doorknob of the back room Shangri-La, they realized the difference—they had not had to duck. They surveyed the path just navigated. Not a feeling, but a lack of one—no head butts into mahogany doorframes; no resultant throbbing skull.

"We had them raised. Just for you." Fox stood at the open door, smiling at their belt buckle. "A fitting tribute to a man of your stature, someone we expect to see in our humble office on a regular basis once you're elected. Do come in, our friend."

There sat Zinger in the calfskin cocoon of his chair, cradling a snifter despite the nine a.m. start time. His lap, however, remained vacant. They scanned quickly to ensure Breeze didn't lurk in a corner and listened in case she might approach from outside the room. As sure as they now were that Zinger had chauffeured her away from exile that night at the Star, they felt almost as certain the old boy would punish her for the incident, make her perform some menial duties to remind her of her place in his world. If she sashayed in wearing a black mini and seamed stockings, carrying a tray of drinks and cigars, they would not have been surprised.

Zinger opened with pleasantries: the calm waters beyond the club's windows, do you sail, and of course, congratulations on your decision to get back in the race after that unfortunate series of events. They did not respond, but the Gray half of them relaxed over the realization the old men did not recognize his former self in this new and goliath-like body.

Still, it felt strange to both of them, sitting in that room of wealth and privilege. Gray had once mused that neither he nor Reason belonged in this pampered world, and now that idea became palpable. In the last few days the memories of Reason's prior life had begun to emerge more clearly: scenes of deprivation and hopelessness, crippling poverty cemented by the attitudes of another century. The hardest years of all come just before rebellion. They thought together now that Fox and Zinger's twenty-first century economic oppressiveness was more subtle, but in its own way, more severe. They resolved to fight it, if they could.

"Why don't we get down to business?" they said. The longer they exposed themselves to the old men's buttering, the more susceptible they might become to suggestions. Besides, Randy wouldn't wait in the parking lot forever.

Fox shut the door. He went to the bar and poured two more snifters, and held one out.

"Too early for that," they said, the monster's voice betrayed by Gray's anxiety, into finishing the sentence with a little squeal.

"Only if you adhere to the useless convention of the clock," Zinger said. "Sit, my boy."

A tinge of the old, subservient Gray came over them, combined with Reason's programmed acquiescence to commands, and they squeezed into a leather chair like a swollen finger into a glove. The sultry arms of the lounger embraced their hips like a lover's. Would they ever feel that kind of touch again?

Fox did not let them dwell on the issue. "I must admit we were quite surprised at the public's reaction to your reentering the race for mayor. We would have thought the people would see you as…how do you say it…a flip-flopper. Yet they have deserted our favored candidate and returned to your camp. Yesterday's poll shows you're only three points behind us now."

"The people are our friends," they said.

"For the moment." Fox sipped his drink and paused, as though the fumes bolstered his belief in his own power. "All things are subject to change."

"We will not change. We are dedicated to this city."

"As are we," Zinger said. "The only difference is in our approach. We tend to look much further into the future than you."

"We do not understand. The problems of the city are in the present."

Fox turned to Zinger. "I like the way he speaks. The royal 'we.' Coupled with that amazing stature, it gives him an air of majesty, don't you agree?"

Zinger nodded his approval.

How small they were. Even if one sat on the other's shoulders they would not meet the stratospheric gaze of Reason's eyes. But their minds were connected. Although they inhabited separate bodies, they functioned with a seamless consistency of purpose. It might be some time before Gray's and Reason's thoughts meshed as well, if ever.

"It almost doesn't make sense for him to run for as lowly an office as mayor," Fox went on.

Zinger lifted his glass in salute. "You're right. There are bigger things in Mr. Wilder's future. Much bigger."

"The mayor's office is all we desire."

"Nonsense," Fox said. "You're a big man, and you should think big."

"There are several opportunities we could discuss, my boy," Zinger added.

"Our place is in Grand River," they said.

"Reverend Hand said that to us, too. And that didn't work out very well for him."

"We have nothing to do with Reverend Hand. We are independent of his actions."

"Of course you are," Fox said. "Of course. We don't blame you for distancing yourself. Any connection to his crimes could deal a serious blow to your campaign. But despite the hard feelings, you're still planning to attend the funeral, yes?"

"He is dead? How do you know this?"

Zinger picked up a remote and pressed a button. A cabinet over the bar slid open to reveal a small flat screen. He tuned to CNN. "They ought to have something on it by now," he said.

The caption indicated a live feed from Fairbanks, Alaska. Police tape cordoned what looked like a makeshift laboratory, more primitive, but not too different from the one at the manse. "...had been a fugitive from charges in Grand River and a lawsuit in Georgia. Hand was found this morning, apparently strangled by an assailant the local police described as 'ridiculously strong.' And the lab you see here contained evidence of human remains that forensics experts—" Zinger clicked it off.

"Interesting," he said. "Apparently there may have been some truth to the implications of Mr. Davenport's article in the *Journal*. It's too bad no one can locate him to see what else he knows. I do hope he hasn't come to harm as well."

"Thank goodness reporters from the dailies have expressed an interest in looking into the situation," Fox said. "The results of their investigation could prove illuminating."

The old men lifted their snifters in unison and sipped. Yes, their two minds were far more coordinated. They had the resources to make well-informed decisions, and they certainly got things done. Maybe they had realized an advantage of a two-man oligarchy over democratic ideals.

But, no. The reborn giant had made their mind up to serve the city and had committed to that goal. "What do you want of us?" they asked.

"Only to allow us to help guide your career to its apex," Fox said.

"What of the people of Grand River?"

"You shouldn't worry too much about them. They will be taken care of, as they have always been."

"The people deserve a voice."

"With us behind you, your voice could represent many more people," Fox said.

"The Senate, my boy!" Zinger said. "The United States Senate. Think of it. You, our hand-picked candidate in the November election. And when you win, you'll be the voice of millions, not just of the rabble of this city."

"We'll even help you work on that voice," Fox said, stifling a chuckle.

"But if we run for Senate, Elvis Vega will be left to plunder the city's accounts."

"He will be in our employ, as well as the city's," Zinger said. "We will see that he doesn't get too out of hand. But a certain amount of extracurricular activity is to be expected."

"As it has always been?"

"As it has always been," Zinger said. "Trust us. We know what we are doing. We know everything."

They probably did. They'd had access to Hand, and who knew what part they'd played in his demise? They had the region's media in their apparently bottomless pocket and could turn their investigations on and off like a kitchen faucet. They wanted to stuff this oversized body into that pocket too. And they had Breeze on their side, again.

"You sent Breeze to our press conference."

"Yes. Of course," Fox said. "I would have thought that was obvious. If she hadn't raised some concerns, you might not have agreed to chat with us today."

"She's become quite accommodating lately," Zinger added. "Much less of a bother."

"You would harm her?" they asked.

The old men smiled and ignored the question.

The great body pushed out of the chair, the suction created by the too-tight fit of their hips making an audible noise. They stood, but looked at the floor, instead of their new masters. "Very well. We will make a speech."

"Bravo, my boy," Zinger said. "You'll soon understand what an epic decision you've made. You won't be disappointed."

Had the doorframes on the way back to the parking lot been of average height, they would not have run into a single one, so hunched were they with disappointment. The posture was a strange one for a senatorial hopeful, but they understood such maneuvering was what brought the rest of the world down to Fox and Zinger's size. Perhaps in time they would come to appreciate the turn of events orchestrated by the powerful little men, but not yet. Too much power in too few hands did not seem like the solution to Grand River's ills. But what could they do? If they didn't play Fox and Zinger's game they'd be exposed. The oldsters would make sure this time the media got the message out about Reason's origins, and maybe now the truth would be too much for the public. The campaign might be shuttered again, this time for good. And then there was Breeze. They shouldn't care about her now. But they did.

True, service in the Senate would potentially benefit many more people than a mayorship here. They had made no promise to the power brokers that they'd follow their dictates once in office. But could they win without the close personal contact that campaigning in Grand River afforded? Would they really be independent? Or would Fox and Zinger go so far as to bring down a sitting senator who displeased them? They put nothing out of the reach of these two now.

They were still thinking about the possibilities when they clomped into the parking lot. Randy had opted for a nap, his head sideways against the seatback. They moved to wake him, but another car rolled into the lot, and they paused to watch the E-class Benz glide into a space reserved for yacht club board members.

Breeze saw the giant body and stayed behind her locked door. But they would not leave without speaking with her. She owed them—him—both hims—that much.

They stood outside her door, waiting, and finally she cracked the window an inch. "I have nothing to say to you," she said.

Her presence said enough. Inside the tank-sized chest, their innards contorted. Within the machine-shop head were such conflicting thoughts as to undo all the two minds had done to get along. Gray's lust still burned for Breeze.

The great hand, that hydraulic vise of a hand, reached down and clamped onto the car door handle. When Breeze saw it was capable of defeating the lock and tearing the door from its hinges, she relented and stepped out.

"You must tell us why," they said.

"I did what I had to do."

"That is not an answer."

"Sorry," she said. "But it will have to do. You know how powerful they are."

Power? She understood power? Gray had had enough. He would take it from here.

"You slept with this body and never gave Gray a chance. And he would have done anything for you, to be with you."

"And what," she said, "are you talking about, Reason?"

"We're talking about how you used him, at every turn." The excitement of the moment pushed the voice toward the donkey bray register, but Gray would not stop. "And you never felt the least remorse about it."

"Why are you so concerned about him?"

"Because..." they paused. "Because he is a friend of ours."

Breeze looked into the jaundiced eyes. "It's you," she said. "It's Gray. I don't know how, but you're in there. In Reason's body."

"You do not know—"

"No, Gray. It's you who doesn't understand. I know what I am. I used you, yes. And all I can say is that I felt guilty about it sometimes."

"And now?"

"I still do."

"Are you saying you could have loved us?"

"It was possible."

But impossible now. The steak-sized hands reached out and held Breeze by the shoulders.

"No," she protested, but a grip like that could not be broken. Try as they might to be gentle, this new body would not permit it, and they knew their touch would injure her. But this would only take a moment. They leaned down, moved that wooly head toward her and parted the once-crooked lips. One first and last kiss might make the memories less painful. She closed her eyes as their lips touched hers. She stopped fighting, stopped moving altogether, and let them have their way. But the moment felt plastic to them. Staged. Just another scene for the cameras.

They let go, and she fell to the asphalt, clutching her shoulder. "I think something's broken," she said.

To be so strong and so weak at the same time.

"We are sorry," they said. "We never meant to cause you pain."

Breeze held herself tightly. "Now maybe you understand what love really is," she said.

Randy was awake now and calling for paramedics.

Lacunae

A sea of faces filled the courtyard, and they watched them from inside the hotel, over the balcony where they would address the crowd. Like a tide, the throng ebbed and swelled, and lapped against the buildings that surrounded the square. They felt a responsibility for these people, for everyone who had come out to support Reason. How they hated to let them all down, but what alternative did they have? Fox and Zinger had rigged the game, eliminated their options.

Once, Reason had convinced the voters he represented the future of Grand River—convinced them without trying, thanks to Reverend Hand's magic. Now, working together, nearly as one mind, Gray and Reason would try to reignite that devotion and redirect it to a larger stage. They'd finished their speech this morning, polished it, agonized over it. All they had to do now was read it and pray the people would follow them in the quest for a senate seat. They would abandon the city to Vega's oily grip, rationalizing they would achieve a higher power. But they knew in their melon-sized heart that they would merely serve as a bigger pawn in the puppet masters' plans.

"Reason..." L'aura stepped in from the hallway to address them. Her hair! The long, straight tresses had been permed and stood almost straight up on her head in a beehive of sine waves. She'd colored it black again, but along the sides, she'd brushed in flashes of white like bolts of electricity. Below, a simple white dress, the kind that, in some primitive ritual, might signify purity. Their attraction to her was instantaneous, as though someone had crafted her just to please them. Still, they couldn't let her onto the balcony like that. They would have to keep her hidden from the crowd before anyone misinterpreted her appearance as something sacrificial.

"I need to talk to you," she said.

They took a step, a clomp, backward as she approached, but she was not dissuaded from coming right up to them, taking their fingers in her hands. "I want to be with you," she said. "I want to share in your life, in your triumph."

"But what of your promise to Tristan? And you are still married to Gray."

"I want you," she said. "Ever since I met you I've been thinking of us together. But I wasn't sure. Lately, there's been a change in you. Something's different. You're more intelligent, more caring. I find it irresistible."

"But how can we—?"

"Take me from Tristan. I am no longer for him. Speak the words of asunder, and I will be yours."

The part that was Gray weakened. If only she'd said these things when they were still a couple, living in the Pollocked halls of their condo and trying to do no more than make ends meet. Look at him now. The knowledge that he could never go back to such a simple existence made his pain over her reawakened desires acute.

The part that was Reason urged him to focus on the task at hand. It would take the efforts of both minds to convince the crowd of their sincerity about switching races, the people's current show of devotion notwithstanding.

They turned to her. "L'aura, you are a beautiful woman. Any man would be proud to be with you. But we were made for another purpose, and we must fulfill that destiny."

L'aura hissed. "It's her, isn't it? It's that Breeze woman. She's poisoned you. You can't trust her."

"We know," they said. "You are right. She was poison. We have no desire for her now. No desire for any companion. We must face our future alone."

L'aura swiped at the once crooked face with a set of fingernails that resembled paring knives. But she could not come close to the stony visage so high above her reach.

Randy had seen. He wrapped his arms around L'aura's, pinning her deadly nails to her sides. "There, there, sweetie," he said. "It's not to be. He's too much man for any of us now." She began to cry, and he led her away, back into the hall.

They watched her go. Now it was Gray's turn to provide memories. He reached back beyond the months of argument and ill feeling, back to when he and L'aura still enjoyed each other's company. Their great body began to relax. A sensation of warmth came over them, and Gray realized it was Reason's sympathy for him.

Outside, the crowd chanted in anticipation: Reason! Reason! Reason!

They would have to go out to the balcony soon and speak, before the people became so worked up they would refuse to allow the switch to another campaign. What was this spell that Hand had used to dupe the public? How was it that it still worked, still bound the people to his cause, even with the reverend gone and dead? Perhaps the madman had slipped a mickey into the city's water supply or encoded a trance into the fumes from the garbage dump that wafted over Grand River.

Reason had said almost nothing of substance throughout the campaign—now one with the beast, Gray understood Hand's master strategy. "Your mind is as yet too weak," the mad reverend had explained. "Until I can teach you what to say, and how, you must speak only in the platitudes I give you. It won't make any difference. The people will adore you."

He'd been right. The part that was Reason recalled the scenes for the part that was Gray: hands and hugs and adulation, vapid praise for banal utterances interpreted, somehow, as statements of incomprehensible beauty and sagacity. Everyone he met acted like a child in his presence, ready to dance or sing or do whatever he asked to win his praise, earn his friendship, his respect.

To know success and respect. To feel appreciated and wanted. So this was what it was like.

And so many said they felt a deeper connection as well, something more than emotional; almost physical, as though a part of each person lived inside Reason. Well, maybe a part of each person's ancestors.

Randy jogged back into the room. He'd managed to calm L'aura with a smoothie and a shoulder massage. "She was pretty upset," he said. "She told me she finally had someone to believe in, but when you turned her down, she felt betrayed."

They did not want to hurt her, despite the way she'd treated Gray over the past year. His doing anyway: who could stand to be with that kind of man?

Their friend reached high to clasp a statue-like shoulder. "This crowd won't wait. Better not disappoint them."

They looked over the parapet again. The crowd had spilled past the square and into the adjacent boulevard, which had closed to traffic. Those drivers caught at the barricades stood on top of their cars to get a better view. People watched from offices in nearby buildings. They held impromptu parties on rooftops. In the throng below, placards screamed for the "Great Things" they had promised. Vendors sold shaggy wigs and Reason masks. Children wore bulky shoes and danced "The Clomp," stumbling into each other and banging their foreheads into imaginary doorframes.

They scanned the sky over the tops of the buildings that ringed downtown. Today it was as blue and clear as the vista that lingered over the beautiful cities to the north and south. They saw it as a metaphor, a promise of possibilities. And as they watched, their minds came closer and something else became clear to them.

"Yes. We see," they said aloud.

There had been no magic. Inchoate Hand had made a giant and infused it with life, and that was all he had done. The people took it from there, despite the reverend's machinations and criminal intentions. They saw in Reason a symbol, someone not controlled by the clique in Island Retreat, someone big enough, imposing enough to make a statement without always having to speak. Someone not so smart as to be unapproachable, but who recognized the value of individual lives and their collective power.

Someone who would do what they would not or could not do for themselves: to stand against their oppressors and lead them out of Grand River's troubled times.

Someone they could call a hero, because the people always need a hero, an underdog to fight their battles, so they can pursue their smaller dreams of middle class life, the ones they believe themselves capable of achieving: the house and two cars; the eight-hour workdays, followed by dinner with the family and sitcoms at night; the weekends in the yard, making things a little nicer so the neighbors would notice, but leaving time to watch the kids at football and ballet practice; and the little nest egg for the golden years when all that effort would seem worthwhile; the kind of dreams Gray had once, the kind that even Reason—whatever his name had been in his past life—may have once dreamed but never dared believe in.

Like the crowd watching a magician, they wanted to believe. And the part that was Gray realized that he and perhaps a thousand other men had imposed that same form of magic upon Breeze, saddling her with the burden of their childish lust, forcing her to play the role of slut and spy, and for that he finally felt sorry. But now he, and Reason, and the people would have to awaken from their dreams. They would give the people over to the old men and allow the waking evil to continue. Perhaps, having known no other existence, the people would not miss an altered future.

Ah, they could have done so much here.

Randy beckoned. Time to get out there.

The speech would only take a minute or two to read. It fluttered in their titan-sized hand as the wind outside the hotel room caught it. They would read, apologize, and then turn and go back to Fox and Zinger, who had called a meeting to get the senate campaign started. Below, they noticed a group of supporters who wore T-shirts with letters and had assembled themselves to spell out their champion's name.

The part that was Reason continued to remember. This time what it was like after the rallies and public events, inside the gloomy hallways of the mansion, where Hand controlled every aspect of the giant's life: the lessons to be learned, who he saw and what he said, when to eat, when to sleep, how often he could indulge in the rejuvenating ooze.

The part that was Gray sensed the other's happiness that the madness had ended, that he was free from Hand's restrictions, free to live another way. And he remembered how Reason had once said he lived in the world, but apart from it, separated by his link to the netherworld. It didn't make sense then, that anyone could exist in such a divergence, but now that they shared consciousness, he understood that his and Reason's new duality was perfect—that their combined natures created an exquisite perspective. Now they would use that distance to think, to make decisions. In fact, it represented the only way for them to go forward.

He was glad he'd played a part in the liberation of this immense spirit, which had made possible his own.

Gray had spent years trying to fit into the world, hoping to find a niche someplace other than in a wall. As he looked out at the happy, trusting faces in the multitude, he knew that place was here, on this balcony, in this city. In this body. He was no longer a slave to the whims of others, or to his own emotions. No need to fit anywhere now. No need when one releases and is released.

They stepped outside and leaned over the parapet. How like the particles of atoms the people seemed, each spinning merrily in its own space and time, connected to the others by nuclear forces, but not by any visible bond. They resembled quantum bits in a solid—the illusion of a solid—the space between the bits far greater than that taken up by its mass. Another duality of sorts. This particular universe was all about dualities. The assumed reality offered Breeze and L'aura, tangible bodies and objects, at one time or another, of Gray's desire. It was Bob and Patsy and Vega and Fox and Zinger and Homer, and their mistaken belief in the religion of the senses, which made it possible for all of them to live without questions, cocooned in self-preservation, always hungry, always wanting. It was, by definition, a conflicted, ironic place, where the key to survival depended on another's failure.

Reason had said he could not die a natural death again. Having been reborn and charged by artificial means, his spirit would diminish, but never extinguish. With Gray inside, providing the missing spark of life, they no longer needed the jolt of the vat. They might live forever in this giant shell. Survival, then, was no longer the primary goal.

As a neutron who had escaped the strong nuclear force of his former existence, Gray could focus on an altered reality, a greater purpose. He perceived that the vast distances between particles, between people, were not vacuums, but perspectives as well, places inhabited not by matter, but by intellect. Those spaces brimmed with dark, invisible energy. And now, he and Reason would live in those gaps.

They stood straight and tall, to allow everyone to see their full stature. They loosened their grip and let the speech fall to the balcony floor. They would not need it to continue the run for mayor.

"Our friends!" they bellowed. They raised their massive hands like flags, and in semaphore, signaled the crowd to quiet.

Acknowledgments

If you've read this far, I'll assume you found at least some part of *Mr. Neutron* mildly amusing, or funny, or maybe even hilarious. That was always the intent. Rather than write a story with a little humor thrown in, I approached *Mr. Neutron* the way I approach most everything in life: from the opposite direction, by putting down the most absurdly funny stuff that came to mind, and reasoning that a story would arise from the chaos. While writing I almost never said no to a joke (which may explain some of the more cringe-worthy lines), because I knew someone, somewhere would laugh, and whether with me or at me hardly matters, since people have been doing both for a long, long time. Despite that philosophy, if I were asked for advice about writing humor, I'd say the best path is not to force the funny stuff. Life (aka people) offers humor in many ways, and all a writer need do is pay attention and the comedy will present itself. Then all you have to do is write it down. David Foster Wallace's essays about cruise ships and state fairs are the best example of that.

The humor in this book is in no small part due to the influence of dozens of writers and comedians whose work I've admired over the last several decades. Here's a partial list, in no particular order, of the people who made me laugh and think:

John Cleese, Eric Idle, Michael Palin, Terry Jones, Graham Chapman, and Terry Gilliam of *Monty Python's Flying Circus*, who by the way once aired a skit called "Mr. Neutron," which seemed like a perfect title for my book; Jerry Seinfeld; David Foster Wallace; Fred Armisen and Carrie Brownstein (*Portlandia*); Dave Chappelle; Philip Roth; Lucille Ball; Richard Jeni; Gary Shteyngart; George Carlin; Chuck Lorre and the writers for The Big Bang Theory; Gilda Radner; George Gobel (who once quipped, "Did you ever get the feeling that the world is a tuxedo and you're a pair of brown shoes?" which is where I got the brown shoes bit.); Eddie Murphy; Mae West; Lars Iyer; Benny Hill; Moe Howard, Curly Howard, Larry Fine (the Three Stooges), and Shemp Howard too; Dan Rowan and Dick Martin of Rowan and Martin's Laugh In (yes, I am that old); Christopher Buckley; Robin Williams; Rodney Dangerfield; Lenny Bruce; Andy Kaufman; Peter Sellers; Charlie Chaplin; Johnny Carson; Buster Keaton; Mel Brooks; David Letterman; Whoopi Goldberg; Larry David; Billy Crystal; Kelsey Grammer; David Hyde-Pierce: Rowan Atkinson; Julia Louis-Dreyfus; Jerry Stiller; Tina Fey; Stephen Fry; Alec Baldwin; Gene Wilder (not where I got the name for the monster, in case you were wondering); Zero Mostel; Dan Aykroyd; Queen Latifah; Bob Newhart; Leslie Nielsen; Jonathan Winters; Martin Short; Kathy Griffin; Sid Caesar; Paul Lynde; Molly Shannon; Jack Benny; Steve Allen; W.C. Fields; Groucho, Chico, Harpo, Zeppo, and Gummo (the Marx Brothers); Allan Sherman; Bob Hope; Woody Allen; Carol Kane; Jane Curtin; Jenna Elfman; Marty Feldman; Mary Tyler Moore; Dick Van Dyke; Soupy Sales; Jimmy Walker; Flip Wilson; Lily Tomlin; David Sedaris; Colin Mochrie; Wayne Brady; Don Adams; Barbara Feldon; Debra Messing; Sean Hayes; Al Franken; Norman Lear; Sinbad; Joan Rivers; Keith Olbermann; Dudley Moore; Harold Lloyd; Eugene Levy; Christopher Guest; Redd Foxx; Phyllis Diller; Sacha Baron Cohen.

Phew.

More seriously, I'm also indebted to some non-comedians,

particularly 7.13 Books Publisher Leland Cheuk, who saw enough promise in *Mr. Neutron* to take a gamble on it, and on a small group of writer friends who laughed often enough at Gray Davenport's antics to keep me writing and revising (so blame them). Thanks Kelly Davio, Christine Daigle, Dora Badger, Stewart Sternberg, and the late Jon Zech.

And a special thank you and love to my wonderful wife, Dona, who not only has put up with twelve years of writing, but also has endured the rants about the writing business, as well as the jokes that were so bad they didn't even make it into the book.

About the Author

Joe Ponepinto is the founding publisher and fiction editor of *Tahoma Literary Review*, a nationally-recognized literary journal that has had selections reproduced in *Best American Poetry, Best American Essays, Best Small Fictions,* and other notable anthologies. He has had short stories published in dozens of literary journals in the U.S. and abroad. A New Yorker by birth, he has lived in many locations around the country, and now resides in Washington State with his wife, Dona, and Henry the coffee-drinking dog.

7.13
BOOKS

CPSIA information can be obtained
at www.ICGtesting.com
Printed in the USA
FSOW03n1324150318
45767FS